THE
LAST
KARANKAWAS

THE
LAST
KARANKAWAS

a Novel

KIMBERLY GARZA

Henry Holt and Company
New York

Henry Holt and Company
Publishers since 1866
120 Broadway
New York, New York 10271
www.henryholt.com

Henry Holt® and ❶® are registered trademarks of
Macmillan Publishing Group, LLC.

Portions of this book have appeared in different forms. "The Queens of
Santo Niño" originally appeared in *Copper Nickel* in 2019; "Red Zone"
originally appeared in *TriQuarterly* in 2017; "The Last Karankawas"
originally appeared in *CutBank* in 2016; "Caballeros" originally appeared
as "Caballero" in *Huizache* in 2017; "Galveston: A Glossary & Guide for
the Uninitiated Traveler" originally appeared in *Puerto del Sol* in 2017.

Yona Harvey, excerpt from "Hurricane" from *Hemming the Water*.
Copyright © 2013 by Yona Harvey. Reprinted with the permission
of The Permissions Company, LLC on behalf of Four Way Books,
fourwaybooks.com.

Library of Congress Cataloging-in-Publication Data

Names: Garza, Kimberly, 1985– author.
Title: The last Karankawas : a novel / Kimberly Garza.
Description: First edition. | New York : Henry Holt and Company, 2022.
Identifiers: LCCN 2021060827 (print) | LCCN 2021060828 (ebook) |
    ISBN 9781250819857 (hardcover) | ISBN 9781250819864 (ebook)
Subjects: LCGFT: Novels.
Classification: LCC PS3607.A7834 L37 2022 (print) | LCC PS3607.
    A7834 (ebook) | DDC 813/.6—dc23
LC record available at https://lccn.loc.gov/2021060827
LC ebook record available at https://lccn.loc.gov/2021060828

Our books may be purchased in bulk for promotional, educational, or
business use. Please contact your local bookseller or the Macmillan
Corporate and Premium Sales Department at (800) 221-7945, extension
5442, or by e-mail at MacmillanSpecialMarkets@macmillan.com.

First Edition 2022

Designed by Meryl Sussman Levavi

Printed in the United States of America

1   3   5   7   9   10   8   6   4   2

for Dad,
for Lindsay,
and especially for Mom

List of Characters

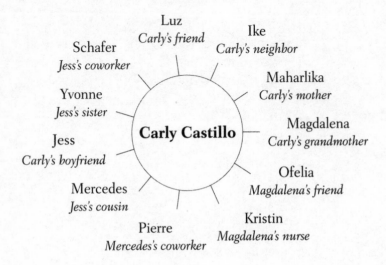

Carly Castillo

Luz
Carly's friend

Ike
Carly's neighbor

Schafer
Jess's coworker

Maharlika
Carly's mother

Yvonne
Jess's sister

Magdalena
Carly's grandmother

Jess
Carly's boyfriend

Ofelia
Magdalena's friend

Mercedes
Jess's cousin

Kristin
Magdalena's nurse

Pierre
Mercedes's coworker

Mama, let me go—she speaks

What every smart child knows—
To get grown you unlatch

Your hands from the grown
& up & up & up & up
She turns—latched in the seat

Of a hurricane. You let
Your girl what? You let

Your girl what?
I did so she do I did
so she do so—

Girl, you can ride
A hurricane & she do
& she do & she do & she do

—YONA HARVEY, "HURRICANE"

THE
LAST
KARANKAWAS

THE QUEENS OF
SANTO NIÑO

In the parking lot of Sacred Heart Catholic Church, in the cool dusk—which is a lie already, because it is never really cool, not even on this January evening, since this is Texas and, more specifically, this is Galveston—we wait. We stand on the concrete, ducking into windows of one another's parked cars to chat, or we sit inside with the AC blasting, or we lean against the walls and watch twilight draw shadows like a dark veil around the church. We are there before even the priest arrives to unlock the doors or the volunteer choir sets up their amps and microphone stands.

We prowl for things to do, tasks to help with. Some of us, like Yoli Sandoval and Tagay Macasantos, cart in vases of flowers from our new Buicks. Some of us, like Gloria Rivera or Marlo Suayan, arrive in hand-me-down Hondas with roses clipped from our backyard bushes—red, always red, for the holy day. We arrange flowers on the altar, or at the feet of the Blessed Mother's statue, or beside the portrait of the Sacred Heart of Jesus for whom this church is named. (When we think about that, we place more flowers by the portrait.) Some of us, humming with the energy of Santo Niño feast day, buzz about distributing paper programs—the programs we have used since we started this event many years ago. The pamphlets are battered, creased from our hands, pocked by inkblots and typos where we list the schedule of the Mass, the Tagalog prayers we will say together, the Tagalog songs we will sing. We place copies in each pew. We sit or kneel on the cushions, our fingers pressed to rosary beads. We tune our guitars and warble a few chords of the opening song. *O Santo Niñong marikit, sanggol na handog ng langit.*

Our voices—in song or in gossip—echo in every corner of the Catholic church on Broadway and 13th, which had been quiet before we arrived. We do very little quietly. And yet we quiet when Maharlika Castillo walks in. We turn to watch. She has that effect. She strides into Sacred Heart purposefully, with her daughter—Carly, is that her name? yes—by the hand.

Hello, we call out to them, and ask Maharlika, *Kumusta ka na?*

"I'm fine," she replies in pointed English. We flinch. We can't help it. Her English is sharp, intentional, a knife aimed at us. From her new crooked smile that shows teeth to this language she chooses in place of ours, she has built an arsenal; she wages war against us and the world.

Once she was kind to us. When she arrived, she found us almost immediately, as every FOB does—bonding first with the ones who worked at the hospital. We walked her through the corridors and buildings of John Sealy and the larger complex, taught her where the supply closets and cafeterias were, where to purchase scrubs, how to update charts and input medical data for UTMB system-wide. We instructed her on the Spanish phrases she would need to learn (*¿Cómo se escribe su nombre? ¿Tienes seguro médico?*). In our homes we passed her platters of sticky rice and whole fish fried crisp; when she wept with homesickness, we rubbed her shoulders, shushing her as we, too, had once needed. And on this feast day, the one day of the year when the Filipino community emerges from every sweaty corner of Galveston to unite and honor our patron saint, Maharlika was always there. She read at the podium. Sang in the choir. Served plates of pancit and adobo at the after-party. Was it just two years ago that she was last here? That she was one of us?

Maharlika, we used to say with admiration, marveling at the rare, beautiful name that means in our tongue something akin to nobility, to being of a line with royal blood. *Maharlika*.

But she is exalted now, or thinks she is. That is probably our fault.

She washed up on this island with a nursing degree and a job at the hospital despite having never set foot in America before. We thought she was embracing a new life, as we had. Unlike us, she had family here—her mother, who had immigrated long before. We did not really know her mother, and when she died of cancer not long after Maharlika arrived, we felt no sorrow, but we went dutifully to her funeral Mass, prayed the novena for her in Maharlika's apartment in Fish Village.

We should have noticed it then, but we didn't. Should have seen the shape Maharlika's grief took—curled up sideways on the couch, cheek to the padded arm, slippered feet tucked beneath her as if she hadn't the energy to take her shoes off. How she burst into sobs in the middle of shift-change meetings or standing in the Walmart checkout line. We should have seen that her grief was lasting. We did not expect that when the next loss came—her man—it would shift again, reshape itself into a grief for the old ways, her old lives in which she belonged to someone. A mother. A man. A country. When she was a child of something tangible in the world. Years from now, it will seem so obvious to us that she was never meant to be a mother or an immigrant.

"Carly," she says to the daughter, "sit here. Practice the prayers." In the front-row pew she has claimed for herself— Yoli Sandoval sees her coming and scoots her brood of five way down, hissing at them to move faster—she hands the girl our program. Carly clutches a rosary. She is six years old.

"Practice," Maharlika says. She prods her daughter, poking at her.

In the busy quiet of the church, we watch Carly squint at the words.

"Ama . . . Ama namin," she begins the Our Father in Tagalog, painfully slow. We look at her, the little mixed girl. "Sumasa—suma—" It hurts our ears, her accent; from our places at the podium, in the choir, by the entrance, we wince.

"Sumasalangit Ka," Maharlika corrects her. "You know this, Carly. Try again."

The child has grown, we think as we tilt our heads at her. She is taller than our own children, though Maharlika is small, like us. Was the child's father tall? In our memories we find only a hazy image: skin brown as ours, with wide shoulders and an arched nose. He came to one Santo Niño fiesta and sat in the back while Maharlika led us through the First Reading. He was Catholic, we assumed, like most of the Mexicans here, but he seemed to have forgotten even the English prayers, or maybe was simply uninterested in reciting them. During the Our Father when we reached out for one another's hands, he kept his tucked into the pockets of his khaki slacks.

If he was handsome, we did not notice. His slacks fit him poorly and looked ragged. We thought him crude, uncouth. Emblematic of his kind. We dislike Mexicans—the slouch of their posture, the growl of their accents, which sound like those of the peasants in the lower provinces we left across the Pacific. The way they speak Spanish even here, glaring when people insist on English, muttering *gringo* and *Tejas* and *did you know the border crossed us*, and all the while we have killed ourselves to learn the hard, sharp words of America, force our teeth and breathe through our noses to imitate their sounds, refusing to recall colonizers or occupation and instead remembering MacArthur, Kennedy, Elvis. But that is only the start of it. Listen: The important thing for this moment is that her man was Mexican. Maharlika loved him and hated our scorn. That one fiesta when we sneered at him was the first time she looked at us with shadowed eyes and saw something she was not part of.

The girl is speaking, or trying to. She casts her gaze past her mother to us, pleading. Baby Manon-og and Gloria Rivera, who have American grandchildren, take the most pity on her. *You can do it*, we dare to say aloud, *just go more slowly.*

Carly starts again, breaks again. She fumbles through our words, and we are afraid that what we suspect is true, that she has a Filipina mother but no Philippines anywhere in her. That Maharlika has cast us off, truly. That this—flaunting the half-breed child who came from her but knows nothing of our ways—is her simply going through the motions, another weapon she can wield.

———

We named our children traditional names: Rose, Lucia, Yolanda. Virgilio, Esteban, Rudolfo. Paz, Joel. Maria. Lourdes. Maria Lourdes. We named them as Americans: Jessica. Gregory. Belinda. Luke. Kaylee. Hannah. Blake. Madison. David. We named them for saints—Bernadette, Joseph, Catherine—and for political leaders—George, Lyndon, Benigno, Corazón—and for things that sound sweet, that make us smile—Cherry Pie, Little Boy, Honeybaby, Sunshine.

Maharlika did the same. At least we can say that.

We were there after her delivery as soon as the OB nurses would let us in (which, since seven of us work there, was very soon). Maharlika held the bundle of pink, puffy-faced girl to her breast.

Anong pangalan niya? we asked.

"Carly," she said. She smiled; we all did, remembering the first year Maharlika arrived here, 1979, how the only American song she knew the words to was "You're So Vain," she and her mother singing along with Carly Simon on cassette, how that song was the first thing she loved, truly, about America.

Our children were born here, or raised here, and when they are old enough, they will rename themselves. Benigno will not be called Ninoy, for fear that he will share that politician's fate; Corazón is called Cory, in hopes that she will. Yolanda is Yoly, or Yoli, or Yoyo (whichever distinguishes her from the three other Yolandas in her sophomore class). "Call me Birdie," Bernadette will say to her patients. Maria Lourdes's name badge says *Marlo*, or *Maria*, or *Lola*, or, in one confusing instance, *Odette*.

Long after her mother is gone, after she has cut ties with this part of her, Carly will stay Carly.

———

While Carly reads in the pew, we cluck our tongues and turn back to our work. We place the remaining programs and fluff cushions. Near the back of the church, we gather to discuss the order of things. *Rosie, go up to the podium and give the greeting. Make sure, Yoli, that the choir starts with the right song this time—last year maraming mga mistakes. Ihanda ang music. Lolo, your family will bring the bread and wine during the Offertory, can you make sure your husband doesn't wobble the decanter? Hay nako.*

We assign Beeb Macaraeg the honor of bearing the small Santo Niño statue in the procession before Mass. The doll-statue of the child Jesus, our Santo Niño, is waiting at the back of the church as we approach reverently. We part its bronze curls, arranging the ringlets just so. We smooth its crimson robes, spangled with designs of golden leaves, wiping away specks of dust and salt the island air has left.

"Why's he blond?" We turn at the small voice. Carly stares at us, at the Santo Niño statue in the midst of our fussing.

Ano? we ask. *What?*

"The baby Jesus. Why's he blond? He has dark hair when he's grown up, doesn't he? So why's he blond?"

We look to Maharlika. It's her child, after all. But she has turned around from her seat in the pew and faces us calmly, half a smile on her face. She props her chin in her hand and waits for something. For us, we realize. To answer.

The girl watches with steady eyes, no longer frantic. She is different from us. In this church, on this day, is when we look the most alike; gathered together, you see our similarities. Our skins the same mixture of brown and gold, our heights the same ranges (from five two down to an eyelash over four feet), the same broad noses. Beneath heavy lids, our dark eyes peer out; when we smile, our cheeks spread like the curves of a heart. Maharlika's girl has the look of our mixed children—many of us have married American men—but she is darker, more distinct, the skin of her shins marred by scrapes. She looks like a palm tree climber, a jetty jumper. She looks like the child who would challenge our kids to a game of tag and then jeer at them to run faster, to move their goddamn asses why don't they.

He is blond because . . . We trail off, trading glances. *Because he has always been.*

Because this is how he appeared to the people of Cebu, back in the 1800s, some of us chime in. (Is this true? We don't know. We might be making this up.)

"It's weird," Carly says, a six-year-old who has formed a clear opinion that cannot be shifted in the least: The blond child Jesus is weird. The end.

But now Maharlika speaks. "It's not weird." She squints at her daughter, shakes her head. "This is our patron saint, Carly. It's the way it has always been back home."

"Okay," Carly says. She shrugs. "Your home is weird then, Mama."

Maharlika sits back in her pew, the frown still on her face. We do not know what that frown means for her, but we share it, too. For now.

––––––

See us. See: We have put on our best, nothing less will do for Santo Niño. Our best means a dress, a long skirt frilled with lace or adorned with rosettes like Betty Villanueva's. Our best means silk slacks and tops that flutter about Baby Manon-og's arms, drape over Beeb Macaraeg's full breasts. Our best means jeans and sweatshirts for Lolo Diaz and Precious Orocio (*tomboys*, the rest of us hiss, a word more offensive in Tagalog than in English; we don't concern ourselves with that). And we have done our best—what we can—with this coarse, heavy hair of ours. We have curled it around our faces, pulled it back in prim knots, wound it up in braids or ponytails. Some of us, like Rosie Santos, wear bright scarves to cover scalps stripped clean by chemo. Some of us wear hats because the Black ladies of Galveston wear them to the Baptist churches and we find them dazzling. Some of us have retained the black black black of our youths (and some of us, we won't say who, are savvy with L'Oréal bottles).

See how Maharlika's hair, black like ours, is loose around her shoulders. She has a red knit sweater that is too warm for our January; gold glints at her earlobes. See, as we do, without surprise, that she wears men's khaki slacks. They drape too large around her thighs, and she has rolled them at the cuffs to keep from tripping over them. Recognize, as we do, that they are his.

A year ago, when he finally ran off, he left behind three generations of women—his mother, Maharlika, and the girl—plus his dress clothes and a case full of Vitalis hair tonic bottles. We urged Maharlika to donate them to the church, but she took to dabbing Vitalis on her temples or beneath the fall of hair. When she stopped doing that, she began wearing his clothes: a threadbare undershirt, a necktie dangling between her breasts, too-long socks stretched up to her knees. We pursed our lips when she stumbled into meetings red-eyed, reeking of liquor, her man's jeans hitched around her waist with a belt.

We should have said nothing, but we could not help ourselves.

You can't keep doing this, anak, we scolded, narrowing our eyes. *What would the Blessed Mother think? The Santo Niño? You shame them. You shame us.* We said this over and over—we had no sense of the damage we were doing—until one day she crumpled under our voices. She collapsed into a worn-housedress-overlarge-button-down-shirt-and-Crown-Royal-bottle pile on the floor of Marlo Suayan's rec room. She buried her face in the hem of her dress and cried wounded-animal noises.

The Blessed Mother, she wailed. *Iniwan niya ako. Everyone has.*

No one has abandoned you, we snapped. We were impatient, frustrated by her grief. Be stronger, we willed upon her. We had overcome worse back home. What was a vanished husband to the streets of Metro Manila, the slums lining the trash mountains we walked past daily? What was a dead mother—who had died comfortable, in an air-conditioned hospital with tile floors and ketamine—to the crunch of broken glass and rocks beneath bare feet? Here in this country we started anew, our work valued, money—more money than we had ever had—sent home to help the ones we left behind, which we could never do if we had stayed. What is American grief and loss compared to Filipino grief and loss? Smaller. Bearable.

We are lucky, we said aloud. *Your mother was lucky. You do not know how lucky we are.* But she kept sobbing. Everyone was gone, everyone had left her.

So we did, too. We bundled Maharlika into Marlo's husband's car, made him drive her home. We did not call to check on her for a week; we planned the song arrangement for the next Santo Niño reception instead. We needed the space, we thought, and so did she.

We were selfish.

Later we left messages—*Call us back, huh? Anak, we just want you to be well*—that she did not return.

In the months since, as she drifted away, she has left off the Vitalis, the drinking, but apparently not the clothes.

The Mass, for all its extra trappings to make it special, to make it Santo Niño, runs just over an hour. To the tune of *Maligayang araw at oras ng pagdating* (clap clap), *bilang pasalubong sa Santo Niñong giliw* (clap clap clap), we proceed with our husbands, brothers, children, children-in-law, grandchildren, and friends across the lot to the parish center. We emerge from the cold air of the church and step into the heavy warmth of Galveston; it only lasts the length of the parking lot, but our children complain. *Ew. It's so gross out here.* Our skin beads with sweat. Above our heads the palms sway. The air-conditioning, the orderly street signs, and the uncracked asphalt beneath our feet the only things separating this new home of ours from the old one.

Inside, the parish center is a flurry of color and movement: streamers of red and gold swaying from every stationary spot; disposable white-tissue tablecloths we bought from Walmart's clearance section; a disco ball casting dappled light across the still fully lit room. We swarm into the hall and claim spots at the tables. With the priest's help, we bless twenty-six trays of pancit, sinigang, chicken and pork adobo, kare-kare, menudo, and seven tubs of steamed white rice. We eat too much and drink Coke and Big Red mixed with the whiskey and vodka we sneak from the coolers in our cars. Every half hour or so one of us gives the traditional call—*Viva Santo Niño! Mabuhay ang hari ng mga hari!*—and we cry out the response—*Viva! Mabuhay!*

"What does that mean, Mama?" Carly asks.

"Long live the king of kings," her mother replies. "*Mabuhay* means—"

"Mama!" Carly interrupts. "What's *that*?"

At their spot against the wall, Maharlika is sipping a Coke and adjusting the belt around her pants. But Carly has turned to face the other children and is staring, eyes round, as they bring in the poles for the tinikling dance.

The older boys carry them in, two to each pole—ten-foot-long beams of bamboo worn silk-smooth by many hands. Two children carry the blocks of wood that the ends will rest upon, to keep the poles elevated, and to make sure the boy at each end will have room to move his hands during the dance. They lay the poles in parallel fashion, side by side, each resting on two blocks of wood.

The children will not dance for some time, not until

everyone has settled and is ready to watch performances. While we mill around, Maharlika takes Carly by the hand and leads her to where the tinikling poles wait their cue. Maharlika explains how the traditional dance works: Two people, one on each end, take both poles in hand and clap them on the ground, then bring them together with a swift slide and crash. Timed to the beat of the music—*clap-clap-CRASH clap-clap-CRASH clap-clap-CRASH clap-clap-CRASH.*

Within those counts, when the poles are separate entities, clapping on the ground for two beats, the dancers dance. A young man and woman (we have been her, in our day, long ago) step over and in between the poles, facing each other, facing away, twirling around—always lifting their feet out of harm's way before the poles crash together. *Step-step-OUT*, we told ourselves in our heads, *step-step-OUT step-step-OUT.*

Maharlika was the best of us. She does not say this, but we think it. She performed every year before she had the child. We had forgotten the memory.

There is no music. Everyone is talking, laughing, shouting as the fiesta carries on. In the din and the noise, we somehow notice, we turn to watch her—just us—as she shows Carly the steps.

"Here," she tells her daughter. "This is how my inay taught me."

Inay. Since she does not address Maharlika this way, we expect Carly to be unfamiliar with the word. But we blink our surprise when she nods. When she says, "Your mama."

And Maharlika begins to dance.

As she moves, she sings the familiar tune. Carly picks it

up and joins in, mangling our words but carrying the notes well. She claps in time to her mother's feet, darting in and out of the spaces between the still, heavy poles.

Maharlika raises her hands gracefully; she forms beautiful shapes in the air as she steps and twirls. Her bearing is straight, not hunched or rushed. Her face is flushed, and she is laughing. She, like us, remembers dancing the tinikling as a girl, when we learned its rhythm the hard way. Skirts hiked up above our knees with our hands. The crack of the poles on the block, keeping time, or smashing the frame of a careless foot between them. *Crunch.* We yelped, gritted our teeth, kept dancing. We didn't stop. *Yes, we think now, that is how it happened to me, too, just like that.* Maharlika raises her face to the ceiling, not watching the poles as she jumps in, out, spins, knowing where they are by heart. She is smiling, eyes closed, head tilted back.

Carly jumps between the poles with her. She lifts her arms, laughing. "Show me, Mama. Show me."

As one, we let out a sigh, a release. We feel the moment break apart. Maharlika lowers her chin, opens her eyes to her daughter, and takes her hands.

"Step-step-out," she says, slowing her movements from fluid pace to a choppy crawl. "Step-step-out." Her smile has brittled, ready to crack.

And suddenly, as if there were not miles of space between us, we know exactly what she is thinking—we are thinking it, too. We think: We are not ready for this, to be the elders, the teachers, the mothers. We are still daughters and sisters, girlfriends and wives. We have partners who love us, yes? Parents with years yet to pass their words, their stories, down to us. We can still be the girls who dance the tinikling, yes, yes. We will never be old, or we already are.

Viva Santo Niño! one of our husbands shouts, and we turn toward the sound, obedient, accepting.

Viva! we call out.

Mabuhay ang hari ng mga hari!

"Mabuhay!" That is Carly, clapping her hands with joy. Maharlika says nothing; she does not look at us. If she had, we could have told her we understand that she never wanted this role of single parent. In this place we pretend is the Philippines but really is just a steaming island off the American coast with palm trees that are not ours and oyster-shell gravel that is not ours and brown-skinned people who are not us. We were wrong to think that if she had just been stronger, she could learn to love all of it.

Maharlika shoulders her purse, lifts Carly to her hip, and leaves the parish hall without a glance back. We do not try to stop her. We wouldn't know how.

———

Some other things we don't know, at least not yet:

That in two weeks, Precious Orocio will be deported because she lost her job and let her papers lapse. Not an uncommon story, but then she ran a red light and was discovered. Her tears in the airport will ruin us. A month later, Betty Villanueva will follow her back to Manila—her papers were fine, but her father was sick. We are nothing if not dutiful.

That tomorrow, Carly will practice the tinikling with her best friend, a boy—Mexican—named Jess. She will teach him to pound the bamboo poles (they use twigs from the live oak on Dolphin Avenue) in time to the *clap-clap-CRASH clap-clap-CRASH* of the song she sings. She will tap her foot in the space between the sticks as if testing the water in a bath. She will make him practice with her every day after school when he doesn't have Little League.

That two months from now, before her night shift begins, Maharlika will kiss Carly goodbye, lift her mother-in-law's hand to her forehead in blessing, and head out the door for work. Her mother-in-law will find a note, and she and the child will never see her again. Some of us will hear, through our relatives on Mindoro, that Maharlika bought a secret plane ticket home. Carly will grow up under her grandmother's care—learn Mexican and American ways, learn half a history. But she will master the tinikling a month after her mother leaves, the step-shuffle-twirl without smashing her foot between the twigs; she will laugh so brightly that Jess will laugh, too, not understanding what she has gained.

That eighteen years from now, Hurricane Ike will sweep through Galveston, snatching palm trees up by the roots, sending water and refuse from the bay into our homes and the wooden floor of Sacred Heart. We will move the feast day and fiesta to a church in south Houston, one with reliable AC and cushions on all the kneelers. Sacred Heart will be renovated, revitalized, but the Santo Niño fiesta will never come back to it.

That twenty-one years from now, one of us will receive a letter from Precious Orocio, who thinks she saw Maharlika walking into the church in San Teodoro. She can't be sure, Precious, but she would swear it was Maharlika by the man's barong she wore. And her bearing, of course—like something queenly holding her up. Her hair had gone white, ran loose around her thin shoulders. She raised her chin as she entered the room, Precious wrote. When people called out *Kumusta ka na?* she looked right through them.

IGNITION

Carly

She isn't sure what triggers it, why her bubbling anger geysers up and out. At first, the fight is all noise, Carly screaming *I'm going and you can't stop me*, her grandmother hollering back *You're not going anywhere, me entiendes*, their voices spiraling in a shrill kind of harmony. *Yes, I am. No, you're not.* But then something cracks behind Carly's eyes. She leans in close—so close she spots a streak of Pond's cold cream still white on Magdalena's jaw, breathes in the Vicks Magdalena smears nightly on her chest, its sharp smell pricking her lungs—and hisses, *Do not tell me what I can or can't do.*

For that one electric moment, Carly feels infinite. Flames ignite deep in her breast, the words spill like golden smoke between her lips: a woman, she is a woman now, after all, and will claim her own power. But no sooner have the words left her lips than they are replaced with a gasp, her grandmother's palm popping hard against her mouth, quick as lightning from a blue Galveston sky.

It isn't so much the force of the smack but the shock that snaps Carly's head back. Magdalena has not struck her in three years, not since she was twelve, grounded from going with the other junior high cheerleaders to Moody Gardens for the day because she made a C on a social studies test, and she stomped her foot in the doorway of Magdalena's bedroom, declaring *My* real *mom would love me enough to let me go.* The slap she earned that day still reverberates in her muscles on occasion—when they drive past the apartments on Holiday where she knows her parents had lived but Magdalena looks purposefully straight ahead, or when she catches Mrs. Suayan or any of the other Filipina ladies at Sacred Heart watching her during Mass with faces like scales, weighing her against the woman they once knew but of whom Carly has only cobweb shreds of memory. But this has nothing to do with her mother, not this time.

She simply wants to borrow the car and drive herself to Katy, where Jess is playing in a summer baseball league his mom insisted he do to keep his skills up during off-season. And maybe she only has a learner's permit, but hasn't she been driving for nearly a year, all over the island and even into the Bay Area a couple times? Can't she be trusted with this quick trip up for the morning game, bringing the car back before Magdalena's Saturday shift at the school library is over? She makes her case, her voice calm—that won't last long—and she smiles hopefully. *So can I, Grandma?* But her grandmother snorts. *A game? So vas a ir an hour away, through the city, for a game? Because you can't watch Jesusmaría play any day of the week right here?* Laughs and shakes her head, making Carly seethe with the injustice of it, and then the fight, their voices rising and falling, the slap that ends it.

As if Magdalena were not a rebel herself. Carly knows her grandmother's independence like no one else—her *no me digas que no* a famous refrain around Fish Village—and here Carly tries to show her own yet earns nothing but a smack on the mouth. There must be pride in there somewhere, Carly thinks as she huffs and turns away, her lips smarting, listening to her grandmother call *You're not going because I said so y se acabó* through the slammed door. Somewhere deep down, doesn't she feel approval for her granddaughter's grit? Doesn't she marvel?

So the next morning, Carly steals the car. But *steal* is a strong word, really—as she insists later that evening, loudly over Magdalena's howls—for what essentially amounts to slipping the spare key off its hook and coaxing Hector to give her a ride across the island, to where the Harris Elementary staff parking lot sits nearly empty except for her grandmother's Grand Marquis and a handful of cars belonging to the other janitorial staff and library assistants preparing for the start of summer school, then unlocking the Grand Marquis with shaking hands and sliding into the driver's seat, adjusting the mirrors and seat and easing out of the parking lot onto Broadway, heart jackhammering against her ribs with exhilaration and fear.

She feels the slaps already, hears the scolding and screaming she will be in for tonight, but still she believes that Magdalena will admire her spirit—how can she not, when it is hers, the one she gave Carly, the one she fostered when both parents cast her off? And even though Jess's team will lose the game—despite him going three for four and snagging a line drive on a diving catch worthy of *SportsCenter*—and afterwards, under the bleachers as he tangles his hands in her hair and she presses against his sweat-stained uniform, when she confesses about the car and he laughs so hard he almost collapses, telling her *You're gonna be in so much shit, babe, I don't know if this was worth it*, she knows he is wrong. It is worth it. Not his game, not him, but the drive. Pushing down the gas pedal, *on on on*, climbing the causeway with Galveston Bay glinting gray and green beneath her, *forward forward forward*, the hot air whipping her hair, fingers clenched around the wheel. *Please please please*. Drivers zooming past and changing lanes at light speed without a care as she sings loudly along with 97.9's hour of 2Pac to drown out the fear burbling in her throat, focusing instead on the delight, the joy of the road ribboning beneath her and unfurling in the rear-view mirror into familiar shapes, nothing she recognizes up ahead.

THE WAYS OF MEN

Jess

William the Conqueror was a warrior, but according to the book, people called him a bastard. *The* Bastard. Jess doesn't think that is such a bad nickname. Hell, maybe half the other kids in Fish Village are bastards—fathers living in the house but not legally bound to be there, or staying in their own place on the mainland and visiting every other weekend, or working on an Odessa oilfield and sending misspelled birthday e-cards. Or simply an empty space, having split long before, quit, for whatever reason, midway through father duties. So many states of gone.

The driver hits a pothole and the school bus stumbles. With one hand Jess tightens his grip on the book to keep it from falling, with the other grabs the duffel beside him on the seat. The rest of the team is asleep, and they don't wake. Jess presses his fingertips to the window and lets the outside seep through, a slow warmth. He guesses they are on the causeway now; he thinks he can smell salt, but the windows aren't open and he's probably just being romantic, as Carly so often says.

She won't be waiting for him. He told her there was no point—the game was a doubleheader up in Port Arthur and wouldn't be done until midnight, most likely. Then there was an accident that completely blocked 73. Then general stupidity on I-10. And here they are, nearly three a.m. and barely arriving. As rain spits against the windows, he feels better knowing she isn't sitting in her Corolla in the Ball High parking lot. Carly grows cranky and uneasy in the nighttime. She'd be blasting the radio, drumming her fingers impatiently on the wheel, trying to widen her eyes and cursing the bus driver for being so slow. When Jess arrived, she'd make him drive and then she'd be too tired to do anything anyway. Better to see her tomorrow at Sacred Heart for Mass and then fool around after. And in just another year—graduation. Once high school is done, they will have their whole lives to fool around.

About twenty minutes left, he figures, before they pull into the school lot. He opens the book and, with his Nokia as a light, finds his place again some 960 years ago.

He was called William the Bastard for much of his life, usually by his enemies, and always behind his back. He was the product of an affair between Robert I, duke of Normandy, and a woman named Herleva, a tanner's daughter. After Robert died while returning from a pilgrimage to Jerusalem, William became duke of Normandy in his stead. He was only 8 years of age.

Life was rough even then without a father. Rougher, probably. But William's father had left him a legacy worth having. So there was that.

When Mr. Collier began their unit on early British history, Jess thought it looked lame. Who gave a shit about the British? In seventh grade, Ms. Morton had taught them how Galveston held Native roots, Spanish, French, Mexican, Texan. Jess looked up more beyond class, devoured the information he found. The Karankawas roaming up and down the beaches; Cabeza de Vaca shipwrecked on their shores; Jean Lafitte founding his own pirate kingdom; even the weatherman Isaac Cline denying the Great Hurricane of 1900 until it was bearing down. Juneteenth, Jewish immigrants from Eastern Europe, the Maceo mafiosos during Prohibition. Nothing could be as interesting as their own story.

Jess rolled his eyes at Mr. Collier's assigned reading, carelessly flipping through pages with boring kings and queens of varying shades of white. But he paused at the portrait of William the Conqueror. Something intrigued him: how the crown rested in an arrogant tilt on the man's brow, the longsword propped against his shoulder (Jess liked his style, liked the kind of guy who would insist on holding a sword in a royal portrait). The way he faced left but aimed his eyes boldly to the right, directly at the viewer, as if he had overhead Jess muttering an insult and cut sharply back to confront him. Jess went to the Galveston library after practice that week and checked out a biography on William the Conqueror. When the other guys teased him about reading for fun, he said it was for a paper.

He reads until the bus lurches to a stop in front of the school, near the team's collective pickups and sedans; then he steps off into the slanting rain, carrying his duffel in one hand and the book in the other, tucked close to keep it dry on the quick jog to his truck. He takes Avenue O, then cuts over 33rd to Harborside, a slight detour but worth it.

He prefers the bayside to the Gulf, the scrolled-up sails of yachts and the occasional hulking mass of a cruise ship more interesting to him than the brown-sand beaches or the San Luis or the Seawall.

Jess spots the smoking engine on 16th before he sees the small man leaning over his open hood. The bend of his back, the stained gray hoodie, look vaguely familiar. Jess slows to a stop and lowers the passenger window, already knowing how Carly would mock him, say it was cold out, and raining, and fucking late. And she'd be right. He is tired. He should go straight home. But he knows this guy, he thinks.

"Hey, man, you good?"

The man turns, looks out from within his soaked hoodie, and Jess sees he is right. A neighbor from one of the houses near where Carlos Saldivar lives, next to the Black family with two Chihuahuas. He is Vietnamese or Korean or something.

"Don't you live on Marlin?" Jess calls out, squinting in the cool rain.

"Yes," the man says. "I know you?"

"Jess Rivera. I live on Dolphin."

"Ah." He nods. "Yes, I've seen your sisters running around."

Jess has four younger sisters, energetic, social. "They like running around."

"And a mother, right?"

"She doesn't really leave the house." Jess clears his throat. "Look, you need to use the phone? A ride or something?"

"I'm on my way to work, I can call to get this towed when I get there. I'm going to the pier."

Jess sighs. It isn't too far, and this late, there is almost no one else on the road. "I can take you."

The man nods again, as if deigning to accept this favor. He leans into his car to grab a black backpack, then locks it and climbs into Jess's passenger seat. He shivers the wet off him, quick like a dog. "I'm Vinh," he says. "Pham."

They shake hands; the man's palm is calloused, rough, and Jess wonders how his own palm feels to him. Soft? Should he tighten his grip? He pulls a U-turn.

"So you work at the pier?" he asks.

His radio is set on 97.9 The Box as usual. A Bone Thugs-N-Harmony song kicks in and Mr. Pham grimaces. Without a word he reaches over and turns the knob, spins to a country station, then, satisfied, leans back again. Jess doesn't know if he should be offended, insulted, angry—he settles on amused. Mr. Pham gives him a sidelong glance and smiles.

"I'm a fisherman," he says.

"Oh." Jess went fishing with Ramiro and Carlos once, years ago; Ram's dad had a buddy with a boat they borrowed. They took it out on the Gulf and caught nothing but sunburns. "What do you fish for?"

"I have two boats, a shrimper and an oyster boat. But right now is oyster season."

Jess knows nothing about oysters, other than he likes them fried and in po'boys, while Mrs. Castillo and Carly prefer to slurp them raw. "Cool."

He pulls into the pier where Mr. Pham says his boat is moored. Casts an eye over the one he points out. A wide, flat-bottomed, squatty-looking vessel—almost like a houseboat. Dingy, stained with rust and grime. The roof is wide and flat. A faded *Miss Saigon* script on the side of it. "That's yours?"

"Yes. Thank you for the ride." Mr. Pham gathers his backpack and glances back at Jess critically. "You're on spring break?"

"School got out yesterday."

"And you are a strong boy. Athlete, right?"

Jess wonders where this is going, tightening his shoulders slightly. "I play baseball."

"Have you ever worked on a boat?"

"No."

He nods. "You decide you want some extra money, you come see me. We are going out every day this week. We could use you in dredging." He nods again—a man of few words, Jess is learning—and slams the car door.

Jess expects everyone to be asleep when he pulls into the house, but the light in his mother's room is on. He closes the front door carefully, steps into the Pine-Sol-and-old-carpet smell. Hints, too, of whatever his sister Yvonne cooked for dinner, something spicy enough to lace each breath you took with tears.

He moves quietly, but not quiet enough. The bedroom door creaks—he has time for a quick inhale to brace himself—and his mother steps out. A mug of coffee in one hand, her hair loose and waving around her shoulders, the brown shot through with gray. As always, she wears the same robe, the green-gone-gray one Dad gave her long ago.

"So," she says. "You're back."

Because it is expected, he walks over and bends to kiss her. The skin of her cheek dry, tasting of cold beneath the quick sweep of his lips.

"Sorry it's so late. We got in and then I stopped because this man—"

"The game went well? You started?"

Of course, she only cares about the game. "Yes. They replaced me in the seventh when we were up by six."

"Saving you." She nods with approval. "Playoffs coming soon. How did you bat?" she asks, voice gone suddenly sharp.

"I went two for four, a double and an RBI single. But—"

"Two for four, chinga'o. Just because it's spring break doesn't mean you can slack off. More batting practice is what you need. Un tonto, this only son of mine."

They shouldn't hurt anymore, her comments; he knows to be ready for them, to let them roll off. But every time she calls him a fool it stings, makes it so he is no longer a man of seventeen but a small boy, her words clinging like barbs under the skin. "Come on, Mama."

"And you left your cleats on. See, now you've got dirt everywhere." She points. Jess looks down. When he raises his eyes, she is lifting the mug to her mouth and walking back into the room. The door closes with a groan behind her.

His fists hurt from where he is clenching them; his throat burns. He won't cry, goddamn it. What is he, six?

He showers, weary, puts his face to the tile as the heat beats down on his shoulders. And finally, the sanctuary of his room. As the only boy, he gets his own; the girls each share, two on two. His baseball trophies are piled on the bottom shelf of the closet. Spines of Hank the Cowdog paperbacks and Tom Clancy hardcovers—he paid for the former, swiped the latter from the library—lean drunkenly against the mirror on his dresser. Empty beer bottles take up place of pride on the windowsill, remnants from the party last year after he hit a walk-off double and the Torna-dos won bi-district. Jess saved some of the bottles, rinsed them out, lined them up. They stand straight as a regiment, a few with peeling labels.

There are letters beside them, too, a small, unopened stack. He knows without looking that the postmark says Huntsville, Texas. Texas State Penitentiary. That they are addressed to Jesusmaría Rivera; his dad always calls him by his full name, which was his own father's. Jess hates it.

Stretching out on the bed, a long, long sigh escaping him as his back muscles flatten on the mattress, he blinks into the darkness. Oystering seems like hard work. He doesn't know much, but he's seen boats coming in from the bay in the early mornings or at night, their nets up like butterfly wings. Were those oyster boats or shrimpers? Fuck, who knows the difference. But maybe he can learn. Mr. Pham was nice, and he could use the extra money as long as it doesn't interfere with baseball. Jess does okay on water. He never gets seasick on the ferry over to Bolivar, not even that time fishing with Mr. Jackson when the boat hit choppy waters on the Gulf and Ram threw up all over the deck. He will go by Mr. Pham's house the next evening after he sees Carly, he decides, and accept.

Restless now, he switches on his light. He ignores the letters, reaches for the book instead. Opens to the year 1045.

Young William's early reign was uneasy, riddled with violence and corruption as feudal barons fought to steal his lands. Several of William's guards died and his teacher was murdered. King Henry I of France came to William's aid in those early years by knighting him when he was a teenager.

Jess envisions the sword, a flash of silver in the sunlight, coming down to tap the boy's thin shoulders. You were a man then, weren't you? You were respected, you were prized. A ceremonial touch was all it took. You had honor then.

———

Yvonne promises to get up early and make him breakfast on the first day; even though he has to report to the pier well before sunrise, Yvonne insists. He knows better than to argue once her mind is set. She is sixteen, but it is her nature these days to take charge. Since their father's departure, and their mother's slow drifting away, Yvonne has become the matriarch. She dresses Sarita in the mornings and braids her hair how she likes, helps Ana Laura with her English homework, makes sure Francie's softball uniform is always washed. "Mama won't like the noise of us getting up that early," Jess says, and Yvonne responds as he expected: "Mama can suck it."

So at 4:30 a.m. Monday Yvonne is throwing tortillas on the comal, waiting until they blister black on one side, the way he likes. She snatches them off the skillet bare-fingered—Jess remembers his mother's hands, deftly turning the masa, unscathed from the heat. *It's a woman thing*, she said when little Jess and Yvonne asked, *pura mexicana*. Pride and laughter warmed her voice; later she soothed Yvonne's small, singed fingertips on ice cubes when she wasn't quite womanly or mexicana enough.

By 5:15 a.m. he is climbing aboard the *Miss Saigon*, with Mr. Pham watching to check his balance. Whatever Jess does seems to work. Mr. Pham nods—that nod—and introduces him to the other crew member, a moreno named Rey with an eagle tattoo on his arm and a gold tooth that flashes when he smiles. Normally the deckhand crew includes at least one other, but their regular guy picked up a construction job inland. "We can use the help," Mr. Pham says. "And call me Vinh."

"Here." Rey tosses him blue rubber work gloves, damp with the early-morning cool and bay water. Jess pulls them on, flexing his fingers. They smell of dirt and brine.

The engine rumbles, spitting out diesel fumes and exhaust; then the boat is puttering out from the marina into the waters of the bay. The sun, unseen, casts weak light over the horizon, the white tiled roofs and bright pink and green houses of the island's east side. Jess regrets not bringing a thermos of coffee like the one Rey gulps from. Instead, he pulls the hood of his sweatshirt up over his hair and sits on the bench, damp seeping into his jeans, watching the sparkle of sunlight on the brown water.

There isn't much to do while the *Saigon* heads out to the reef where Vinh has a lease to dredge. Jess sits, grabs the seat occasionally to keep from falling when the boat pitches. Sits, and looks at the water, and thinks.

He didn't tell his mother about the job, or where he would even be that day. Before Dad went away, she used to kiss Jess's forehead when he went anywhere. *Ten cuidado, Jesusmaría*, she'd say and make a cross on his forehead with her thumb. She would attend his baseball and football and soccer games, before he focused on baseball for good, brushing the curling strands of dark hair over his brow after games for no reason. That stopped the night gunshots cracked near their house, when tires squealed and Dad screamed at them to get down get down get *down*, when the girls stopped crying and no bullets had come for them. In the chaos, his heart pounding, Jess ran to his parents' mattress and flipped it, grabbed the bags of pot and cocaine tucked beneath, then locked himself in the bathroom and flushed them down. He had known for a while, his friends always talked about it, and maybe Mama just refused to see it. She was the one pounding on the bathroom door, screaming at Jess to open it, to let her in, to stop what he was doing, but Dad stayed silent, even when the cops came and took him away. Three years later, Yvonne is the one crossing foreheads and giving kisses. Mama still talking about how important it is to have a real man in the house. Looking at Jess with heavy eyes and a heavier mouth, as if he were a bronze statue that could never be gold.

They arrive where Vinh's lease begins. Vinh guides the boat into a slow, loping circle around the bay. "This is the dredge," he announces, pointing to the chain-and-metal basket, about four feet wide, suspended from an arm over the side. He moves some levers, and the dredge drops with a splash. As Vinh eases the boat in circles, the dredge dredges. Jess listens to the scrape, feels it rumbling and stuttering over unseen rock and reef, in his feet, shuddering up through the deck.

The men move without explanation, stopping to talk Jess through the process only when it is clear he doesn't understand. He learns the rhythm quickly, more quickly than even he expected. Once Vinh decides the dredge is full, he uses the winch to lift its dripping mass into the air. Jess and Rey pull it in and over the stainless steel table between them, where it drops its haul. Soon his jeans are soaked from the spray; Rey wears rubber overalls, which he eyes enviously. "You should get some," Rey says, but Jess shrugs and responds, "I'm only here for the week."

Rey hands him a hatchet. He stares at it. The short,

squat blade in his hand, his brown fingers around the smooth handle. Medieval, this weapon, this tool. Ancient, even.

"Focus, chamaco." Rey snaps his fingers, and he blinks up at him. "Like this, ves."

Jess hacks at a small clump of oysters the way Rey shows him; he works carefully, mindfully. Rey has been doing this for dozens of years—his hands a blur of fingers and blade. Rey shows him how to feel for the oyster, how to sense the different textures and shapes of shell versus reef. Jess feels like a stone carver, creating a lumpy orb from a knot of dark mud. When the oysters appear in his hand, seemingly from nowhere, he tosses them into the pail at the end of the table. Anything smaller than three inches goes back overboard; Rey says they need to keep growing so the reefs won't die out. Jess smiles at the idea that these little clods of dirt and shell will spawn, grow larger, create worlds beneath the dark water.

It is a kind of dance, set to the oily drone of the diesel engine and the Tejano music Vinh blasts on his little radio. The motions of it spark in Jess's mind, sing in his muscles like the 6–4–3 double play. Vinh lifting the dredge, dumping its haul; Rey and Jess culling out oysters, sliding them this way or that; the empty mouth of the dredge swinging back out and disappearing into the water again. Shortstop to second to first, smooth as sea glass. On the field, he is the six; out here, he is part of the cycle, too. The wind picks up, but he doesn't notice. He reaches for another clump of mud and reef.

He has baseball practice Wednesday morning, so Vinh gives him the day off. Hector's cousin from Dallas is in town, and the guys gather at the park that afternoon to play a game of touch football. Though Jess is bone-tired, between practice and the bay, he doesn't want to miss a fun part of his spring break.

The wind off the Gulf is unnaturally cold, tinged with salt but no hint of its usual damp warmth; it gnaws at his lips, his ears, as he jogs from Carly's house on Albacore to Lindale Park. He makes out a knot of bodies away from the playground equipment, clustered around the stretch of empty field. Ramiro is already there, cornrows like black seams along his scalp, with Carlos and Hector and Hector's cousin Freddy, a skinny guy in a blue zip-up hoodie and wifebeater. Jess grabs a beer from the cooler; they haven't bothered with ice.

After shooting the shit and stamping their feet to warm up, they get down to business. I-formation, with Carlos at QB for both sides. Jess takes up a post in the back; familiar energy hums in the tips of his fingers and the balls of his feet, or maybe it is the beer. He hasn't played football in so long the thrill feels illicit, as if he is cheating on baseball.

"Hike!" Carlos turns for the handoff. The ball slides into Jess's grip and he is gone. He spins past Hector and makes it as far as the rusty merry-go-round before Freddy wraps him up and out of bounds. The next play, Carlos has the option and pitches it; Jess takes it all the way. They win, naturally.

Later they sit on the merry-go-round, chugging from the cans, warmed enough from the exercise to sweat in the chill wind. Ram wipes his mouth with the back of his hand. "You hear from your dad at all, Jess?" he asks. He has fond memories of Orlando Rivera, who once open-hand-slapped one of Jess's cousins from the Valley for calling Ram the N-word.

"Not really." The beer tastes sour, but Jess swallows.

"Where's your dad at?" Freddy wants to know.

Jess stays still, doesn't meet his eyes. "He's in Huntsville."

"Locked up," Hector adds. "For running drugs."

"No shit?" Freddy's brows lift. "Respect."

Hector pops the top on another. "Stone-cold baller, Mr. Rivera. You should've seen him, primo. Running them right out of his house, even the Bloods."

"Aren't there cartels and shit down here?" Freddy asks.

"No," says Carlos, rolling his eyes.

"*Yes*," says Hector. His voice carries a hint of drama, of relish. He's like that. Jess's skin crawls; rare temper rises in his throat. "Mr. Rivera wasn't scared of them, either. Just kept running his whole chunk of the east side with balls of steel until the cops busted him."

"Shut the fuck *up*, Hector," Ram says, snatching Hector's untouched beer from his hand and glaring. "Why are we even talking about this?"

"Jess doesn't care. Do you, guey?"

"He's right," Jess snaps. He fights to keep his voice and face calm. "Shut the fuck up, dude."

Hector looks annoyed at being chastised in front of the cousin he is trying to impress. He mutters, "Shit, bro, didn't think you'd be *touchy* about it." Ram leans over and passes Hector another beer, brings up something that happened in history class last week, and they all begin to laugh. Even Jess, fingers vised around his beer can—remembering the way he grips the hatchet on the boat—telling himself inwardly, *Laugh*.

The trouble began for William in the year 1066. It is believed that he visited England and met with his cousin Edward the Confessor, the childless English king, where Edward prom-

ised to make William his heir. William planned to take over the English throne upon Edward's death, only to be betrayed: On his deathbed, Edward instead granted the kingdom to Harold Godwinson, head of a powerful noble family. In January 1066, Edward died and Harold was proclaimed King Harold II. William began making plans to invade.

The stack of letters glints in the dim light. It has been two weeks, but he hasn't moved it. Jess switches off the lamp and closes his eyes.

The girls usually watch TV in the evenings, but this time only Yvonne and Ana Laura stay up. Jess arrives home after a long day of dredging and unloading their haul—thirty-eight sacks—at Johansson Oysters. Both girls are snoring in front of Jay Leno. In the kitchen, a plate of arroz con pollo sits on the stove for him, covered with a paper towel.

He opens the fridge for a drink, and she speaks from behind, startling him, as she usually does these days. "Your sister left that for you," Mama says. "The least you can do is eat it."

The skin around her eyes is loose, as if too weary to fasten to her bones. The bar stool gives a creak as she settles in, even though she is little more than a ratty robe and what once was the best ass on the block according to his shithead friends.

"Pour me an iced tea," she says quietly.

"Yes, ma'am."

When he slides the full cup to her, she doesn't drink from it, only runs her finger around the lip.

"You're getting skinny out there on the bay." She tilts her chin, a gesture he has seen in Sarita. "They feed you o qué?"

He pauses with his hand on the covered plate, surprised. He didn't know she knew about his job. Yvonne must have told her, or one of the girls. "We bring food sometimes. Mostly snacks. We eat when we get back on land."

She stares into her tea, appearing not to hear him, and when she speaks again, he knows she wasn't listening. "Those letters. His. You haven't read them, have you." It wasn't a question.

Jess pushes buttons on the microwave and watches the plate spin, the numbers blink down. How long can he stay this way, his back to her, her question unanswered? Avoiding the conflict. He wishes for peace; he longs for it. He is tired of every brief exchange becoming a battle.

But he steadies his shoulders. "No." He waits.

She scoffs. "Can't forgive, can you, even for a father who loves you, who provided for you." Her tone has an edge now. "Maybe you can't make time to visit, but you can at least read what he's taken time to say."

"Why should I?" Jess asks over the beeping of the microwave, hearing his voice rising in anger. Again. "Why should I read anything he sends? He fucking screwed us—"

"*Watch your mouth.*"

"He *freaking* screwed us, whatever." He turns, repeats the same words he has used for three years. They fall easily off his tongue. "He did it to himself, Mama. *He's* the reason he's not here, okay?" Can she not see how weary they both are, how rote this conflict? Same refrain. Same wounds. They dredge it over and over.

The fire dies from her eyes and she lowers them to the counter.

The microwave beeps, finished. He sighs, takes the hot

plate, and holds it out to her. "Want some?" he asks, more softly.

"He'll be calling Saturday, you know. You don't have a game this time, so you'll talk to him. You owe him that."

I don't owe him shit, he thinks.

"You're a good player, Jesusmaría, a strong hitter, but you don't have the discipline for the pros. You need to stop wasting time on the bay when you could be getting ready for the playoffs. There will be scouts there. You need to work harder, think less selfishly. Be better than you are."

There is no heat in her voice. Only the weary. Somehow that hurts worse, and this time he feels tears well up despite his best efforts. She takes her mug and walks into her room, closing the door behind her.

Jess swipes at his eyes. William the Conqueror once cut off the hands and feet of citizens who had mocked his mother—the daughter of a tanner—by hanging animal hides on their walls in insult. The book said nothing set off his rage like disrespect to his mother.

His sisters sleep soundly on the couch. Blue light flickers beneath Mama's bedroom door. She will be sitting upright in front of the TV, a cigarette smoking in the ashtray on the nightstand, the portrait from her wedding day propped beside it. In another life, he would kneel at her feet, lift her knuckles to the corners of his eyes, and promise to be better, to conquer every field he set foot on.

———

The Friday sun, bright despite the chill, beats down as Jess stands at the back of *Miss Saigon*. Country music thumps through the speakers, and Rey hums along. Vinh turns the boat in slow circles, dragging the dredge. They cull, Jess not nearly as quickly as Rey but getting faster. The pile of oysters in the pails at their feet grows steadily larger. They will make their quota, fifty sacks, by ten a.m. easily.

"Have you ever brought in only a few sacks?" Jess asks. "Or nothing at all?"

Vinh chuckles without humor. "Oh, sure. Usually red tide." When the waters become too warm, too salty, red tide algae blooms. Jess is an islander, knows red tide means you can't eat bay shellfish. "And hurricanes, of course," Vinh says. "They wipe out reefs. Alicia was bad. We're back to normal now, but it took years. Hurricanes"—he shakes his head, makes a gesture like a sloppy sign of the cross—"are very, very bad for oystermen."

Jess loves the work at this point, the routine of it. Like baseball, a soothing ritual, one his body could settle into and remember. *Muscle memory*, his father used to call it, when he was in Little League working on his swing. *Get your muscles to remember, mijo.*

When they tie up at the pier, Vinh holds up a hand to stop him from jumping off. "You do good work."

"Thanks." Jess glances at Rey, who smiles.

"Back to school next week?"

"Yeah."

Vinh's eyes, squinting in his leathered face beneath his trucker hat, are direct. "Rey and I like you. You're a steady worker, you don't complain, and you learn fast. And the bay is good for you, I think. Watermen are meant to be on the water." He indicates himself and Rey in a short nod. "Just so you know, you can come back and work for me, whenever you want."

It is high praise from Vinh, and a flush of pleasure creeps up Jess's face. "Thanks, but this was just temporary. I play ball, you know. I'm pretty good—I'm getting recruited to go college or pro."

"Okay. You finish school. You play ball." Vinh shrugs as if he doesn't care about those things, and Jess knows he probably doesn't. "But if you change your mind, you come see me."

———

A descendant of Vikings, William of Normandy had a family tree made up of raiders and warriors; his great-great-great-grandfather raided and pillaged northern France in the early 10th century. Perhaps it was this heritage that drove him to land on Britain's southeast coast at Pevensey on Sept. 28, 1066. William assembled a fleet and an army, but their advance was delayed for several weeks due to bitterly cold northern winds. Meanwhile, the Norwegian army invaded England from the North Sea, and King Harold rapidly moved his army north to defend against them. After defeating the Norwegians, Harold unwisely marched his troops back down to meet William, without a break, without any rest. This would be a key decision in his downfall.

William must have been frightened, Jess thinks as he closes the book that night. But he wouldn't have let anyone see—not the soldiers who looked to him for strength, not the people who whispered *bastard* behind his back. He would have set his shoulders and raised his chin for war. If anyone saw him tremble, he would have said it was simply the cold.

They are coming to the battle scene now.

———

"A prisoner from the Texas State Penitentiary at Huntsville is attempting to contact you. If accepted, this call will be charged collect and may not exceed twenty minutes. Do you wish to accept this call?"

Jess adjusts his grip on the landline. His palms have gone sweaty, which irritates him and thickens his voice. "Yeah. Yes."

Some clicking noises, a mechanical whir. Jess thinks how stupid this is. No one is there; his sisters gone on various errands; even Mama, who rarely leaves the house unless it's for her janitorial day shifts at UTMB, has disappeared. He should just hang up. No one would know, and it would serve the asshole right—

"Hello, Eva? Can you hear me?"

The voice. His voice. Higher than Jess remembers, a bit rougher, too. Was that time? Nervousness? Some mysterious prison reason?

"Hello?" he asks again, and Jess answers before he can think about it.

"It's me, Dad."

"Mijo?" The high voice pitches a degree higher. "Jesusmaría?"

"Yeah."

"Well, wow. Oh, wow, son. I haven't talked—it's been a long time. You—you sound so grown."

What can he possibly say to that? "Thanks."

Some 150 miles away, his father clears his throat, and Jess recognizes the nervous habit he has apparently never been able to shake. "Well, you sound real good. Healthy. How you been?"

"Fine." Another silence. Jess feels no urge to break it. Instead he strains to hear background noises. If he listens hard enough, can he hear prisoners yelling? Fights? Screams and orders from the guards? But there is only his father, only their dual breaths mingling through the line.

"I sent you letters, mijo."

"Yeah, I haven't read them." The bitterness flares up. He knows he sounds like a child, but in that moment he doesn't care. "I don't really give a shit what you've got to say to me."

"Aha." His father laughs. *Laughs*, and Jess's anger surges. "There it is. Go on, son, get it out. Just get it out the way."

"Fuck you."

"Nah, none of that. You say what you got to say straight. Like a man."

"You want me to say it straight? Fine." Conqueror. Child of Vikings. He sucks in a breath and speaks through clenched teeth. "I don't want to read any letters or talk to you, period. I don't fucking forgive you. *You* put us in danger, and *you* went to jail, and *you're* why Ma had to go back to work all these years. She should hate you for that, but she doesn't. She hates me." The words feel like oyster shells, ragged, caught in his throat. "You made me the bad guy."

"Whoa, hold on now. I didn't make you no kind of bad. She doesn't think that."

"Bullshit," he spits. "She thinks it's my fault you're there."

"She doesn't, boy. She's the one who called the cops on me."

A moment ago, fast in the grip of his own fury, Jess would have thought there was nothing his father could say to quiet him. But this does. His mother? Devoted, loyal to her husband to the end, wasn't she? It cannot be true. But of course it is. Of course.

His heart gives a dull, plodding thud, one he feels behind his teeth.

His father continues. "The gunshots were the last straw, she said. Meant to scare us and they worked. She called the cops next morning. I was in the room when she did it. She never blamed it on you, son. She wanted the bags as evidence, sabes? You there?"

"Yeah, I'm here."

"Your mom and I had problems, we still do. But I'm not gonna fucking pretend like I danced on in here just because of her. It's been rough. I get it. But I promise, you didn't do nothing. Understand?"

Jess stares at the coiled wire of the landline in his hand. The man left. He is gone, sent away, and does nothing—can do nothing—to help the family he left behind. The family he threw away. It is always on Jess, on Yvonne, on the girls even, each of them looking after one another and themselves because of a father who carried on crimes and a mother who'd given in to her own guilt. He should be furious; he is.

Ridiculous, then, this sudden urge he feels to lay his head down on his father's shoulder. To look between his parents and know that one of them, even one, would have his back no matter the battle, that he was no longer fighting alone.

"Jess? Understand?"

"Yeah. Okay."

"And some things I know, even from in here. She needs you—your mom. She's shit at saying it, but she needs you."

"I don't think so."

"Show some respect. She loves you, son. She needs you to be a man—"

Jess jolts at the sound of the recorded voice, cutting in, announcing they have one minute remaining before the call will be disconnected.

"Putamadre. Look, mijo, just know that I'm counting on you. We all are. Your mom says you're doing real good with ball. That you're getting scouted. Already getting scouted." Jess's stomach tightens, but he says nothing, listening to the rush of his father's voice, letting the warmth slide over him. "That you're gonna make it big for us. I'm so proud of you, you know. A real man."

When they hang up, Jess twines the cord through his fingers. He should have told him about the oystering, how he has found another thing he is good at, that isn't just the sport his father groomed him for. How he discovered it on his own and is considering doing it full-time. There was a moment when he felt the words form, the shape of them in his mouth. But he let them sit there, and the time on the call ran out until the dial tone hummed in his ear. Now he roots inside himself for a pang of regret, shame—but he feels only sparkling within his veins, an angry sort of pride. Like William being crowned king on Christmas Day 1066, standing before the crowd at Westminster Abbey, snow blanketing the lawn, icicles hanging from the arches. Like standing on a mountaintop that had previously been unsummitable and, looking down at the tiny bodies of his father, mother, friends, everyone he knows, finally recognizing the exact distance between them.

RED ZONE

Mercedes

First rule of the ballpark, at least for girls like Mercedes: Don't sit with fans in the bleachers. Don't crowd along the baseline fences. Don't mix with the kids running in ball caps and too-big gloves. Look at her there. From where she stands in the entrance, she sees that for this playoff game, the Brownsville Vaqueros versus the Corpus Christi Sharks, people have brought lawn chairs and towels to sit even in the scraggly grass beyond the park. Perfect spots for catching homers, or for heckling the visiting outfielders. Her father taught her this, in another country, so close to Brownsville that on some evenings she can smell the smoke from their fires. So close that from the uppermost bleachers she can see buildings in the city where, on his good days, her father took her and her baby sister shopping. She doesn't ever sit there—believe that.

Instead she climbs to the first row of right field bleachers, directly behind the home dugout. See how the girls like her grin, greet her with little hugs? Their seats are behind the players, a good view of the field, but she's been told (by Jessica, whose fiancé is the veteran shortstop and who's been here the longest) that the boys like it that way. De veras, the girls sit here *because* the boys can't see them. They told them so, their boys, and they have obeyed. They sit in these spots so the boys can't shoot them quick glances from the dugout, where they sprawl on benches or lean on railings, spitting into paper cups streams of dip juice or sunflower seeds chewed to pulp. Can't get a glimpse of the girls when they're at the plate, either, adjusting their grip, digging in once, twice, trying to follow and then disrupt the path of the ball. At least most of them can't.

Mercedes's guy, though—he can see her. He's on the mound now with that ball in his glove, glove lifted to his lips, scanning the plate and the bleachers beyond. She loves him, but he brings her a whole different set of worries.

Please rise for the national anthem. She loves this moment, too, when the show starts and the lights don't dim but brighten. Two flags ripple in the evening breeze— warm still because this is the Valley—and they stand as one, together. Even she, mojada that she is. Yes, she is. She will say it. Every game she sings the words, sweeter to her because they are stolen.

Play ball.

The team spreads into their defense positions, as choreographed as the tentacles of a firework. Jessica watches Andrew M. warming up in the hot corner. Bee-short-for-Beatrice keeps her eyes on Valentín in left field. Anita, José at catcher. Even their gazes belong to these boys.

Mercedes's boy takes off his Vaqueros cap and wipes his brow, settles it back over the sweaty pile of dark hair.

Sweaty from the bullpen since this is his start for the night. Which means he is ready. He buries the ball in his glove, and though she can't see it, she knows he spins it in his hand to get the feel of the seams, the bumps and the white space in between speaking to him like braille. He leans in to check the signs José flashes. Straightens, side-eyes the empty bases out of habit.

He will see her if he looks this way, but he won't. He has told her a thousand times since they were kids. *Nah, I don't even notice y'all there. Just don't sit behind home plate. Red zone. Never sit in the red zone.* So she doesn't. Like I said, homegirl knows her place. I ought to know, she's me.

———

I met Luis eight years ago, when he and I were both ball-players, before he became an independent league pitcher and I his girl in the bleachers behind the dugout. Not long after I'd crossed.

Some people cross on jet skis now, tú sabes? In broad daylight. I've seen them. The last time I was in Mission visiting my aunt Flor, we took my cousins to Anzalduas Park on a bright blue Saturday, and I watched them climb off the back of the machine and step onto Texas soil that looked just like the Mexico across the water, scrambling behind scrawny mesquites we knew from home. The migra agents—in their olive green and khaki, their mirrored sunglasses—barked into radios and ran after a few who disappeared into the brush. The rest, the mass of them, gave themselves up by choice. They raised their hands high over their heads and walked straight at the agents, babies bound to their chests, children beside them. Things are bad in Honduras, in Gua-

temala, I know. But I couldn't for the life of me, for the freedom I've taken, understand the urge to come so far and cross
so many fences and, finally, cross the last one—which is just
a fence of dirty water—only to see the men who want to
send you back to all that and run straight at them, fall to your
knees before them. *Let's go back to Tía*, I said and led my
cousins away, but not before I looked in the eyes of a woman
who was trying to hug a border patrol agent and I spit on the
ground in front of her.

No, not by jet ski, not me. Same place: near Anzalduas
Park, outside Reynosa, across Mission. I was newly twelve,
and it was night. It had rained in recent days, so the river
was running high and fast. Some crossers, my mother and
sister among them, crouched low in plastic rafts patched
by duct tape and barely inflated enough to hold them up.
The rest, like me, stripped down and put our things in garbage bags looped about our necks and swam. The coyotes
hissed at us to hurry up, to not breathe or splash so fucking
loud and putamadre, shut that baby up.

When we reached America, crawling up through the
mud and tree roots and clumps of grass, I remember bodies
drifting in the current, or lying still and swollen with the
river inside them. Some of the others became bodies, too—
live ones, weeping silently, vibrating with sorrow. Not me,
though, because none of them were me or mine.

That makes me cruel, doesn't it. I felt bad for them, but
I no longer wasted time on grief. Another thing my father
taught me with his fists, between the skin on my back and
the buckle of his belt.

An electric squawk ripped apart the night: a radio.
Immediately an owl hooted, an owl that was not an owl

but instead a coyote crouched behind the tree next to me. Then a responding yelp, a cry that could have been a real coyote this time but was the two-legged kind. We ran.

I knew where my tío's truck would be, where he'd said over the phone it would be. I sprinted in that direction. Around me the silence became a thunder of footsteps, heaving breaths, bodies slamming into one another, babies howling, men's voices yelling *Alto alto*. The darkness shattered into beams from flashlights and headlights that bounced off us, our sodden clothes, onto them, their green and tan. I kept my eyes on the far brush line where I knew the blue pickup would be, and as people one by one dropped away from me, I didn't look back until I was there, until I lifted one foot onto the bumper and hurled myself over the tailgate. Screaming *Go Tío go go*. And like magic my mother was next to me, facedown in the bed of the truck with her hands wrapped around my baby sister's head to protect it. The truck squealed and bounced beneath us, picking up speed. I pressed my face into my mother's neck so the tears she cried mingled with mine; we laughed together. It's a rare story, I know now, how we crossed—as if the violence and rape and death decided not to touch us, as if it could sense we had seen enough of them in the house we left.

We had family throughout Texas, as far as Galveston Island up the coast near Houston. But my mother chose to keep us in the Valley. We moved into Tía Flor's house in Mission for a couple of months while we settled. Really, there wasn't much to settle. We were from Matamoros, border twin to Brownsville, a grand total of 1.45 hours away. I spoke English—Mama insisted I learn—but I hardly needed it. Here we walked on streets like those from home, christened with names like Allende and San Juan, narrower in some places, wider in others, only slightly better paved. Buildings with bars on the windows and the red-white-green flag of Mexico pasted on the doors. Signs reading *Cristian Ortega, Abogado. Ydania Gonzalez y Cruz, Médica. Se Aceptan Cash. Se Habla Español.* Norteño music blasting from old Chevys: horns triumphant, the barrump-barrump of the bass and the cumbia throbbing a heartbeat in the pathways of our bodies.

We moved to Brownsville, joined up with my other aunts and uncles and cousins there off Rentfro Boulevard. Tía Medora threw us a party and invited most of the neighborhood. Spanish all around me with the music I'd known my whole life in a new place that was not new at all. I sulked in the front yard, picking at the grass poking through the sidewalk. Through the press of bodies and the smoke from the grill and my uncles' cigarettes, a boy my age eased over, sat down beside me on the sidewalk, and offered me a Coke. Beads of condensation like diamonds on its side. When he smiled, he flashed a missing incisor, dimples in his cheeks sweet as my baby sister's. *I'm Luis,* he said. *You play ball?*

I borrowed my cousin's glove and spent the rest of the day playing catch with Luis. He'd learned the curve, but his would hover and hang too long; mine, on the other hand— yeah, I'll say it—mine had the nastiest 12–6 drop this side of Sandy Koufax. I said, *Let me.* And he did. I showed him the grip on the seams, the arc of the elbow, the way the palm turns inward as you snap your wrist, as my father had shown me a year before. I didn't tell Luis that he'd shown me one week, then broken my arm in a drunken rage the next. That it was still in a cast when Mama made the phone call to her sisters in Texas about crossing.

Luis came again the next day, bringing his old glove for

me to use. We played catch in the street to work on his distance. I knew his fastball would really be something. He'd throw and I'd think *putamadre*, like my father would say when Nolan Ryan took the mound for the Rangers. When Luis was ready to go home, I offered him his glove and he said, *You keep it. For tomorrow.* I set the glove on my nightstand; the part of my heart that cried constantly for something strange and unfamiliar quieted a little.

Some days, Luis took me to the international bridge and we watched the cars cross. Gasoline and scorched asphalt and humidity weighing the air heavy. I could see the city from there, the curls of smoke and exhaust rise above the streets. One day, I brought the baby; I was watching her while Mama worked at the convenience store. *Look, Celia,* I said, *there's the shitpile where we used to live. And here's the one where we live now.* I lifted her chubby arm and used her fingers to point across the water, and back again.

For months we moved carefully, fearing not INS but the hulking shape of my father. We looked over our shoulders in the driver's seat of unmarked vans, over the top of Celia's head in the grocery store. He knew where my tías lived; when the phone rang, the skin on the backs of our necks itched. We waited for shadows, movement in the corners of our eyes, but there was nothing. He never came after us.

I couldn't have been happier, and I searched for that happiness in my mother. Mama's bruises faded; the cut above her eye fused back, though she'll bear a rift in her left brow forever, a lilt upward that even today makes her look slightly surprised. I wanted to see relief on her healing face, radiant beams of joy and recognition that we were free, that the river we'd climbed out of and the ground we stood upon had provided that for us. I saw it some days. Others, I recognized disappointment when she looked around and he wasn't waiting there, tears in his eyes, wildflowers in his fist.

On those days I hated her, and she knew it. I would run to Luis's house and throw baseballs at his plywood fence until my arm gave out, until the balls ran out and I was just picking up rocks and chunks of dirt and flinging them. He patted me on the back when I cried.

My uncles tried, too. They tinkered with our car and the pipes that acted up. They found my mother jobs at the convenience store and cleaning the houses of some faculty at UTB. On Sundays, we'd gather at Tía Medora's, and while I washed dishes, they'd recline in front of the TV and watch ball games for hours, all of us shouting praise and curses at the screen by turns. As Luis earned starting spots on the junior high team, then Hanna, then UTB, we watched the games in real life. They sat with me in the stands. They bought me chili dogs and snuck me beer. They pounded Luis on the back after a win and reminded him to ice that arm, winked at me and said, *Don't you aggravate it too much, mija, that's the money right there, Mercedes, that's your ticket.*

I kissed their cheeks when I wanted to say, Jesus Christ, don't I know that already. I'd known since freshman year that on game nights I sleep on the left side, the blistering scent of IcyHot drawing tears from my eyes. I know to place a towel beneath the right half of him to catch the runoff from ice packs, the clumsy way his left fingers will part through my hair, that if we want to fuck that night I'll have to be on top.

And I know he'll never give up that goddamn number

he wears: 11. No matter how much I beg him to change it. He's worn it since grade school. It's lucky, he says. *Come on, M. Just because it was your dad's doesn't mean it's bad for me.*

Maybe he's right. Luis is my ticket to many things. To my uncles, he's fame, small fortunes, a paycheck with our non-MLB league now but a few good seasons away from getting noticed, from that call over to the minors. To my aunts, he's citizenship, a ticket printed in green. But my mother, she looks at him and sees my father. I can tell by the way her eyes gleam when he bears the number 11 on the field, when he walks into our house all shoulder and leg at six foot four. He could hurt me is what she's thinking. He doesn't—I don't think he ever would—but he could. The *could* is enough to both please and frighten her.

I wonder about the life we'll lead, about the engagement ring he put on my finger a few months ago that I sometimes stare at for hours, trying to read shapes in the cubic zirconia like a crystal ball. In my mind the number 11 has never been his; it belongs to my father, it's the one he wore through school and his time in the Mexican minors, it's the one he insisted I wear in our own city club. I hate it, but sometimes I wonder what my father would think about the space I occupy now—in a city like Matamoros, in a ballpark, but not on the field or in a center-section row, rather behind the dugout between girls named Anita and Jessica and Teresa, all of us like gloves and bats and caps, another piece that belongs to the players. Like my mother, a piece of a man who exists across a river, both of them incomplete.

Most nights when Luis and I lie in bed, these thoughts drift through my mind, fragile as the dandelion threads Celia blows in the backyard. I shouldn't think them, should I.

I should be happy, content with what I have. Shouldn't imagine reversing my life, starting in Mexico and doing it over again, only this time I cross the river into a New World rather than more of the same.

Before we drift off, Luis will tell me he loves me, and he'll mean it. He never means it so much as win nights. And I never mean it so much as when he loses. Tell me what to think about that.

———

The air has cooled slightly. Sixth inning, and Luis stays on the mound. Not too many pitches thrown, so his arm is still loose. His changeup's got brakes on it, his curve dropping like it's falling off a table. He could put more heat on the two-seamer, but his coach doesn't want his arm to give, and neither do I, not yet, not so early in the series. He shakes off José's first sign and then sees the one he wants; his shoulders straighten, then bunch as he rises into the windup. Lifts his left leg. Snaps it down as the right arm comes around to pronate—it's both his fault and my father's that I know this fucking word—and hurls.

Fastball on the inside corner. Swing and a miss, batter goes down. Vaqueros, 4–0, heading to the bottom of the sixth.

We hoot and clap. With a great play, some girls, like Anita or Teresa, shout their guys' numbers, shit like *Way to go, 14* and *Attaway, three-oh*. Not me. I clap and whoop his name. I call out no numbers. I don't like the taste of that number in my mouth.

Luis trots back from the mound, and the rest of the guys spill out of the dugout, gloved hands ready to pound Luis's back. Someone hands him a jacket, and he drapes it over his right arm. In our bullpen there is no reliever in sight, not even Henry or Martín stretching out. Three more innings and he'll have thrown a complete game, and if he keeps it scoreless, a shutout—his first of the season. A big deal for the scouts I've spotted behind home plate with their clipboards, crisp ball caps, radar guns.

Luis turns slightly toward me on his way back to the dugout. I smile and wave, trying to catch his eye, but he is fixed on the guys around him, on the brotherhood. The brothers come first. I know this, by now I swear I know this. I put my hand down.

———

He didn't like when I brought up Galveston again. For a place I've never been—it's halfway up the coast, a good six hours away—I've been thinking about it a lot. Some of my family is around Houston, and one of my tías lives on the island with her kids. My cousin is there, too, working a fishing boat. We've kept in touch. Jess invites me out to stay with them. He says it's good money, a good town. The ocean for miles; well, the Gulf, en serio, but still an ocean. There's a diner he knows on the bay that turns a blind eye to the proper papers. And his neighborhood is safe, he says. Mojados from many countries, as I think of us, filling homes in a place called Fish Village.

Luis and I were lying in bed, in the quiet after sex, before sleep, when I mentioned it. I told him that to me, Galveston is new. Fresh. Salt in the air instead of diesel and concrete. There's ball clubs for days in the Houston area: independent, minor league, the Astros—the team he and I both grew up idolizing from different sides of the river.

He'd have to start over, but that's what tryouts are for. I told Luis all of that. I led with the teams.

But he frowned, his palm still stroking my hip. *I have the starting spot here. I'm building a brand. Coach thinks I've got my whole career ahead of me. Why would I go anywhere else?*

Because there's no future for us in the Valley. I gritted my teeth against the weight of what I was saying, a truth I've known since cars wheezed past me on the international bridge. We will live here and die here, minutes from the spot where I climbed out of the river, where my mother cleaned houses and covered up bruises. Shouting distance from the place where my father still works, fucks women, coaches a kids' baseball team.

I said this, but Luis laughed. *We* have *a future, M. Mine is yours.*

Outside, the Valley air pushed against the windows, drawing sweat beads against the glass. A car alarm went off down the street. It could have been my mother's car. It could be my cousin's, or my tía's, or mine, or belong to any of the people in this town that Luis and I know and have always known.

That's not enough, I thought, and finally found the courage to say out loud, *Luis, I want my own.* But he was asleep by then.

———

Mija. Someone taps my arm and I look over. Tío Raúl stands in the aisle, grinning. Behind him, three more of my uncles hold flimsy plates of nachos, popcorn bags, tall plastic cups of beer. They lean in, and their cheeks where I kiss them are pink, flushed with drink and the thrill of a winning game. *We're not gonna bother you here, we just wanted to say hi.*

Where are you sitting, Tío?

He points to a spot in the center section. *Got us some good seats this time. Front row to your boy. Hell of a show so far.*

Boy's throwing the shit out these pendejos, Tío Carl says around a mouthful of popcorn. *See that fastball he's got?*

The curve, Tío Steve adds. *Drops like no fucking thing. Almost as good as yours, 'jita.*

Anyway. Tío Raúl glances over at the other girls and nods; they smile politely. *We'll see you later, Mercedes.*

They make their way into the aisle, curving around the field, back into the center section where people have given up on seats in general and are crowding the rails right up against the netting to protect against foul balls. I watch my uncles take their seats in full sight of the field. They holler as loud as they want because they can.

Like them, I rise for the seventh-inning stretch. Sling an arm around Teresa and Jessica and sway to "Take Me Out to the Ball Game." Clap my hands to "Deep in the Heart of Texas." Luis is in the dugout, and try as I might, I can't see him from here. I can't see him, so he can't see me. The realization that this is all I want surges into me as if I touched an electric fence. As if I held fast to one and climbed.

We're at *one, two, three strikes you're out* when I pull away. It's time, you see. Or maybe you don't.

Ves: This is not the moment I've been waiting for. Just the latest in a series, times where I am faced with a choice I decided on long ago. I made this choice years ago while the doctor set my arm, my father's face grimacing and red above me, sobbing, *Lo siento, mija, mi vida querida, lo siento*. I decided again with the flashlight of border patrol screaming in my eyes. And again, last night: Luis's breath ruffling my hair, my words of wanting more hanging in the air between us like the hanging curve he used to throw. Before I showed him how.

The other girls look up, startled, as I take my purse and jacket and climb through them. *Excuse me, excuse me*, I apologize as I pass. *I need to go. I'm sorry.* I'm smiling. *I need to go.*

Because I do. As I make my way down the aisle, I feel stronger for the knowledge. This spot, this space, this fucking city. If I stay here, yo voy a morir. Or, worse, live a whole other life just like the one I left across the Rio Grande: mindful of how I move, what I do and say, how it affects and represents a man.

I'm going, with or without Luis. He doesn't know yet, but he will.

Walking around the dugout feels illicit. No river here, no one waiting to point me away from the red zone and back toward the bleachers behind the dugout. Invisible lines dissipate beneath my sneakers. I cross, already feeling like I belong.

My uncles cheer as I climb the steps to them, a few rows up behind home plate. They laugh and scoot over on the bleachers to make space for me. They call me mija. They call me babygirl. *Your boy's gonna close this puta out, babygirl.* I kiss their cheeks and take the beer they pass.

The bottom of the seventh goes scoreless, although Andrew M. gets in a good double to right. From here, I can look straight into the dugout. I chew sunflower seeds, sucking the salt from their gritty shells, and watch Luis adjust the jacket over his pitching arm.

He doesn't notice me until they take the field at the top of the eighth and he once again strides over to the mound. He punches the toes of his cleats into the dirt as if planting a flag. He removes his cap to wipe his brow and looks behind home plate. Directly at me.

The batter raises his shoulders and readies. José adjusts his mask, crouches in the dirt. The girls behind the dugout clap and call out encouragement. My uncles mutter. I look straight ahead into Luis's eyes and the 11 on his chest and, for once, I don't think of my father. Instead, it's Galveston, and Jess, a little house with a porch on a street named after a fish. Me, bussing tables in a diner on a bay I've never seen.

Luis glances down at José's fingers, flashing signs; then his eyes dart back up to me. *See me*, I tell him. Look at me, existing here, in a place you've said I don't belong. You forgot que soy una mojada. Give me lines to cross, why don't you.

OPHELIA OF THE SAINTS

Ofelia

Her first thought as she gazes upon the image of the Grim Reaper is this: *Childish*. Ofelia de los Santos almost laughs, looking at him. A bright cartoon figure, not at all in line with the professional, serious look she assumes the Society would want to achieve. For one, the Grim Reaper is grinning. Yes, El Muerte, whom Ofelia de los Santos has feared since girlhood, sports a cheerful, gap-toothed smile on the flyer, next to several exclamation points.

That is her second thought—the exclamation points. *Demasiados*. The capital letters hurt her eyes.

As she studies the flyer, taped up to one of the Victorian columns surrounding Old City Cemetery, Ofelia de los Santos begins to sweat. The night air is warm, humid against the windbreaker her grandson insists she wear despite the fact that it is August and 85 degrees. But she is safely, finally, alone now. Ofelia removes the windbreaker and ties it around her hips.

When she first told Magdalena she was attending a

meeting of the Spiritualistic and Supernatural Society, her friend laughed so hard she choked on her coffee. *En serio, comadre*, Magdalena scoffed, signaling the long-haired waiter for a refill. *Not that nonsense. You know better. You are better.* Hector's reaction that evening was the complete opposite—her grandson wanted badly to come, had even offered to drive. *Come on, Abuelita*, he said with an enthusiasm that made her laugh. *It'll be fun!* But by the time he came home from the construction site, reeking of sweat and dust, he was so tired he had to brace both hands against the wall to stay upright. *Shower and bed*, Ofelia ordered, and he was too exhausted to argue. He was asleep when she walked out the door.

Ofelia de los Santos adjusts her glasses on the end of her nose, hoping that will help her read the flyer. She is not sure exactly where the meeting is being held, and the cemetery spans six blocks. But the smudged paper gives no specific location:

MEETING!!!
THE SPIRITUALISTIC AND SUPERNATURAL SOCIETY
OF THE GREATER GALVESTON AREA—
Just ahead!
10 p.m.–11 p.m., "The Witching Hour"*
COME ONE, COME ALL, BUT COME <u>QUIETLY</u>!**
*The Witching Hour starts at midnight, but we reserve the right to use this term loosely.
**This is a place of eternal rest for bodies of those who have passed into the afterlife peacefully. Please be quiet out of respect to those souls. The ones who haven't passed will make themselves known—KEEP YOUR EYES OPEN!

Ever the rule follower, Ofelia de los Santos keeps her eyes open as she walks along the sidewalk parallel to 43rd Street. She sees her sedan beyond the boundaries of the Old City Cemetery. It is parked across from the corner bodega that she decided, yes, she likes after all. The bodega has bars on the windows, but that comforts her—back home in Brownsville, lots of buildings have those. Back home in Brownsville, everything, even bars on the windows, is a comfort to her.

"Excuse me? Ma'am?"

Ofelia de los Santos turns—doesn't jump or jolt, despite the darkness of the cemetery, hasn't she always prided herself on her unflappability?—and faces a woman smaller and browner than she. The newcomer wears a short-sleeved dress, galoshes, and a knit cap over her short dark hair. She lowers the flashlight in her hand so the beam hits Ofelia at chest level; the woman grins at her.

"Are you coming to the meeting?" Ofelia hears the woman's accent, the way the *T*s became hard *D*s, the rise and fall of the vowels that sound to her like the clucking of a chicken. A Filipino voice. She recognizes them now. In Brownsville, she never needed to, was required only to know the way bolillos spoke versus mexicanos, because everyone spoke Spanglish, kept the same mother tongue in their mouths.

"Yes, I am."

The woman grins, a smile that splits her face into creases and teeth. "Oh, good! Someone new. I'm Beeb! Genebeeb"—it takes a moment for Ofelia to translate that as Genevieve—"but you can call me Beeb!" Unlike the flyer, her tone seems made for exclamation points.

She shakes the hand that is offered. "Ofelia."

"Come with me, I'll show you where to go. Your first time here?" Beeb asks. She takes Ofelia's elbow; Ofelia pretends she doesn't mind.

They walk together. And Beeb begins to talk, a fluid, unceasing current of words.

"I love this cemetery. So old and with such big white stones. Beautiful! Look!"

Ofelia de los Santos peels away from her thoughts. She is not quite sure what she should be looking at. Beeb gestures with a wide scoop of her hand. Everything, apparently.

"Do you know this was once *seven* cemeteries? And it got so big they began to bleed together. They built a newer one, a few blocks away, but this is the heart of the island. These are nice ones, these headstones here. You can tell they are new, though."

Yes, thinks Ofelia de los Santos as she looks at the graves Beeb means. The gleaming and unchipped look of them. She admires the way they sprout from the ground in symmetrical rows, neat as false teeth. Ofelia approaches one that is clearly ancient, lying flat against the dirt and grass. She has to stand over it to read the words, the white marble streaked with the darkness of age. A medallion of a crucifix emblazoned at the top. CHRISTOPHORUS EDUARDUS BYRNE. She squints at the Latin beneath, words like *natus*, *ordenatus*, *consecratus*. A priest.

Perhaps Roland, ever the fearful Roman Catholic, should have had Latin on his headstone. His looks nothing like this one, though that was not her decision. Once they learned the prognosis, he insisted Ofelia go with him so they could pick one out together. But he ended up choosing it himself. The end came quickly, and now he rests beneath a granite headstone in a corner of the pretty Catholic cemetery behind St. Luke's, in a section of east Brownsville about a mile from the house where she and he spent forty-four years, just off Boca Chica Boulevard. He is four hundred miles away, alone. And she is here.

When Roland died, their son Oscar decided his widowed mother shouldn't be down in the Valley anymore. *You'll come to Galveston and live with us,* Oscar said. *Mama. No arguments. Let us take care of you.*

She resisted for months. In the Valley, she had her church, her weekly games of Rummikub and Chalupa, her monthly bingo mixers. Pachangas, quinceañeras, barbecues. A community built on decades of stories lying thick, seventy-two years' worth of threads passing from one person to another, then back to her in a pattern they could recognize. But her son and daughter-in-law had insisted, and on their last visit to the Valley, Hector smiled so sweetly at her. He was what did it. Ofelia de los Santos loves her grandson. He is a big, strong boy; at twenty-one, he already reminds her so much of her own father, un buen hombre. And he introduced her to Magdalena Castillo, the grandmother of his classmate. Ofelia's first new friend in years, her only friend on Galveston. *You'll like Mrs. Castillo, she can be a crazy viejita, but she's nice,* his only description.

Now she and Magdalena meet for breakfast once a week, walking together to the taqueria a few blocks away. Ofelia likes the crazy viejita with the long, gray-streaked dark hair that makes her look like a fortune-teller. She orders her sausage-and-egg tacos a la mexicana and her coffee black, like Ofelia, and though Magdalena has only ever known Galveston, she understands roots, patterns of threads, and stories. In her eagle-sharp black eyes, Ofelia sees an understanding and respect for el otro mundo—the unseen senses people have long feared, denied, burned women for.

Her friend and her grandson are the only things Ofelia loves about this island.

"I like this one," Beeb is saying, and Ofelia looks again at Father Byrne's marker. "So pretty, the cross."

"Yes," Ofelia agrees. She crosses herself and murmurs a quick Apostles' Creed in Spanish. It is still habit, despite all these years without the craft. Her mother used to say demons could withstand much, but not the Creed. *A healer's first tools are her hands and her tongue.* Ofelia de los Santos had been Ofelia Vaca then, watching her mother trace a cross on her own forehead, her lips, her breasts, mimicking. *Yo creo en Dios, Padre todopoderoso, creador del Cielo y de la Tierra. Say it, mija.*

Beside her, Beeb crosses herself, mumbles a prayer under her breath. Many Filipinos were Catholics, too, Ofelia remembers, deciding she likes the woman a bit better.

"Rest in peace, amen," Beeb finishes in a loud voice. She squints at Christophorus Eduardus Byrne. "Do you know him?"

Ofelia shakes her head.

"That's nice. So the spirit moved you to pray? Or I should say the *spirits* moved you!" Beeb laughs. "That's what Xander says. Oh, of *course* you don't know Xander yet, but you will. He's just up ahead." Beeb steers her around a chunk of sidewalk jutting up from the ground. "Xander founded the whole Society! Xander is the Galveston Ghost Whisperer. You've heard of him, yes?"

She recognizes the name, but only because of the Society website. Hector found it for her. He laughed as he pulled it up on his computer, but when he saw the seriousness of her face, he quieted. *Something like this could be pretty cool, Abuelita. The Spiritualistic and Supernatural Society? They could learn a lot from you*, he said. *I know how strong you are now.*

Ofelia de los Santos stared at the picture of the Society's founder: *Xander Reeves, the Galveston Ghost Whisperer*. He of the long, bleached hair, white as a sunbeam, and the pitch-black sunglasses. He looked the way Ofelia imagined young serial killers looked—high boots, dark clothes, a black trench coat lapping at his ankles.

Xander Reeves appeared nothing like the ghost speakers Ofelia once knew, two tías and her grandfather among them. The Vacas were average people; they had white hair that puffed around their faces like bolls of cotton. Even their trances were sensible, lacking drama. They simply stopped what they were doing—stirring a bowl of cereal, turning the radio dial, opening a door—as their eyes rolled back in their heads. They did not shake when Ofelia Vaca or the others led them to a chair, flinching at the cold air seeping from their skin. Their arms would come up above their heads as if pulled by the sky, or as if they reached for other invisible hands.

This Xander had his hands on his hips, chin lifted at an arrogant angle. Ofelia de los Santos doubted spirits reached down to him from anywhere.

"Xander is a medium," Beeb explains as they walk. "He's lived on the island all his life, so he knows the best places to find spirits. This cemetery is full of Civil War soldiers— did you know that? It was the first cemetery when the city was founded. Many of the people who died during the big hurricane, they're buried here. The ones they could find,

you know." She clucks her tongue in sympathy, and Ofelia finds herself doing the same. "Xander says there were
so many dead they built funeral pyres on the beaches and
burned them all day and all night for weeks. We have meetings there sometimes, where the pyres were, on Stewart
Beach—over there by Fish Village. That's where I live."

Ofelia de los Santos nods but doesn't say that, yes, she,
too, lives in Fish Village. The name makes her wince, though
Hector is particularly proud of his neighborhood, where every
street is named after a different fish. Albacore, Barracuda,
Marlin, Tuna. They live on Bonita. She looked up bonita
once and saw something sneering, full of stripes and fins with
jagged edges. It was ugly. She thinks Galveston ugly, too—
its faded brick buildings, tourist surf shops and cantinas in
gaudy colors along the waterfront, the waves of silty brown,
and the smell of salt seeping in everywhere. She knows, deep
in her heart, that she is being stubborn. That it is her longing
for the Valley churning, driving her scorn for this new place.
And still.

But it is not ugly to her Hectorcito. He loves it, this
island where he has grown up so far away from his father's
family in the Valley. (Ofelia blames his mother.) Hector
told her Galveston's story was like that of New Orleans, a
shipping port that became the beating heart of the coast.
Hub for sea trade of cotton, farming equipment, yellow
fever, immigrants. First place in Texas to have electricity,
and a telephone, and baseball. Decimated by a hurricane
in 1900 that killed eight thousand people. A site of tragedy.
He speaks of the city's history and beauty when he takes
her on walks around Fish Village, or down the Seawall, or
west along the Strand district. Up until now, Ofelia only
saw tourists with ill-fitting bathing suits and wilting brown

leaves of palm trees. (She admits to herself that this is all she really wants to see.)

"Oleanders!" Ofelia de los Santos, she of the steady constitution, jumps at Beeb's shout. Beeb reaches out to a tree and plucks a white blossom, tucking it beneath her cap.

"You should wipe off your hands now," Ofelia says absently. Memory bites like a needle prick. The oleanders of Brownsville. The bright blooms and slender green leaves calling for fingers to reach out and break them apart and come away with gummy sap. Fingers that could be sucked on. Leaves mangled like lettuce between baby teeth.

Beeb nods. "Yes, they're poisonous, aren't they?"

"Yes."

The parents brought him to her, the curandera of Boca Chica Boulevard, as her mother had been before her. She recalls the toddler, the tousled dark hair and gray-blue tinge to his skin. He was cooling in his father's arms as Ofelia Vaca scanned frantically the remedios behind her— eggs white and brown, jars of albahaca and palma Christi, crucifixes of wood and leaf and steel—but she was moving quickly as performance, already knowing none would help, that no gift could bring the dead to life. His father was screaming.

It was fifty years ago. It was yesterday.

Venenoso, Magdalena said one day as they walked down Albacore; she pointed to a pink-blossomed tree in the front yard of the house across from hers. The owner, an older man Ofelia had not met, stood by the tree and saw her pointing. When he raised a hand in greeting, Magdalena only lifted her chin in response. Ofelia simply replied, *Yo sé*. She did not tell her friend she had made un veneno once, just once, for a man who paid heavily and brought her oleanders. Do no harm, she had sworn before her mother and the Virgin Mary. But he begged, and she needed the money.

She touches an oleander now and envisions the flowers sitting in the bowl of Ofelia Vaca's molcajete, soft petals against the bite and grit of volcanic rock. When she crushed them with the pestle, they curled into wet ribbons and cast off a damp, sweet scent. The man watched Ofelia Vaca pound the flowers down into a paste, and then he began to shake vigorously. He fled from the shed and never came back. She buried the paste in the lot behind her house, dousing the ground in holy water and yerba buena. She went to confession every day for a month.

Oleanders—yes, she supposes she loves those about Galveston, too. How they bear both beauty and death.

"Oh, this one is lovely, don't you think?" Beeb asks, tugging on her elbow. She is gesturing to a marble grave marker twelve feet tall and half again as wide; Beeb flicks her flashlight beam to the top. A winged woman with a crown on her head clasps a robed baby in one arm, hugs a young girl in the other. They stand upon a columned pedestal flanked by cherubs. GRESHAM—JOSEPHINE ARDETH. 1848–1933.

Beeb swats at mosquitoes. "That's us up there, by the tall tower."

Ahead, candles flicker; flashlight beams bob. Ofelia sees the shift of bodies—living ones—in a huddle near a fifteen-foot obelisk that seems the center of the graveyard. Did that obelisk exist during Josephine Gresham's time, in Old Galveston? Had she looked at it as she walked through this cemetery, laying flowers on someone's grave, contemplating her own?

"That's a pretty name, Ardeth," Beeb murmurs, still eyeing the monument. "Nice for a middle name."

"It was her maiden name," Ofelia says. She is sure of it, doesn't need a whisper to tell her so. She knows without a doubt that Josephine Ardeth gave up her life to be a Gresham. That she had propped her past life upon the windowsill of her husband's house, her chin in one hand, staring out at the buggies and riders passing on what would soon be Broadway.

Beeb looks at Ofelia from the sides of her eyes. "Pretty name," she repeats. "My married name is Macaraeg—not pretty, but it means *brave*. What's yours?"

"De los Santos."

Beeb nods solemnly. "Ophelia of the Saints. That's a blessed name. A holy name."

Is it? wonders Ofelia. De los Santos was Roland's name, which she took when they got married, when she had given up healing. Before that, she had only ever been Ofelia Vaca, curandera of Boca Chica Boulevard. Roland had been Of the Saints but also a lawyer, well regarded, and though he respected the old ways, he did not want to be married to them. *Basta, querida. We're in a better time, aren't we? We can come out from the Dark Ages.*

She loved him. It was simple. So along with her maiden name, Ofelia put aside her salves and remedios, the jars, the matas. Her molcajete she cleansed and packed away; she bought a new one in Matamoros for grinding chiles and spices for cooking. If neighbors came to Ofelia's door in the night—whispering of their wife's susto or their infant son's caída de mollera—she shook her head, *I can't help you*, but passed a slip of paper with the proper measurements of la ruda or a diagram of where to place their hands for the ritual.

Eventually the whispers in the night stopped. Friends who had known her as a teenager grew old, moved out of the Valley, or died. Until all that was left of Ofelia in Brownsville was wife of Roland, woman of the saints.

She hated it, Ofelia realizes now, feeling a pang in her stomach, a short, deep stab. She loved Roland, but she had mourned no longer being Ofelia Vaca. She had lost herself.

"This way, this way! Xander and everyone are waiting." Beeb gives a little skip.

Ofelia allows herself to be led along the cracking sidewalk with black-eyed Susans peeking through the rifts. Roland picked them when he was courting her. He knew she loved black eyed-Susans—he'd gather them along Boca Chica and the resaca near her house. He'd show up at her door with them bunched in his fist, a sheepish smile on his face, sweat stains at the collar and armpits of his shirt. He still brought them once they were married, usually after a fight but sometimes for no reason other than to make her smile. He was holding some the day he came home with a fever.

Ofelia asked what happened, and he said he didn't know. He had been at court for a trial and felt fine until the last few hours. His forehead scorched the palm of her hand when she pressed it there; he had sweat through his entire shirt and suit jacket. By the time she lowered him to the bed, he was near convulsing.

Roland, tell me what you did today.

I was in a trial. He was a prosecutor, and often put

away violent criminals—a lot of immigrants but mostly just malos, Ofelia thought, trash no matter which side of the Rio Grande they came from. *He was convicted. I—I felt sick.*

She could see it, the defendant staring at the prosecutor with such envy and hate they bubbled into brujería. The strongest emotions become power; enough desire, fury, grief make mystics of us all. Roland wouldn't admit it, but Ofelia Vaca could see. Mal puesto.

Te dio el mal de ojo, she said. The evil eye. He stared and shook his head until he fell asleep. She fetched an egg and a bowl of water, her vial of agua bendita. She washed her hands and said a quick prayer for La Virgen's blessing and guiding of her actions.

He slept and tossed. She rubbed the egg over his head, his face, *Yo creo en Dios*, across the bones of his shoulders and down his chest, *Padre todopoderoso*, in circles across his belly and groin, along the lengths of his legs, *creador del Cielo y de la Tierra*, vigorously against the soles of his feet. Once again, all over, and once more: three times total for the Trinity. When Ofelia Vaca broke the egg into the bowl of water, the whites sizzled and crisped as if by a flame beneath; that was the fever. She peered at the intact yolk, saw clearly the outline of the eye. She sprinkled the cracked egg with holy water. She spat in it for good measure. His sweat would abate now.

Roland woke later and smiled. But as she told him what had happened, fear crept into his eyes and turned them feverish again. *Ofelia*, he said, *don't ever do that again. We don't believe that brujería anymore. You understand, don't you?* His hand tightened on hers. *We're not the mojados with common ways and common beliefs that they think we*

*are. This is the twentieth century. You don't give them cause
to think like that.* He lifted her hand, Ofelia de los Santos's
hand, to his lips.

"Ofelia, you're shivering." Beeb pats her on the arm,
concerned. "Are you cold? Put your jacket on, ma'am!"

"I'm not cold," Ofelia de los Santos replies. She heard
her Hector—*No, Abuelita, I'm not cold*—yesterday as he
lay on the living room floor with her hands on his abdomen.
She had been sitting on the couch with Magdalena, sipping té de manzanilla when he had walked in from evening
practice wincing, hissing. He clutched his side; all day he
had been in pain from the stitch in his stomach. *Like I can't
breathe.*

Ofelia hesitated. It had been years. She was no soba-
dora. And Oscar was his father's son—their medicine
cabinet full of antibiotics and Pepto Bismol. But he wasn't
there, Roland wasn't there, only Hector and Magdalena,
only she. Magdalena was watching her with those eyes,
sharp and dark, nodding as if she could read Ofelia's
thoughts.

Like a snap, a flicker of the candle flame she would
soon light, Ofelia could see it as she once did: quick slips
of images, shimmers like the rainbow on a puddle of oil.
Hector lying on his back on the floor, his shirt off. Ofelia
holding a jar, a lighter, a tea candle for the ventosa. The
flame of the candle atop Hector's stomach quivered, a yellow flame with a blue heart dancing. When she placed the
jar over the candle, its mouth against Hector's skin, trap-
ping the candle within the jar, the candle flame shook. It
drew into that blue heart the offending air from beneath
layers of Hector's skin and fat and muscle. The skin within

the jar puckered, lifted as if pulled, and the flame went out. Hector expelled the long breath of the cured.

Magdalena crossed herself, grabbed the salt shaker, and tossed salt over her left shoulder, muttering words in a language Ofelia didn't know. *Healer woman*, she said. *Such fuerza you've hidden from us.* Hector flexed his stomach and laughed. *Awesome! How did you do that?* So different from his father, his grandfather, that Ofelia Vaca began to cry. Hector patted her shoulder while the tears came down, and Magdalena shushed her like one does a baby. *'Ta bueno, comadre. Estás bien.*

"I think I might be a medium, but I don't know yet." Beeb has continued speaking as they walk, closing in on the obelisk. The candlelight grows brighter; Ofelia makes out the shapes of four or five people. "I've been trying, but I haven't had any encounters yet. Xander says I will soon, though! I've only been coming for about six months. We're a small group, but we are true believers, every one of us! What about you, Ofelia? Do you believe?"

She stops, and Beeb, startled, does, too. Ofelia stares at Beeb, her smile so earnest beneath her bright knit cap.

"I believe in many things," Ofelia says, allowing—for the first time in so many years—the pride and power of her rank to echo in her voice. *Curandera. Soy la curandera.* She need not explain herself to this amateur; the elements that mattered understood.

Beeb nods. She is unaware of the magnitude of the moment. Ofelia has named herself, renewed herself. Her body reacts now, reawakening as if from a long sleep. She senses fire in her fingertips and a tingling in her feet, the pooling of heat between her legs; she has the sudden urge to urinate, or maybe to shake her hips, to throw her head back and howl. She knows what to do.

"It was very nice meeting you, Beeb," she says, "I think I'm going to go."

"Oh! But we're almost there!" Beeb gives a cry of dismay when Ofelia steps backward on the path. "You're not going to stay for the meeting? You won't even meet everyone?"

Ofelia shakes her head. She feels herself smiling. "No, gracias."

The walk back along the path is quicker; she knows where the dangerous spots were now. She passes the black-eyed Susans, and Josephine Ardeth Gresham, and the white oleander tree. She makes the sign of the cross at Father Byrne's headstone, *Requiescat en pace*, keeps walking. Somewhere in Brownsville, Roland's is like the many modern ones here, with husbands and wives buried together. At the top in large, elegant print DE LOS SANTOS. Beneath it to the left, Roland's first and middle names and the years that bracketed his life. To the right, a blank space. It will stay blank at least a little while longer, Ofelia knows. Let it.

WELCOME, WON'T YOU STAY AWHILE?

Luz

When Luz learned her grandmother died, she was floating the river, snug inside a cheap inner tube stolen years ago from the Rio Frio General Store. She was ten, and things were simple: school, sunshine, the river. Looking back now, Luz recognizes this young version of herself as a girl who grinned, leaping off into dark, deep water without regard for rocks beneath. That Luz never would have predicted a life for her grown self hundreds of miles away in Galveston—had she even heard of Galveston back then?—nor would have predicted a life so full of death. She remembers the June sun beating down that day as she drifted in the appaloosa shade of cypress patches. A few yards ahead thundered the first set of rapids, and as she prepared for the drop, she heard her mother—*Luz*, she cried, *Luz, come back.* Her mother stood on the banks sloping up from the water, the oversize T-shirt she wore as a bathing suit cover-up bunched in her hands, clutched to her mouth. Luz saw the grief in her eyes before she lowered the T-shirt and let it loose in a long wail.

Now, fourteen years later, death again. Mere miles from that spot on the Frio, in her parents' house in Uvalde. Luz sits beside her mother, curled up in the hospice bed, smoothing the patchy dark hair against her scalp. Her mother has not spoken in days. Luz watches her chest rise and fall. Until it just falls, and she waits for the rise, but it doesn't come. Finally, it doesn't come. She presses her cheek to her mother's cooling collarbone, sharp and frail beneath the nightgown; the circular ridge of the port-a-cath digs into her skin, but she does not care. Beside her, her father weeps into the pillow by her mother's face. Gone. She is gone. No fanfare, no warning. Just days of this waiting. And now they are over.

Sorrow and relief course through her, twin currents. The relief shames her; Luz bites her tongue and bears down hard.

By the time her husband, Carlos, walks in after the seven-hour drive from Galveston, the men from Suarez Funeral Home have come and gone. Her dad speaks softly into his cell phone. Luz watches him from her seat on the couch as she folds the bed linens—she has washed, dried, and ironed each one, shoved the hospice bed against the wall, and returned her parents' bed back where it used to be.

Carlos reaches out to touch her face. His eyes are red and raw; he must have cried the entire drive. *You okay?*

He seems surprised she isn't crying. He doesn't understand. Unlike these men, she doesn't expel her grief through tears or noises. No bargaining, no anger. Instead she feels focused, sharper somehow. What Luz knows is simple: Her mother is dead, and she wants her back. She wants her back whole, the way she was before that stubborn tumor wormed in, lodging first in her breasts and then, once those were gone, reappearing where it had with her mother before her in the soft hollow of an ovary. But Luz knows, too, that she can't have these things; simple, again. She is not stupid. She feels electrified in a way she has not been in years, alive and thrumming with the need to work, and work, piecing all this back the way it was.

She waits for Carlos to hug her dad, and when he sits beside her on the couch, moving to enfold her in his arms, she pulls back. In a clear voice tells him, *I don't want to go back to Galveston. I want to move back home. Not here—to Concan, really. And the river.*

His jaw drops. It's a sudden move. They've had a few good years in Galveston just steps from where his parents and childhood friends still live. But he reads something in the shadows of her face and nods. *Okay, baby, we can do that.* Luz knows he is thinking about her own breasts and ovaries, about the children he wants in the future. He'd have promised her anything.

The way she feels about river country—it's the same way Carlos feels about the Gulf. Luz cannot understand his near-feverish devotion to Galveston's brown sand, brown sea, the hordes of people who clog the beaches and leave Styrofoam cups and ripped chanclas amid knots of blood-colored seaweed. Who would choose that, she wonders—that tiny slice of a tiny sea—when all around you beats the heartblood of Texas, its green veins?

That's where they met: college students at a ranch party on the Nueces, a stretch of the river where fresh water sinks into dark pools so deep she couldn't swim to the bottom in one breath. Carlos Saldivar, he said, his full name, shaking her hand like she was a man. Luz liked that. He had a city look about him—when he said he attended UT Dallas, she laughed with the superiority she'd been taught as a Longhorn in Austin—and she felt like impressing him, or rather shocking him. Still the reckless ten-year-old rock scaler, cliff jumper. She climbed to the top of the bluff and leapt, spiraling through the air before slicing the water in a dive. She broke the surface, grinning, her friends cheering, and Carlos Saldivar stared with her beer in his hand and his mouth open, admiration in his eyes. He called her ballsy. He kissed her that night; he proposed a year later.

They were married a month after they both graduated college. Carlos suggested they move back to Galveston while he earned his real estate license, and she reluctantly agreed. His face lit up at the thought of going home, so bright she couldn't bear to dampen it by telling him it wasn't her home. What argument did she have, after all? His roots were buried deep in the town he loved, a sprawling weave of family and friends and history; unlike hers, from the southwestern wedge of the state, where the family tree consisted of her and her parents, both transplants from frontera towns. *It's nothing*, she told herself again and again. *It's easy.* Easy to uproot and move to the island with him, take a job as an office manager for a church rectory, grab drinks with his friends Hector and Carly and Jess at one of the dive bars lining the Seawall. He had a place, had people.

On Galveston she found salt water for miles and miles, heat and sweat in the air stinging her eyes, coating the insides of her mouth. All Luz had ever known in her twenty-one years was the rich damp-muck scent of cypress trees and chalky rocks and a cool green river. Carlos added a pool to the backyard of their bungalow on Pompano Avenue, but it wasn't enough—the bottom scraped clean against her soles, the water felt lukewarm instead of spring-chilled. The drive became too far for her parents to make once the cancer metastasized a year later. She spent so much time back home that the thought of Galveston, of speeding her car past the potholes and semis and fast-food joints of 10 and 45, made her as queasy as Cytoxan made her mother. Not to mention the constant reminders—every clump of hair falling out, every purple ring in the bed of her mother's fingernails—that this could happen to her as well, that she carried the same faulty coding in the genes.

No more, she thinks. She is still in her parents' home, listening to the mockingbirds chatter and chase, watching through the kitchen window as they race around her mother's jasmine, star-studded vines creeping up the porch posts. She hears Carlos watching TV in the living room, the strains of some TNT crime procedural. Upstairs her father is napping—Luz realizes he does that a lot now; they both do. They have learned it requires a new kind of energy, this living without her.

She flexes her fingers as they start to cramp. She has been writing thank-yous for an hour, responses to the many condolence cards, prayer and donation booklets, food deliveries. Someone has to. Luz closes her eyes briefly, reminds herself she is coming home, that Carlos has said yes. *It's nothing. It's easy.*

Her father descends, sleepy-eyed, gray-stubbled, in a T-shirt and the Longhorn pajama pants she gave him three Christmases ago. When she tells him they are moving to Concan, he calls her mija and cries a little. *It's going to be different, so you know. Things are changing,* he says. *It's not how it used to be.*

I know. The world before her eyes and beneath her feet fits wrong now, like two halves of a photo that don't quite line up. She finds herself tripping over her own shoes or running her hips into the sharp edges of tables. Her own body has stopped making sense. But she doesn't say that.

———

Carlos heads back to Galveston after the funeral to arrange their move, and Luz stays an extra week. Her father spends hours poring over the realty listings in Concan, Utopia, even Leakey. She wants a new place, their own, no matter how much he claims it wouldn't bother him to have them both at the house. She bristles imagining Carlos crammed into her old bed, as fun as he jokes it would be. She doesn't want him near her old things; she can't explain why.

On the first calm day, she makes the twenty-minute drive north from Uvalde into the foothills, to where the rivers run. As she winds, speeding up on the two-lane roads, she thinks how Carlos flinches at the sudden drops, the turns, while she delights in them. The wax and wane of the hills. The mesquites and shrub grass melting into cedar trees stretching tall. Paved roads that become the crunch of crushed rock or caliche beneath tires.

Her father mentioned their friends' general store on Highway 83 needs a manager. So she stops in front of the small wooden building, admiring the hand-carved goods for sale, the thorny bougainvillea spilling pink and red out of clay pots. The owners are both inside at the counter; seeing Luz, Mrs. Caballero begins to cry, *Pobrecita mija*, and Mr. Caballero pulls her in for a hug. When she says she's moving home, Mrs. Caballero cries harder. Luz signs the paperwork for the job that afternoon.

She knows she should go back to Galveston even briefly, but she cannot. Carlos soothes her over the phone: *I can handle it, don't worry.* She cannot bring herself to feel guilty that he is processing their move, his own uprooting, alone. She sleeps in her old room, tucked between the shadows thrown by her cheerleading megaphone and framed diplomas and stuffed animals, the photos of her and her mother smiling.

It takes negotiating over the next few months, but eventually, Carlos signs on with a Utopia brokerage. He puts their Galveston house on the market—Jess promises to trim the yard, Carly to look after the stray tabby cat Luz leaves scraps for—and they spend their savings on a two-acre plot with an old cabin about a mile downriver from the tourist area, nestled among ancient pecan trees and a stagnant, marshy part of the Frio where nobody wants to swim. It is only a quarter mile to where the current picks up, and Luz can walk down there any time she wants. She moves in immediately; Carlos joins her with the rest of their things soon after.

In May, she takes him to the river.

When she slides down the mucky slope, stepping between rock and cypress roots to dip her foot in, Luz gasps with pleasure: still steal-your-breath cold, the water, Texas not quite hot enough yet to want it that way. Some locals are there—she recognizes them as swiftly as she does the tourists with their broad-brimmed hats and waterproof stereos. She braces herself and cannonballs in, Carlos's laugh ringing in her ears. Beneath the water, she opens her eyes to watch minnows and the occasional striped fish slip past. *Home. I'm home.*

That night she gets her period, and she sees the disappointment in his eyes when she unpacks the tampons.

In bed he slides an arm around her, and she burrows in, puts her cheek against his tense shoulders and knows he's thinking, as she is, of that mutation coded into her DNA. Given to her by her mother, by her grandmother, generations ago. Thinking, too, how some researchers speculate her staggering chances of getting cancer will decrease once she's had children. Decrease. Decrease. The risk like a blaze weakening, folding into itself if she'd just get pregnant. *It would be simple*, Carlos has said before. She can conceive, after all. BRCA doesn't prevent that. And they want children eventually, don't they?

She agreed, but she lied. She doesn't know how to say she is afraid of a baby. She hates the idea of being a mother now that she is stumbling without hers, when she knows very well how quickly a mother leaves her child behind.

Don't worry, baby, he says. *It'll happen if it's meant to happen*. Luz imagines the thread of her life unspooled, extended just for giving birth. Have a baby, live longer. *Simple*, they say—doctor, father, husband. He strokes the small of her back, and she hates him so much in that moment that she has to remind herself she loves him.

———

He gets used to river-country ways, her man from the Gulf. Luz tells him how she has been coming here since before here was here. How back then there were only a handful of cabins along the banks, one general store with tubes and sunblock, one tiny dive with greasy hamburgers and lukewarm Cokes. How the campsites were mostly empty, the water high and fast and worthy of the name Frio; the drought has brought the levels lower these days. She used to hurl out of the backseat, ripping off clothes to the bathing suit underneath, despite her mother shouting to put her things in the car, and racing to the rope swing—before it was frayed from so many city fists closing around it—and whooping as she let go.

Carlos tries it, too, one day, the jump from the rope swing. He doesn't get very high, but his half flip is admirable.

A family of tourists clambers onto the banks. A white boy with red hair takes his turn on the rope swing, attempting a somersault. He hits the water back-first. Luz laughs at his yelp, his flat, smacking splash, but Carlos winces in sympathy.

That rope is damn near falling apart. Safety hazard, I bet.

She says, *It's been there since I was a kid.*

He swipes water from his eyes. *Yeah, Luz, that's the point.*

———

One evening they eat at the Cattle Prod, the big bar and grill. Carlos sits on the patio with a view overlooking the stretch where people place lawn chairs in the river and listen to George Strait. Luz walks to the bar, tells the bartender their order, and he squints at her, saying her name. She doesn't recognize him at first. But he says it again, and as she stares, he smiles.

Josh? she asks, and he laughs.

I knew it was you.

The Josh in front of her is slightly shorter than the wide receiver she dated all through high school—plumper around the waist and shoulders, narrower in the legs. The tangled dark curls she used to run her hands through have been cropped away close to his head. But the eyes are the same, green as the Frio.

You work here?

A while now, he says, nodding. *I came back to town a year or so after we graduated.* Their high school graduation, he means. The last time she saw him.

He asks what she's doing here, and when she says she's moved back, she and her husband—she mentions Carlos almost by reflex—Josh shakes his head.

What?

Nothing. Just . . . He pauses, filling their glasses from the tap. *I never thought you'd be the kind who came back.*

She's about to say something, maybe that he thought wrong, or that she could say the same of him, but someone else walks up and orders a pitcher of Bud. Josh winks at her, steps away.

She returns to the table and hands Carlos his drink. He glances at it—*Baby, where's yours?*—and she looks down. He'd wanted a Shiner, she a rum and Diet. But she was so distracted by Josh she brought back two Shiners. *It's okay*, Carlos says. *We'll make it work.*

———

They visit her dad once a week, making the drive into Uvalde to meet him at the Catholic church. She attends Mass and mouths the words, asking for forgiveness from the God she isn't sure she believes in anymore, and then she takes her dad to lunch. He's concerned about the developers making their way into town—reps from various businesses have been spotted in Sabinal, Utopia, and Uvalde. Carlos thinks it's a good idea to bring in new money and venues to the area. She and her dad trade sorrowful glances. *City boy*, her dad says, and they chuckle.

Carlos mentions their active hurricane season this year—some formations way out on the Gulf. His parents have made plans to stay with his brother in Katy if they're forced to evacuate.

We're so far out now that probably no one will come stay. But I figured we could offer anyway, in case. He glances once at Luz and away quickly, but she can read his thoughts, his sorrow, at being so far from home. *His* home.

Like who? she asks.

Carly and her grandmother. Jess, maybe. Hector's in Sealy now, so he's probably fine, but I'm thinking of the ones still on the island. If that's okay with you?

Luz sips her iced tea, considers. She didn't like Carly at first. Carlos's only female friend, a girl he'd known all his life, an islander, bound to be rough. And she was. Loud and blunt, her dark waves of hair frizzing in the humidity. The way she drank whiskey with the guys, still wore lip liner a shade too dark. But when her mother's cancer metastasized, Luz found herself calling Carly almost every day. She was in nursing school and she answered Luz's questions, asked around for the answers if she didn't know them. Sent over Domino's and Wingstop and, once, King Ranch casserole—*Hector's grandmother's recipe*, she said. *She's from Brownsville, so you know it's legit.*

Yes, Luz says. *Tell them they can come here if they need a place to stay.*

Later her dad asks if she has seen anyone from school, and she mentions Josh. *Yeah*, he says, *he's been back a little while now. I saw his mom the other day, she said he couldn't get his grades up to keep that football scholarship. Bounced*

*around to a few other schools, then finally packed it in. Qué
lástima. Hell of a receiver, that boy.*

Carlos looks at her. *Friend of yours?*

Just a guy I knew growing up.

She wonders about cycles. What leaves, what returns. In
her mind flickers a bright cartoon diagram of the water
cycle from elementary school science: rain, groundwater,
evaporation, rain again. Over and over and over, repeating
through the years. People are born, grow up, build lives by
the water, die, are replaced by other people. The current
flows down to some larger body she can't see, and the river
refills.

She pauses reshelving sunblock and bug spray on the
general store shelves to reach for her phone and type a text.
Want to hang tonight?

Minutes later: *Sure. I'm off at 7.* Josh sends a smiley
face.

She tucks her phone back in her pocket. Karma. Sending something out into the world that will ultimately come
back to her.

In the fading light Luz inhales the scent of rock and wet
ground thick in her nostrils, getting thicker as she and Josh
draw nearer to the water. She notices—with small delight—
that despite the new bridges there are still crossings in
Concan like this one in front of them, where the current
flows right over the road, the paving worn ice-smooth by
moss and water. She and Josh laugh about the special san-
dals in the general store she has to stock for tourists; they

two, like the other river rats, don't wear them. The grip of her toes, the crevices in her calloused soles, these are all she needs. Josh rolls up his jeans, slips off his shoes, and she follows suit. Crosses the road barefoot with him. Steps over gnarled cypress roots that have snaked their way up out of the ground where they belong and into the water.

He says how sorry he is about her mom, chokes up a little. She thanks him, doesn't mention that her mother never liked him. They pass the crescent curl of the river, downstream from the waterfall where they once spent a whole summer making out. She doesn't mention that, either.

He tells her about TCU. *I tried, Luz—you feel me? I really did. I could've done it. I had some good seasons left in me.* She pats him on the shoulder because she does; she knows just how hard that must have been for him. In a rural area like this, in a state like this, where boys play sports and launch as high as they can to the pros, only to fall short and spend their lives welding pipes, digging in the dirt, firing a gun in Afghanistan. How that is life, even if they wish it were different. Josh was closer than most, the fall to earth more heartbreaking, people in town say, because *that boy had such potential*. And because he is white, of course: unspoken.

It's nearly an hour before he mentions he has a three-year-old daughter. It happens at a moment she is bending to scoop up skipping stones. He says it so casually—mentions his daughter, Kayla or Layla—that the words feel like a branding iron on Luz's skin, a sear that strips her bare as it closes her back again.

He and Kayla/Layla's mother aren't together, he says, but he sees her every weekend. Luz turns the stone around in her hand. She didn't know Josh had wanted kids. Things are so different from when he last walked with her by the river, she realizes. He has a child now, and no wife, and she has Carlos and no child. A minute ago she would have said she was pleased with that, but now she is unreasonably angry—she realizes that, too.

The sounds of Josh's fingers tapping on his phone, swiping for pictures of his daughter to show her. Miles away, her father sits in an empty house, watching a World War II documentary, growing older by the second. Carlos, checking the latest weather forecasts online, waiting at home for her.

She skips her stone against the flat surface of the river. *It's getting late.*

He walks her to the parking lot. *This was great, catching up*, he says. *Maybe I'll see you around.*

Cycles, karma. The girl she was who left; this woman, returning.

She presses her lips to his.

He jerks in surprise, draws back from her—just an inch—but she grips his hips and pulls him in. Doesn't let him step away. Murmurs that she has missed him all these years, a lie, but she makes it convincing: calls him baby, says his name.

When he relents and says hers—when he softens his mouth and hardens his hands—she feels only a glittering kind of triumph. Push down the shame, she tells herself. Push down, too, these things: the metal of his truck door handle beneath her palm; the bitter, mouth-warm smell of Skoal from the spit cup in its holder; the clatter of beer cans and baby toys and goldfish cracker crumbs falling to the floormats as he shoves them from his backseat with one swipe; the cold nose of what might be a stuffed dog digging into the bare skin of her ass; his daughter's Minnie Mouse toddler seat against the top of her head where she slams it there again and again until she flips, pushes him down on the seat and the stuffed dog, and rides him with her eyes closed so she can't see Minnie, can't see his hands on her. This does not work. Carlos's face burns in her mind, and she opens her eyes, wide as she can. Focus: Josh's hair curling damply against his brow in the way she remembers. The sounds Josh makes, like sobbing.

On Fourth of July weekend, she takes Carlos to Utopia to see the fireworks.

Some people bring lawn chairs and picnic blankets, but most just bring a truck, lower the tailgate, perch on the edge. They arrive at the park an hour early and still have to battle over space for Carlos's Tacoma. New, this traffic— Luz remembers visiting as a child, spreading blankets over a largely empty field. Her father handing her an electric-blue cloud of cotton candy. Her mother wiping her sticky cheeks, pulling her head down to rest in her lap.

You okay? Carlos has opened the cooler and is digging around in the ice for a beer.

I'm fine. She takes a can from him, snaps it open.

You're not, though, he says, and his voice makes her stop, look closely at him for the first time in a while. She notices now that he is looking at her that way, too: closely. *Are we okay?*

What do you mean? Do not blush, she wills herself. Do not show him the shade of any of the lies inside.

I don't know, Luz. I feel like we . . . He exhales, says again, *I don't know.* She opens her mouth to respond, but he raises a hand, dripping from the ice. *Forget it. Let's just enjoy this.*

Her husband leans back next to her, pulling his knees up like a little boy. Automatically she tips her head against his shoulder; her cheek rises with the movement of his long sigh. *Baby*, he says quietly; then he doesn't say anything more.

There are a lot of people; the fireworks show had become a big deal while she was away. The park is packed with the tourists who have spent a long day on the Frio or the Nueces and now want to see colorful things blow up. So many unfamiliar faces, trucks with license plates from Oklahoma or Tamaulipas. She spots the red-haired boy. He and his family have set up lawn chairs in the grass; he has a fresh sunburn nearly the shade of his hair across his nose and a *Welcome to Concan, the Cancún of Texas* T-shirt. To the west, the sound of running water, corners of the rivers that will be discovered soon, but right now the tourists are all here in the park, so the corners remain quiet, remain hers.

A black F-250 catches her eye, and she spots Josh on the tailgate, sharing cotton candy with a blond toddler. He bounces her on his lap and wipes her cheek with his sleeve. She is giggling. Something tells Luz he has seen her, too, but they both keep their gazes fixed straight.

The girl is holding a stuffed dog with a black nose, and Luz remembers the cold, hard shape of it on her skin. She pictures texting Josh later tonight, *Meet me at the first crossing.* She is sure he will come, imagines slipping into the backseat of his 250 again and again, continuing to do so until one of them finally stops—but what she can't imagine is when that will be, why she wants him at all, why she feels so much pleasure being cruel. She should feel regret, but she doesn't allow herself to feel much anymore—only to act, to move and keep moving. Because she can. She has to.

———

Most nights, when they're not both too tired, they have sex. It's still good; Luz enjoys it. Carlos falls asleep after, but she lies beside him with one hand on his chest, the other pressed to her pelvis. Imagining the activity there, grainy health-class VHS-style sperm seeking out an egg. In this private moment, she allows herself honesty, some truth she can share with her own body. *Go away*, she whispers. *Go away*.

———

After Labor Day, the season dies down. The tourists and campers drift away, back east to the big cities, to traffic and Red Lobsters and stories-high overpasses. Luz doesn't miss the many hours renting out tubes and canoes, slinging snorkels and Off to an onslaught of tourists. She spends time instead doing the books, reading a paperback romance in between the occasional visit from someone looking for a cabin rental, a quiet weekend for their family. Carlos is busy showing around a team of developers from Houston who have *big plans for the area*, he says, *a great new vision for what Concan could be*.

A hurricane called Rita forms, miles away, out on the Gulf. Luz doesn't miss caring about hurricanes; around here, farmers speak of needing *one good hurricane* and the downpour it would bring to the crops. No worries of evacuation, of flooding or wind damage: rain the only element of a hurricane, and an always desirable one. But Rita shifts her path to Galveston. Carlos calls his parents, ensures they are evacuating, and then Carly calls, and a day later she and Jess and her grandmother, Mrs. Castillo, arrive.

At midnight, Luz watches their headlights pull into the drive. Jess rubs his face wearily before he climbs out of the car. Carly is red-eyed, Mrs. Castillo half asleep still. It should have been a six-hour drive; it had taken them eleven, inching along I-10 in bumper-to-bumper traffic, then Highway 90, north through the back roads and winding paths studded with occasional whitetail or armadillo. Inside the cabin, she lit jasmine-scented candles, warming the guest room where Carly and Mrs. Castillo would sleep, beside the pullout sofa made with extra pillows for Jess.

Señora, Luz says, reaching a hand out for Mrs. Castillo. *Let me help you.*

She supports the woman with an arm around her stiff back. *Ah. Gracias, mija*, Mrs. Castillo murmurs as Luz helps her to the guest bed. *Gracias. You're a good girl.* She pats her cheek, stares into Luz's eyes for what feels like far too long, until Luz pulls away.

You look good, Carly says in the living room, after Carlos passes out glasses of Jack on ice and he and Jess head outside to smoke cigars. She swipes a strand of waving hair out of her face, raises her bourbon. *You seem better, being home.*

I am. It's been good for me.

Luz's phone chimes, lights up with a text. Josh. She hopes Carly doesn't notice the way she shifts it out of view, but Carly's tired eyes flicker, sharpen. She sips bourbon. They both fidget, aware of the new, viscous space between them. The next day they order food from the Prod, and though Luz insists she can get it herself, Carly goes with her to pick it

up. Josh is waiting at the bar with their order. Goddamn it.
He eyes her, shakes Carly's hand; they smile too brightly, talk
about being old friends too loudly. Carly says nothing until
the car doors close, and then she sighs. *Luz, you bitch.* She
sighs again. *Fuck.* There's no heat in it, only something sorrowful, something like grief.

Luz wants to scream. Snap, What right do you have
to judge me, what could you possibly know. She wants to
explain cycles, circles. How what she has lost made her this
way, this brittle, hollow thing. What would she know, this girl
who has only ever been on the island where she was born?
Who has never left or been left, never had to weigh her own
wants against the world?

But she drives on in silence. Carly turns her face to the
window, out toward the river running, and Luz bites her
lip against the sudden prick of tears. The pain startles her.
How sharp, how deep, this loss of Carly, whom she had not
known was so dear a friend.

They leave the next morning, after the news shows
Rita veering away from Galveston, heading northeast to the
Louisiana border instead. Mrs. Castillo pats Luz's cheek
again, climbs in the backseat of the Corolla. The hug Carly
gives Luz is perfunctory, for show, her arms stiff and brittle. When she puts her arms around Carlos, she holds on.
Carly rests her chin on his shoulder and stays, so long he
laughs and Jess makes a joke about being jealous, but she
hangs on anyway.

———————

All for nothing, que no? Carlos's father laughs, and even
over the phone his laughter is booming, a cheerful sound.
Carlos's cell is on speaker, resting on the kitchen counter

as he scrapes leftover barbecue and salad into containers, scoops uneaten dill pickles back into the jar. *Rita turns anyway. Pobrecito Louisiana.* Beside him, Luz replaces the throw pillows on the couch and plumps them carefully. She has stripped the sheets and pillowcases from the guest bed and couch, carried the bundle to the laundry room. She will wash, dry, fold tonight. She will put this back the way it was.

Such a hassle, Carlos's mother says loudly. Luz visualizes her leaning over to shout into the phone. *We went all the way to your brother's for nothing. Pero at least we went early and didn't get stuck like your friends. Gracias a Dios. At least they made it.*

What a terrible drive, his father says. He snorts. *They tell us to evacuate, and we do, y por qué? So we can boil in our cars on the freeway, and run out of gas, and not move for hours. So the storm can turn and miss us altogether. We should have stayed.*

Carlos shakes his head, and frustration rises in Luz's throat. She reaches for the phone. *We can't think like that, Roy. You were lucky this time. Look at New Orleans, not even a month ago.* Choices, storms, genes: it only takes one bad one, she wants to say. *We were lucky.*

Roy starts to respond, but Irene speaks over him. *Sí, mija.* Her mother-in-law's voice is strong, sure. *You're right. You're right*, she repeats. And Luz hears—or imagines she hears—the iron agreement, the knowledge they share that their men do not: Things can go wrong, and will, and this world is cruel, but we move through it anyway. *Maybe the next one will not swerve to Mexico or Louisiana, but head right for us. Diosito*, Irene swears, *what a storm that will be.*

Yes, Luz agrees. She thinks of the Fourth of July, her

head on Carlos's shoulder, her lover a few yards away, and the moment when the grainy strains of Sousa pushed through the park's speakers and the first crack of a rocket echoed. How as one the whole park lifted their faces and watched the streak of light rise higher, waiting for the burst they knew was coming.

THE LAST KARANKAWAS

Carly

Carly finally admits something is wrong the day her grand-mother brings home a whole pompano and tries to eat it raw. She walks in off her night shift to find Magdalena crouched on the living room floor, tearing strips of fish flesh with her fingers. The linen pantsuit she wore to six a.m. Mass bunches at her crotch, her waist, and tightens at the thighs and hips. Juice worms down her hand; bone and meat snag beneath her manicure. She looks up and with her mouth full says, "This is the way of our people." When Carly snatches up the newspaper-and-fish bundle, Magda-lena sits back on her haunches and hisses.

Carly drops the thing in the kitchen trash, then leans against the stove and presses the heels of her hands into her eyes. She waits a few moments, until she no longer feels the burn of tears threatening, or the urge to scream churning in her throat.

Weeks, months, they blur together; how long Magdalena has been this way. Signs recognized and ignored, perhaps denied—Carly has worked only NICU in the two years since graduating from nursing school, but some things you don't forget, like a rotation at a nursing home in Texas City. Even Jess senses it on the nights he sleeps over ("Babe, your grandma called me Lando today"—the name of his father, years gone—"that's weird, right?"). The slow but steady trudge into dementia—she can deny it no longer. Her grandmother is moving away from her, as surely as if she were crossing the causeway.

Carly opens her eyes, and the pompano stares back up at her from the open trash can. Its face is ravaged—Magdalena likes the head best. Still, one eye is intact, black as a piece of tar, Gulf-polished. Fixed on the fragments of a life she can't see anymore.

Carly slams the lid down, bracing herself as her grandmother storms into the kitchen.

There have been bad days in Magdalena's decline, but none like this. Today Magdalena thrusts her face into Carly's and battles. Her breath smells of brine and coffee still warm in the pot and the Listerine she gargles each morning before Mass. In her anger, she slips fully into Spanish. Carly stays motionless, recalling the training from that one rotation, when she thought she would never need it. The aggression is coming from a place of fear or physical discomfort. She doesn't mean it. Don't touch her. Relax your face; keep your hands loose and nonthreatening in front of you even though they want to rise up, fist. Accept the flecks of spit on your chin. Translate. Imagine the words as toy blocks, the ones kids in the hospital pedi wing play with—turning over from Spanish to English. One side A, one side *a*. One side *yo sé lo que piensas de mí*, one side *I know what you think of me*. *Niña ingrata: you ungrateful child*.

———

Carly can't blame the dementia. Well, not for all of it. For the vitriol, yes, her grandmother was always firm but not hateful, has never been hateful. But not for the fish, not for eating it raw. Magdalena thinks it the way of their people. Their people, the Karankawas.

Her grandmother has believed they are descendants of the vanished Texas tribe since before Carly was born—long before she grew old enough to witness the threads of Magdalena's mind fray, then fuse again in the wrong places. She offered up her musings as fact over breakfast ("Our people went days without food, and look at you, wasting scrambled eggs"); at Mass ("Sí, somos católicas, niña, pero it's not sacrilege to offer prayers up to the wind and the sun. It's hurricane season"); walking around Galveston ("Oleanders, yes, they are dangerous, but our grandmothers wore them *because* they are dangerous"). Her own father told her they had Karankawa blood, Magdalena claimed, and his father before him, and she came from a tradition where elders were believed.

So as a child, Carly believed, too. In the stillness before bedtime, soothed by the humming of the window AC, she listened to her grandmother's murmured tales. Their Karankawa ancestors were as real as Lafitte, as steeped in legend as his buried treasure, the one tourists search for but none as yet have found. They became real to Carly, real as the uneven brown coils of her hair and the freckles that fireworked her shoulders and cheeks. She sensed centuries of stories running in her veins: a presence of secrets that the body and not the mind could remember.

She believed. Even when her mother scolded her. "Don't be silly," Maharlika said, hands planted on hips, whenever Carly walked into the house with mud smeared across her cheeks or white oleanders twined into the band of her ponytail. She snapped the words at her, not caring if her mother-in-law could hear. "Your grandmother's people are from Texas, from Mexico. *I* am from the Philippines. You have no Indian in you anywhere. And the Indians left anyway. They could not last here."

As it turned out, neither could Maharlika, who one day packed a small bag and left without any word. They assumed she returned to the Philippines, to her island just south of Manila and the extended family they had never met. "Some people are not fighters," Magdalena had said, stroking six-year-old Carly's hair where it lay tear-tangled in her lap. "For some people that is not their way. Ya. Enough crying, Carly Elena." Carly wiped her face, thinking for the first time, *People run away. I could, too.*

She didn't run. But she kept the thought tucked close, in the years after as grandmother and granddaughter crafted their own rituals. Became a tribe of two.

Bay Pines Care Center looks more like a luxe condo building than a nursing home, all soothing beachscape paintings and plush armchairs in clusters atop wide, clean floors. After the pompano incident, Carly pulled strings for weeks. She persuaded a few of the UTMB doctors who liked her to call in favors. It was worth it, she decided, on the day she toured the place. There was a doorman and an intern at the check-in desk to escort visitors to their family member's room. The room itself is spacious; she paid extra for a solo room, ignoring the twinge of resentment she felt writing the check. She can afford it, but just barely.

The TV has HBO, so Magdalena won't miss *True Blood*, and Telemundo, so she won't miss *Más Sabe el Diablo*. Carly makes a note to bring the colcha from home to lay on the bed. She will stick a neon-green *BOI: Born On the Island!* bumper sticker in a place of pride on the mirror, where Magdalena can see it every day and remember she holds that coveted status among islanders. She will hang the replica of the Virgen de Guadalupe on the wall beside the door, ready for the touch of fingers kissed in reverence.

But on the day Carly and Jess bring her to the home, Magdalena takes one look and shakes her head. "I can't see the beach from here." She pulls at the ends of her long braid, black shot through with sterile-swab white since Carly's infancy.

"There's no beach here, Grandma," Carly reminds her. "We're in League City, not Galveston."

"No. That won't work. I need to be on the island."

"Well, there aren't any good homes there."

"*Our* home is there."

"Grandma, please." Carly's fingernails bite into her own palms.

"I'll wait outside," says Jess, reading her eyes, and bends down almost double to kiss Magdalena's cheek. "See you soon, Señora. Have fun here."

"You're a good boy, Jesusmaría," she responds, patting him on the arm. "I'll see you at home."

Carly sighs.

"I belong on the island," Magdalena says in a cheerful voice to the young nurse who escorted them—*K. Caballero, RN*, it reads on her name tag, as noted with approval by C. Castillo, RN. "Somos las últimas Karankawas."

"This is only temporary, Grandma." Carly gives the lie she prepared, expecting Magdalena's stubborn refusal. "Hurricane season, remember?"

"Ah, yes. Our home is going to be very damaged," Magdalena tells the nurse. "I know these things."

"I see," the nurse says politely.

"My granddaughter thinks I'll be safe here. There is a storm coming."

"Is there?" the nurse asks. "I moved here a few months ago, so this is my first hurricane season. But I haven't heard about any coming close." Her dark eyebrows lift, disappearing beneath a thick fringe of bangs.

"There isn't one yet," Carly assures her.

"No, there is. A big one. It's out there, on its way. Lo sé." Magdalena turns her head, sends Carly a beaming smile. "My granddaughter has everything handled. She's very smart. She's going to be a nurse, too, like you."

"I *am* a nurse, Grandma."

"You will be, niña. I wouldn't miss that graduation for anything."

It was a pinning ceremony, not a graduation. And Magdalena hadn't missed it. Carly looked over from her spot on the stage and saw her sitting proudly next to Jess, sandwiched between his six-foot-three frame and another, smaller man. Jess told her later that when Magdalena complained because she couldn't see Carly walking across to get her pin, he had taken her camera and snapped the picture himself. "Jess's-eye view," Magdalena said of the picture later, and the three of them laughed.

Carly rubs the aching spot over her left eye, and the nurse steps back. "I'll give you some privacy, let you get settled in. If you need anything, my name is Kristin. I'm days around here." She pauses behind Carly and places a soft hand on her shoulder, pats. She closes the door behind her.

Carly shows her grandmother how to work the remote for the TV, how to adjust the mechanical bed to her liking. Together they arrange the framed photos Carly brought on the dresser, the nightstand, the windowsill that looks out at a tidy courtyard. Carly as a red-cheeked, nearly bald infant; as a child playing on the beach, with frizzy curls and a tan line; with Magdalena at her First Communion wearing a frilled white dress and borrowed lipstick. Magdalena's wedding photo beside Carly's grandfather, dead before Carly was born. Magdalena's hair gleams black as a raven's wing beneath her veil, her hand, resting gently on her husband's arm, gloved in lace. Neither smiles.

Carly leans in and kisses the paper-thin skin of her cheek. "It's going to be fine, Grandma. I love you."

"I'll see you soon," Magdalena says, nodding. "When you finish up at work, come take me home so we can prepare for this storm."

Jess is waiting for her by the car, beneath the cloudless sky that holds no hint of a storm, only the steam from the sea, a hurricane-less Gulf. He walks around to the driver's side, snatching the keys from her cold hands.

The great thing about Jess is that if he doesn't know what to say, he doesn't say anything. He laces his fingers through hers as they drive. Keeps quiet the whole way back down I-45 while she leans her face against his shoulder, tears and snot soaking into the sleeve of his Astros T-shirt.

Jess never minded the lies. Even now that they are older, now that Carly recognizes how absurd the idea is that she comes from a long-vanished tribe, he shrugs off her bitter rants. Shrugs off whether Magdalena's theories are dropped into conversation offhandedly ("Put on your shirt, Jesusmaría, only my people could walk around the beach naked") or with the detail of delusion ("This is the spot, here, míralo, Jess, this is where my fathers made landfall when they arrived, here is where they sacrificed a sea turtle they'd found on the journey across the bay"). When Magdalena uses his full name, which Carly knows he hates, he always smiles. He has delighted in Magdalena's stories since he and Carly were kids, running wild from Trout to Tuna or playing pickup ball in Lindale Park with the rest of the Fish Village children.

Stories, he calls them, but Carly knows them by another name.

She did a history project in seventh grade on the Karankawas. She stood in front of the class and restated what her peers—most of them BOIs like her—already knew: that the tribe of Indians had inhabited the swath of coastline from Galveston to Corpus Christi; that they'd broken up and dissolved long ago; that no one really knew what had happened to them. Some historians theorized they'd joined up with the Tonkawas, abandoned the Gulf, and moved farther inland. Or they'd migrated down to Mexico and the Coahuiltecans. Or they'd died out, killed or driven away by white settlers. Or they were everywhere, looking brown and black and white, their Native blood running beneath the skin.

Her teacher smiled indulgently at the presentation, until Carly added, "That's what I think. My grandma says we are descended from the Karankawas, too." She looked over as her classmates began to giggle, and she caught the disappointed frown on Ms. Morton's face.

Afterwards, Ms. Morton pulled Carly outside. "I want you to know that it's a tale—a nice tale," the teacher said firmly. "And I'm sure it's fun to believe as a kid. But history class is not the place for wild theories."

Through the glass window of the door, the rest of the class watched.

"She's a bitch," Jess said valiantly, kicking strewn palm fronds out of his path on the sidewalk as they walked home after school. "It could still be true. Your grandma wouldn't lie." He thought Magdalena's belief about their ancestry was wonderful, that Carly was rooted here in a way he, the child of Valley Mexicans, wasn't. He was jealous.

"Hey, Carly!"

They turned to watch Carlos Saldivar jogging past them.

He grinned, pointed. "You're so stupid. Who'd ever think something dumb like being a Karankawa when everyone knows they're dead? You're just Mexican like the rest of us, Castillo, and a chink, too, 'cause of your mom."

"Shut your fucking mouth, Carlos!" she hollered, and Jess threw off his backpack to chase him, but Carlos was the third-best sprinter in their grade, and he was well down the block laughing, calling "Estúpida" over his shoulder. "No, screw it, Jess." Neither of them aware yet that Carlos would apologize a day later and Carly would forgive him, that he would play catcher for as long as Jess was shortstop, teaching him how to spot and hit a slider.

They neared Jess's house on Dolphin, but Carly knew he wouldn't turn—he'd walk her to Albacore first, then backtrack the two blocks. He could be a good boyfriend, she realized. He'd been a steady best friend all these years.

"Carlos is a piece of shit."

"Yeah, but he's right. That's what Ms. Morton was saying." A dark heaviness settled in Carly's chest. "That my grandma's just making it all up."

Wild theories, Ms. Morton said. The same thought that had crept in on the night Carly's mother left, a thought piercing as a knife: *We are wild. Wild things run away.*

Jess shook his head. His cheeks were flushed, his face sorrowful. To comfort him, as much as herself, Carly slipped her hand into his. Held fast.

Sad as she still feels to look around the Galveston house, to not see Magdalena chattering on the phone with her comadres, sipping her daily Coke on the overstuffed sofa or emerging from the bathroom with her shower cap in place, having Jess move in helps. The studio apartment he rents on Mackeral is a half step up from shitty, but it is his—the first place he's called his own—so it matters. He stays in the apartment for a few weeks after Magdalena moves into Bay Pines, and then he moves into the Albacore house, choosing to pay out the remaining four months on the lease rather than give it up just yet. The shrimping has been good so far, and what is left of his earnings after he drops some off to his mother helps. When oyster season starts in the fall, the boat will be going out regularly, and he is counting on more.

This is their first time sharing a room, a home, for real. Carly imagined it would be gleaming and new to combine their things, to make space in her closet for his jeans and superhero T-shirts, to have one nightstand for her lip balm, one for his glasses. But they have been together so long they already feel broken in. She knows how far left in the driveway she must park her Corolla so she won't clip his truck leaving in the morning; he knows that on days she trains a new nurse she'll be too annoyed to cook and they'll order pizza that night.

In high school it was different, wasn't it? He was the ace shortstop, a crappy student in everything except history, popular in every circle. But quiet, more comfortable sitting with her on a tailgate than tapping a keg somewhere. Their date nights usually ended on the western stretches of the beach, past the city limits, parked on an access point only islanders knew about. He opened every beer bottle for her, even the twist-offs. He still does.

Back then he was getting scouted by schools, big schools like UT and Tech. And though Carly was pushing for them hard, Jess started working weekends out on Mr. Pham's oyster boat. If he wasn't there or playing ball, Jess was talking about oystering. He told her how they tossed shells and too-small oysters overboard, back into the bay, where maybe, just maybe, some alchemy of salt and spore would help them find one another. They might fuse to a sunken car or ship and form a new reef. Jess never spoke so much as when he spoke of working the bay. "I can do this full-time once school is over, be out every day during the oyster season. Get work on Mr. Pham's shrimp boat during the summer. Why would I go anywhere?"

She'd smile, but what she really wanted to do was shake him. He could have left the island for a place as far away as Lubbock, as exotic. Could have driven north on 45 or west on 10 and kept going, going, couldn't he see that? She pictured it countless nights as she crossed the causeway to take nursing classes inland, fantasized about driving between the fringe of tall trees north of the loop, flanking the interstate like guardians, welcoming her to Something Else. Anything Else.

The Karankawas had been built for moving. Expert swimmers and lithe, powerful runners, they would wait for a clear day, load their lives into canoes carved from the hollows of a large oak, and paddle into the shallows off the coast. Make their way from one craggy pile of Texas sand to another, season by season, chasing the food sources and the weather. On these solo drives to and from the mainland, Carly wondered if this was how her grandmother saw their past: as something shaped from delusion.

She'd return from classes and turn onto Albacore to see the drapes her grandmother hung. Usually there was Jess's truck in the drive, tires coated with the grit of the docks, beside the space where Carly should be.

A churning in her blood would start, an urge branching like lightning through her muscles: to wheel, to paddle, to sprint. Between the Karankawas and her wayward mother, wasn't she built for moving, too? She had always thought so.

But she imagined her grandmother behind those curtains stirring chicken and rice. Jess, practicing his rusty Spanish with her, pouring Carly's beer into a glass because she liked it that way. She would remind herself that her people were here, were here, were *here*, open her car door and step out.

––––––

The hurricane—a real one—begins taking shape in August, a few weeks after Magdalena is situated in Bay Pines. On the overhead TV in a patient's room, Carly marks its projected path across Haiti, Cuba, the Gulf, to Galveston and nearly drops her blood pressure cuff, hearing her grandmother's voice. *It's out there, on its way.* Storms are typical, she reminds herself. No need to worry yet, to fret. Until days later, when the weather service replaces its number with a name: Ike.

Jess has heard an Ike Turner joke somewhere, naturally, and he repeats it for Magdalena during their visit to Bay Pines that afternoon. She cackles while Carly rolls her eyes. They eat cookies she has brought from Magdalena's favorite panadería. A good day, she notes. Her grandmother's clothes are pressed and clean, her hair neatly pinned back. Her eyes are sharp, lighting on every movement Jess and Carly make, a bird hopping from branch to branch.

"Tell me about this Ike," she says with an encouraging smile. "Will he be big?"

"They think so." Carly flips the TV to the Weather Channel. As one, they watch the swirl of silver out on the Gulf, far from them, still a screen's worth of space between it and the crescent curve of the coast. "They say it's headed our way."

"Gonna hit Cuba first," says Jess, "do some damage there, then pick up speed in the Gulf from the air. It's been

damn hot on the water this summer." He snatches the last
of the macadamia nuts.

Magdalena nods thoughtfully, eyes fixed on the wind
and water that has been named. "I'll need to find some
palm fronds."

"For what?" asks Jess.

"My blessing. For protection. I need to burn them, we
always burn them. But they don't have palm trees here,
do they? Niña, bring me some from home, next time you
come."

Carly feels her face settle into hard lines, as it always
does when the delusions come on. "You don't have a protection blessing, Grandma. You never have. You usually just
light a candle and pray."

Magdalena clucks her tongue dismissively. "Well, that
won't do any good. I need to burn the palms. They need to
be ones from the island. You know this."

I don't. None of this is real. "You're not allowed to burn
things here. Not even candles. They catch you burning a candle here, you'll be in trouble." Carly presses her lips together,
wills her rising frustration to slow. "I'll go to Sacred Heart and
light one for you, if you want."

"Yes, you'll be on the island, that's good. You won't leave,
will you? Not like last time, look how that turned out."

Two years ago—only a year after Katrina and her devastation of New Orleans, evacuees flooding the Astrodome
and the word *hurricane* instilling a new, healthy fear in even
the hardiest hunker-downers—Hurricane Rita appeared and
veered straight at Galveston. Carlos Saldivar invited them to
stay with him and Luz at their new place in the Hill Country,
and they had not hesitated—for once, not even Magdalena

said a word against a plan of her granddaughter's. Fish Village scattered: Carlos's parents went to his brother in Katy; Ram and his boyfriend crashed in Sealy with Hector's family; Jess's mother and sisters and cousin Mercedes stayed with his tío in Pearland. Only some of the lifers—like Mr. and Mrs. Alvarez across the street, or the Phams on Marlin—remained.

The drive stretched nearly double the amount of time it should have taken, according to Carlos. Magdalena made them all pray the rosary on the way, then ask the earth and the ocean for safety, too, for good measure. At the cabin, Luz had put her mother's quilt on the guest bed, orange with white flowers that looked like the jasmine Magdalena grew by the back patio. Carly fell asleep beneath that quilt, listening to the sounds of cicadas, smelling sun-warmed river cooling into night. Her feet tucked against her grandmother's, breathing her in.

The next day they watched the news together. Jess described the gridlock, how cars ran out of gas left and right, stalled out or overheated in the blistering sun. When they saw a report of a bus carrying nursing home residents that caught fire on the freeway, Magdalena cried.

"You were lucky," Carlos said. They spent two days in the cabin and then Rita, quite contrary, juked northeast. It was almost laughable. "I guess that was all for nothing," Carlos said as they loaded up the car again, and Magdalena had nodded from the backseat. "Next time we stay," she said sternly.

Carly had run her hands through her hair and replied then, as she does now: "Yes, Grandma." Had lied then, as she lies now. "We'll stay."

They stop on Seawall before they head home. It is the middle of the week, and the public beaches aren't swamped yet with late-summer tourists. As a habit, Carly rolls up her jeans and cuffs them mid-calf, then checks her glove compartment for the bottle of baby oil she keeps there to remove tar flecks. They may not need them; these days, tar rarely washes in from the tankers on the bay, not like when they were kids, and she and Jess would walk back to Fish Village with smears of black across their feet and calves.

Clouds have gathered, just enough to break up some of the heat; sunbeams lance through, spotlighting sections of the water. They kick off their flip-flops and leave them on the sand. Jess points to a pelican, yards away. It dives toward the water at high speed and levels out, belly feathers kissing the surface. Low, never wavering. She watches it until it curves around a bend, toward the jetties, and is gone.

Jess disappears, too. When Carly spots him again, he has walked farther down the beach, bending down to gather something, and she realizes he is gathering discarded palm fronds. "You're an idiot," she says as he returns with them, but she reaches out to squeeze his hand, touched in spite of herself.

"Maybe we can burn them," he teases. "Your grandma can tell us how."

He begins brushing the grit and bits of trash away. Carly looks back for pelicans, but she does not see any more.

––––––

"Tell me, Grandma. About the Karankawas." Her voice, trembling in her young throat from terror. Outside thunder and rain—a tropical storm? A hurricane? Carly cannot remember, only recalls the pounding water against the windows, the wind like a woman screaming. The rattle of the roof makes her think of *The Wizard of Oz*, fearing they will lift off the ground and spin in the air, land in a place she cannot imagine, a world unlike any she knows. The horror. She buries her face in the pillow, smelling her grandmother: Vicks and Pond's, Dove soap.

"Our people, niña? Okay. Ven, here." Magdalena draws the girl's head from the pillow, lays it on her own thigh. The cotton and embroidery of her nightgown a comforting scratch on Carly's cheek. "They would not be scared of storms, ves. They never were. They respected them, but they did not let the weather keep them afraid. Storms are part of the world, this world, this place. You love it here, don't you?"

"Yes."

"So did they, and we must, too. To love this place is to love its bad parts también. The brown water, the heat, the zancudos. The storms."

––––––

Carly visits alone on her next day off that week. She brings another box of cookies and the palm fronds she decides she is being silly about: Where is the harm? Certainly Magdalena won't have access to anything causing fire. They both can wind them into crucifix shapes, as they used to every Palm Sunday. But instead Carly walks in to find her grandmother on the floor, curled up in a ball, rocking back and forth, chanting nonsense. The box and palms fall to the ground. A seizure, Carly thinks as she rushes to her side, saying her grandmother's name over and over before realizing this is no seizure. Magdalena is lucid—mostly—telling her, "Stop, niña, stop, I'm fine, it is simply the ancient Karankawa tongue, I am letting the spirits speak through me so they will protect us from the storm." Carly insists no as she shakes her shoulders—"We don't know anything yet, it could move somewhere else, dissipate over Cuba." But Magdalena rises to her knees, slaps her palms against the floor and lowers her forehead to the ground, still muttering words Carly cannot understand. "For protection, niña, we will need it. Ruega conmigo." Tears stream down Carly's cheeks. Part of her wants to. The girl she once was, braiding oleanders into her hair and smearing lard across her shoulders as if it were alligator grease, longs to put her head down beside her grandmother and chant made-up words, believe they mean something, believe they are the kind of people who can control long-ago Indian spirits. But she cannot; it must be the Maharlika in her that keeps her from pretending. Her mother never trusted, and she ran without looking back. Her father, too. Lightning in Carly's blood again, sparking through. *Tell me, Grandma. About the Karankawas.* But she turns away. The grandmother who loved her and raised her, who never left, is praying the rosary in Spanish now, "Dios te salve María, llena eres de gracia." And Carly, full of shame, with shaking hands and a bright knowledge of what she can do, abandons the box where it lies and throws the palm fronds in the trash can by the door, leaving without another word.

THE MIGRANT

Schafer

He doesn't know what he expected, but it wasn't this. Since childhood, he's heard of Galveston: a distant land and, to Schafer, a boy from the rocks-and-river swath of the Hill Country, exotic as Madagascar. From Cab's enthusiastic description—*Beautiful island, man, palm trees and old houses and shit, you'd love it*—he imagined more of an oasis. A postcard beach town.

It is a beach town, sure. He can tell from the air slipping damp fingers beneath the collar of his T-shirt, from the constant cry of gulls, ever-present even when not a bird is in sight, from the throng of pink, flip-flopped tourists weaving through the shops and brightly hued restaurants on Fisherman's Wharf. But the water is all wrong, a murky, silty brown beneath the spiny blanket of seaweed. Sea salt and diesel fill his nostrils—that's probably wrong, too.

Cab was right. Schafer loves it immediately.

He unrolls his shoulders to loosen the knots. It was a long drive, longer still with the I-45 traffic. He parked just past the touristy stretch of Fisherman's Wharf, where there are fewer people and more boats. Past the palm tree tops and roofs of buildings, he can see many masts rising, tall and slim as tally marks. He sweeps the sweaty strands of his hair beneath his ball cap and walks that way.

He is sweating harder by the time he reaches the pier. But there are the boats. Row upon row of shrimpers, trawlers, fishing boats, oyster boats. They bear the badges of hard work: metal glinting beneath a sunburn of rust, wood so battered it is worn soft and feathery as down, splotches where the paint has peeled or faded away, streaks of tar. They are blocky and squat; they were built for hard jobs by hard men and will never be beautiful. Yet they seem to sit atop that brown water so lightly, rocking with the movement like dancers, as if defiant of their shape.

They seem empty, but he spots someone moving on one of the boats farther down the pier. He recognizes it as a shrimper from its long arms that reached out on either side. *That's where the nets would fall,* he thinks, fluttering in the wind and the ocean currents like wings.

"Afternoon."

The guy lifts his head as Schafer calls out, his hands wrapped in coils of rope. "Afternoon."

"Good-looking shrimper you got here."

The guy lifts a forearm, swipes at the sweat collecting beneath the brim of his cap. "She pulls her weight."

"What's the name mean?" Schafer nods at the side of the boat, where the faded letters read *La Cigüeña.*

The guy pauses a moment, then shrugs. "Fuck if I know."

"Oh. Hey. Sorry, I guess I thought—"

"That because I'm brown I know Spanish? Nah." He smiles cheerfully. "I get shit for it all the time. Anyway, she's the *Cig* to us." He wipes his palm on his cargo shorts, then holds it out. "Jess."

"Schafer." They shake. "How long you been on crew?"

Jess returns to untangling the rope. "About six years, I guess. Seems like forever."

"The season just started, right? Y'all hiring?"

Jess pauses again and looks warily at him. "You're looking for work?"

"Always."

"*Shrimping* work?"

"I'll take anything."

Jess thinks a moment, chewing on the inside of his lip. "Vinh's usually looking for more hands in the fall season. It's not regular or nothing, and the pay's shit."

Schafer shrugs.

"You ever worked a shrimper before?"

"No, but I've worked on boats for a while. I learn fast. And I need something—different. From what I was doing before." He can tell Jess is waiting for him to say more, but when he doesn't, the other man nods.

"We're going out again day after tomorrow. Vinh should be here tonight, checking that I did this shit right. Come by around nine and tell him you talked to me."

"I will. Thanks."

"Thank me later." Jess lifts the ropes again. "When you've spent a day on the *Cig*."

———

The best part about being in the Army was the routine—others bristled at the rigorous schedule, but Schafer slipped into it as effortlessly as a bathtub. Four years. Three tours.

When people asked if it was hard over there, he wanted to say, *You know the damnedest thing about it is it's harder here.* Here, no one divided his life into bite-size pieces he wouldn't choke on. Choices he'd once thought normal—go out and watch a movie or just pick one up to rent—now caused the breath to back up in his chest, lodge in his throat. He had forgotten how to ease through a day. But he couldn't say that to anyone; instead he shrugged and gave them the answer they were looking for, something along the lines of *It was hard, but goddamn was I proud to defend my country.*

Laurie liked that response; he could tell from the way she lifted her chin whenever he said it. Since he'd come back to Kerrville after his last tour, when they went any-where, she usually stood beside him in what he thought of as her Jackie pose. Someone would approach—recognizing him from his pictures in the paper or from the bulletin board at the Baptist church—drawing nearer to slap a hand on his shoulder or clasp his palm and say, *Thank-youforyourserviceongodblessyou*, and Laurie's arm would suddenly entwine with his, her face tipped over in a way that emphasized the hollows beneath her cheekbones, her direct gaze, a poised woman both solemn and beautiful in that moment.

He hasn't seen her in seven months, though she calls almost every day. He figures she still has the ring he gave her. He regards her faithful calling and wearing his ring as curiosities, small twinges, as if he observes the habits of an oyster or sea sponge. How interesting, how neat. He wishes it bothered him more. Wishes that when he loaded up his truck to meet Cab and some other ex-military friends in

Marfa and told her he needed time to find himself, but he still loved her, wanted a family, would come back someday, he had been telling the truth.

———————

Shrimping has a rhythm to it, and he just needs to learn its beat. They are a crew of four: Schafer, Jess, a sturdy Mexican named Rey, and the boat's owner, Vinh, a Vietnamese guy who wears a cap that reads *BOI* in proud green letters (Jess assures Schafer that Vinh was not, in fact, "born on the island").

On his first day, they head out to the bay before dawn. Rey and Jess lower the outriggers on both sides; the tall, spindly structures drop slowly until they lie parallel to the water. The *Cig* cruises from the shallows out to the bay, bobbing over choppy water with the outriggers extended on either side. They help with balance, Jess explains, keeping the boat riding the waves instead of tipping into and over them. Schafer watches the shadows of other trawlers move out along the bay and imagines them as track stars: arms outstretched, reaching endlessly for a finish line. They know where they are going. He envies them.

When they reach the area where Vinh figures they'll find shrimp, Rey puts out the small try net, then the main—the big—nets. Schafer steps between ropes and cables so his feet won't get caught up "because then you'd be fucked so hard, man," in Jess's words. He hears names like *transom*, *cathead*, *pin rail*, words that drift into his ears and are just as swiftly gone. The one that sticks is *otter trawl*, the main net. Otters are Laurie's favorite. He can't help but think of her, even now, when it hurts—or should hurt—to do so.

They hoist the doors into position. The boards work as

spreaders, easing the sides of the net apart underwater so it can properly skim the bay floor. The nets themselves sprawl limply across the deck, and Schafer digs a toe under one to lift it slightly. "Not so pretty now," Vinh says. "They're ugly out of water but very pretty in it. Like jellyfish."

Jess's fingers fly skillfully across the thick rope looping the bags where the shrimp will collect, forming half-hitch knots that Rey says can hold up to a thousand pounds of weight and still come undone at a simple tug from a human hand. Schafer doesn't quite believe it until he sees it, nearly an hour later, Jess yanking on the loose line to release the bulging bag of shrimp.

That becomes Schafer's favorite part: popping the bag. It bursts like an abscess, and shrimp foam out in a squirming, hopping mass across the deck of the *Cig*. They release a smell like brine and grit that he figures must be the sea floor where they've spent their lives, one place, never changing, never moving. Even the thought of it makes his chest constrict, his legs itch. He lifts a shrimp between two fingers and stares at the way it wrenches, curling and uncurling in a futile effort to be free.

They teach him to sort the mass, tossing good-size shrimp into the drop tank and tossing bycatch—mostly crabs, mullet, or tiny jellyfish ("sea wasps," Jess calls them)—back overboard. Gulls and pelicans hover above the nets, the gulls shrieking and dive-bombing, the patient pelicans navigating the wind on widespread wings. Vinh flings a small crab high in the air and laughs when a pelican scoops it up into its deep bill. Jess rolls his eyes, but Schafer laughs, too. Again and again the sleek, finned backs of dolphins arc behind them; he learns to recognize the distinctive sound of air spurting from their blowholes as they crest.

It continues that way the rest of the morning, in another section of the bay. Drop nets. Drag. Haul up. Sort. Toss back. Repeat. Again. Again. Again. Again. The rhythm of it bullies everything from his mind. The sun rises higher. It beats down. Schafer is taking orders. He is no longer adrift; he is half-hitched to a purpose once more. Proud horn blares from the Tejano music on Rey's radio. His muscles shift independently of his thoughts. No Laurie, no Army, just movement, just order and purpose to his actions. A gull screams far above him. He closes his eyes in blessed relief.

Weeks go by, and the work with it. Schafer's palms harden from the water, the sandpaper grit of the lines. His sunburn darkens to what could pass for a tan on his pale skin. The press of his sunglasses leaves a groove across the bridge of his nose that lingers for hours.

After finding out he was holed up in the Motel 6, Jess insisted Schafer sublet his place on Mackeral Street instead. He just moved into his girlfriend's home, so it is empty, but he has another four months on it. The Fish Village studio apartment isn't fancy, Jess warns as he passes over the keys, but it is cheap.

He wasn't lying. The place is little more than a hole in the wall, in what Schafer guesses to be one of the rougher complexes of the island's poorer corners. He has moved around often enough that he recognizes the breed. Oversize dumpsters that always seem full no matter the day of the week crowding the edges of a cramped parking lot; someone constantly laughing loudly or playing throbbing bass in the middle of the night. Jess keeps mismatched lawn chairs for living room seating and a simple frame-box-spring-mattress combination. There are clean towels in the relatively clean bathroom and a decorative artificial plant with pink rosebuds atop the toilet. The girlfriend's touch, no doubt. Schafer knows it is fake, but every night he traces his fingers over the cloth petals anyway.

The crew of the *Cig* go out on another run a few days later, then every day for the next four days. They have a string of luck, haul in enough to reach the daily limit a few times, and Vinh wants to take advantage of it. Schafer picks up the names for various Gulf fish that find their way into the catch—shad, drum, croaker. Once there is a small sea turtle, even though Rey says every net has the required TED, turtle excluder device. Schafer lifts it carefully, peering at its beak, its wedged spotted flippers. He thinks of Laurie, the veterinary tech: how she would beam at this turtle, point out the scars along its olive-colored shell, before tossing it back into the Gulf.

She still calls every few days, right at 5:15, when he knows she is climbing back into her car after her work at the clinic. He pictures her at a stop light on North Street, drumming her polished nails on the steering wheel, saying aloud, *Please please just pick up.* He watches her name blink on his phone until it finally disappears. She won't leave a voicemail.

He feels like shit, right on time. He should just answer. He should just call her back, talk to her. But he opens the fridge instead, thinking, *Coward.* Knowing two Bud Lights won't be enough. When Schafer does pick up the phone this time, he calls Jess.

They meet at a bar on the Gulf side, one Jess swears is touristy enough to get the hot girls from Houston but local enough they won't frown on sunburned, sweat-stained watermen who wear caps indoors. It has a patio where they can sit and watch the foot traffic on the Seawall—joggers, families out for a stroll, people on obnoxious tandem bicycles—but all those tables are taken so they post up inside. Schafer buys the first round, Jess the second, and they alternate from there until Jess's grin stretches wider than usual and Schafer no longer hears Laurie whispering his name.

It becomes another routine, one he settles into, one he relishes. Every couple of days, he and Jess—and sometimes Rey, and once even Vinh—meet at a dive bar along the Seawall. Pound beers, take shots. Sometimes Schafer catches a woman's eye and smiles. Twice he leaves with someone. But usually he is content to sit with the men, listening to them talk about family, baseball, the water, letting their voices and laughter push through the murk of his memories.

He hasn't dreamed about Iraq or Kerrville once since arriving on the island. At night, if he wakes up drenched in sweat, it is because the AC has cut out. He can handle that. He can fall back asleep after that.

In late August, Laurie stops calling.

———————

"So how do you like being a shrimper?" Jess asks. They have made their way down a set of steps carved into the Seawall, leading to the beach. The sun is going down, the boulevard still bustling with evening strollers. The air has cooled, slightly, and now sits lukewarm on their exposed skin. Schafer pulls out his Camels and lights a cigarette; he offers the pack to Jess, who shakes his head.

He takes a drag and blows it out. "It's good labor—you do this, then you do this, and if you do it all in the right order, and you're lucky, you get shrimp. I like the routine."

"It clears your head, right?" Jess gestures vaguely to his forehead in a waving motion. "My girl doesn't get that. How it is out on the water." He pauses. "You're pretty white for a migrant worker."

Schafer has to laugh.

"We get plenty of drifters—it's a bay town. You're not from here, you seem like a good dude, and you're white as fuck." He smiles when he said it. "What's your deal?"

Jess slips off his flip-flops, digging his toes in the sand. Schafer follows suit.

"I like making my way around places," Schafer says. He draws on the cigarette. "Finding something new to do, learning how. I've been doing it years now."

"What were you doing before?"

He doesn't plan to say it. He has made it this far, weeks and many trips out on the water, hours spent with the men, without saying it. He doesn't like telling anyone because, as Cab likes to say, that is when their faces change. *Watch, güey, just watch the patriotic pity shit take over.* A person hears *Army* or *Iraq* or *tour of duty,* and their eyes glint. They shift their smile into what they always think is a look of admiration, but instead is relief. A *thank God it was you and not me, pal* look.

But Jess waits with the patience of a waterman. And he has been a friend, Schafer knows. Steady, these weeks. So he tells him. "I was in Iraq."

He watches for Jess's face to change, but it doesn't. He purses his lips, nods seriously. "Shit" is all he says. "Did you kill anyone?"

"I was an MP, did mostly convoy security. I was a gunner."

"So . . . yeah?"

Some memory wants to rise up, maybe the swirling desert sand in his mouth, maybe the crack of bullets or the thud as they burrow into a body. Whatever it is, Schafer pushes it away. He's gotten good at that. It isn't important, he tells himself. It isn't the stuff that matters in his story.

"A few," he says, just to move the conversation along.

"Shit, man," Jess says again. "That's heavy."

They stay quiet a while, and he is grateful—Jess knows how to let him sit in silence. So many people fear it, worry what he might be thinking, and fill the void with chatter. But he and Jess sit, let the passersby, the seagulls, and the murmuring waves do the talking.

Jess's phone buzzes, and he glances at it, sighs. "I should go. My girl's off work." A nurse, Schafer knows, at UTMB. They stand and brush the sand from their asses. "You got a girl or anything back home?"

"I did. We were engaged."

"No shit?"

"She cheated on me while I was gone." Unlike the truth, this lie falls easily from his tongue. He has used it for so long.

Jess stops, stares with his mouth slightly agape. "Seriously? Bitch."

"Yeah."

"Sorry, man."

"It happens." They walk back to the parking lot of the bar.

"What about family? You got parents?"

"We're not that close. We didn't keep in touch much while I was gone, and they don't really care that I'm back. I didn't have a lot to keep me home, you know? So I lit out. Just the way it is."

Schafer likes the way it sounds. He has said this—some version of it—many times at this point, in many places. Marfa, Odessa. Houma, Biloxi. Corpus Christi, Carrizo Springs. Better to focus, he decided, crafting the story he would tell, on the lack of roots. Better not to open up and reveal the inner guts of it: the restlessness, ever-present, sparking through his bones and muscles, urging him to move and keep moving. The way his stomach dropped when he looked around at his home, the sight of his parents, brother, and Laurie, every hair in place, every part of them unchanged as if he had sketched them from memory before he enlisted. The way picking up his life in Kerrville felt like another kind of mission, requiring training he hadn't received. With every H-E-B shopping trip, or Sunday barbecue at his father's grill, or night with Laurie's hands on his shoulders and her mouth on his, he felt only adrenaline rising up. *Run. Take cover.*

Jess hums sympathetically. "Are you glad to be back?"

Schafer flicks the butt of his cigarette away; it arcs like a tiny red drone, hits the gravel, and goes out. "I don't know yet."

Back in the apartment, he closes the door, deadbolts it. As always, he paces quickly through the rooms, scanning the corners, behind the stained shower curtain, stilling to hear the sounds of any breathing or footfalls. He sits with one of the Bud Lights in a lawn chair and flicks on Jess's TV.

A weatherman in Houston is pointing to his green screen, to a white spiraling swirl on the Gulf. *Hurricane Ike*, the text reads. Schafer watches the swirl's projected path swoop out, a cone of purple, over the word *Galveston*.

Vinh sends them to stock up on extra lines. The marine store is about cleaned out, so Jess and Schafer have to head inland to find supplies. Bay watermen of all kinds crowd the aisles, clearing the shelves of rope, rigging, cables, plywood, buoys. They grab what they can and bring it back to the island. Schafer asks why boats on the bayside should fret about a Gulf hurricane. "The surge," Vinh says, "is what to worry about."

The news reports make it sound like a nasty one heading their way; whoever named it Ike was, Schafer thinks, a genius. He makes a crack about Ike Turner, and Jess laughs so hard he nearly swerves off the causeway.

They pull up to the marina and begin unloading supplies. Schafer has his arms full of extra rope when he hears someone call out his name—his first name, not the last, which he has preferred since the Army—and his spine instantly stiffens. He turns. Laurie stands on the pier.

She has cut her hair; now it skims her bare shoulders, a golden-brown sweep. She wears a blue dress and strappy shoes that are all wrong on the gravel and the wood. A purse is slung crossways over her body, and she grips it tightly with both hands, so tightly that the ring he gave her at nineteen flashes in the sun.

"Adam," she says again. She is not smiling.

He freezes. Ahead of him, on the *Cig*, Rey and Vinh have stopped working. Jess is behind him, and he hears the slam of his truck door.

"What are you doing here?" It is all he can ask. Looking at her makes him ill, reminds him of home, family, duties he has shirked. *Run*, he thinks again. *Take cover.*

"Your dad told me where you were. On a shrimp boat in

Galveston, all he knew. I've been circling the parking lot for hours." She straightens her shoulders, and he recognizes her fighting stance. "A hurricane's coming and—and we were worried. Your mom is a mess."

Jess clears his throat, and Schafer is sure he's recalling the story—the lie—about not speaking to his parents. Fuck fuck fuck. "So you just, what? Figured you'd drive over and visit every shrimping boat until you found me?" His tone is harsh; he wants it to be. Wants her to leave, to not have been here at all.

She raises her chin. "If I had to."

"I'ma give y'all a minute." Jess tries to move around Schafer, toward the boat, but Laurie turns sharply to him.

"No, it's all right. You can stay. I won't be here long. I just came to say something."

"What do you want, Laurie?"

"I had a different plan, you know. Driving down here. All those hours, I thought about it, getting here and seeing you and begging you to come home. That it's been five years. *Enough already, Adam,* I would say. But I changed my mind. I'm not going to beg anymore."

When she laughs, bitterly, watery, it stings. He isn't a complete monster.

She goes on. "You wanted to join the Army, that's fine. Wanted to do three tours, I didn't say a thing. But now you're home, and you could be with us, people who love you, people who've built a life with you, but you leave."

He says nothing. In truth, he doesn't know what he could say.

She keeps her eyes on his, waves her hand to the *Cig.* "Did you tell them about us? That we are waiting? That you ignore our calls and keep going away, further and further every time?" If she feels the tears sliding down her cheeks, she ignores them. "Your family will wait forever. But I won't. Not anymore. That's what I decided to tell you."

Vinh and Rey have not budged; Rey still holds the rope of a buoy he is lashing down. Beside him, Jess shifts, a slight movement. Away from Schafer.

"Okay," Schafer says. Even he wants to flinch at the dead sound of his voice. So dry, so brittle.

Laurie nods, as if she has expected this. She wipes her face and takes a deep breath. "And here, of all places, Adam. Why here? The coast, in hurricane season? You know they're saying this will be another Katrina, turn into New Orleans again."

"I'm evacuating."

"And then you'll keep going. Some other coast, maybe. Some labor job. Just when these people have gotten used to you."

"Or maybe I'll stay," he interrupts her, his voice thick with annoyance, defiance. She doesn't know him, not anymore. He could stay here, in Jess's apartment, sipping warm beers on the Seawall, pulling half-hitches on the *Cig* with these men. "Maybe I like it here, Lore. I'm happy here."

"Liar," she replies in a weary voice. And he can see now that the fight has gone out of her. "You're not happy anywhere. I don't know if you know how to be happy anymore." When she raises a hand, gestures limply at him, he sees himself as she must. Sun-bleached, bearded, toughened. Years and miles away from the running back she dated, lost her virginity to, accepted a ring from. Both of them strangers.

"I'm sorry," he hears himself say as she turns away. This lie offering false closure they could work with, pretend to move on.

It takes two days to finish storm prep on the boat. They lash it firmly, with extra lines, to the surrounding pilings and dock cleats. They wrap the machinery, lock up or tie down everything that can move. On the first day, after Laurie left, Vinh and Rey pester him about her, asking about Iraq, about his life, where he's been. He gives blunt answers about Iraq and moving around; the questions about his family or Laurie, he doesn't answer, and eventually they stop asking. Meanwhile, Jess stays silent, speaking only to give directions or respond to a command. If any of them notice Schafer drawing in ragged breaths or swiping at his eyes beneath his sunglasses, they say nothing of it.

He and Jess are the only ones there to finish up the last morning. Ike, the news says, will make landfall in a few days. The evacuation order has come down from the mayor. On the pier, they rinse salt and sweat from their faces and hands in the freshwater hose. Jess swishes water around in his mouth, spits. Schafer lifts the hose over his head. Beside him lie the *Cig's* nets, crumpled and shriveled in the sun, reeking of salt and dead fish.

"You've got someplace to ride out Ike?" Jess asks. It's one of the first times he's spoken to him since Laurie.

Schafer shakes water from his eyes and nods. "Yeah. My buddy up in Conroe. I'm heading up there now. Already storm-prepped your place last night."

"Good." Jess rinses off his sunglasses. "Carly and me are going to Sealy tomorrow. You could come, if you need to."

"Thanks. I'm okay. Cab will let me crash as long as I need."

"Cab?"

"That's what our unit called him, because Caballero was too long."

Jess cracks a smile this time. "And I thought my name was rough. So, will you be back? When all this is over?"

"Sure," Schafer says. "I'll come back."

Like Laurie, Jess recognizes the lie. Unlike her, he looks past it. He shuts off the water and coils up the hose. Shrugs. "Guess I'll see you on the other side of this shit."

They shake hands, and in a sudden move, Jess leans in and claps him on the back with his free hand.

Schafer pulls away and smiles. "On the other side, brother."

He follows Jess's truck out of the parking lot, back to Harborside; where Jess cuts east, toward Fish Village, Schafer heads west. His duffel bag, stuffed neatly once again, rests in the backseat. He merges with the already swelling traffic on Broadway and turns on the radio, flipping stations. Everything is either commercials or Christian, so he turns it back off.

Broadway becomes I-45. I-45 becomes the causeway. He drives high above the bay and watches flecks of sunlight dance across the brown water. It looks like a calm day, but he has learned that this can change in a heartbeat. The traffic moves slowly on the road, and he pauses for long moments to sweep his eyes over the shipping channel. A shrimping boat is coming in from the bay, its arms wide, the nets cast down. The nets. If he squints hard enough, he thinks he can see them billowing, beautiful and open in their element, dazzling with fulfilled purpose, reaching out.

CABALLEROS

Kristin

Her brother, Pete, has his Oakleys on—Kristin sees them as his truck pulls into the Bay Pines Care Center parking lot, where she's been waiting for ten minutes. Through the windshield, light glints off the titanium rims, the polarized lenses he's replaced so many times. They were his first sunglasses that weren't two-for-$10 off some cart in the San Antonio mall, affordable only because of his active military discount, special.

Across the way, Mrs. Castillo is watching the parking lot from her window of Room 21, as she usually does in the afternoons, before dinner and whatever evening entertainment Mrs. Reyes has planned. Tonight is a Rummikub tournament, but Mrs. Castillo hates the game, so she will skip it. Kristin has learned her routine these past months. When she waves goodbye, she sees the old woman hesitate, then lift a hand in return. Her hair is pulled back, the two French braids Kristin did for her still tidy down her shoulders, strands of white and black woven together like a basket. She's watching Pete with trepidation, like he's driving a chariot of death instead of a newish Silverado that their mother scraped up the money to pay a deposit for. Kristin wonders what Mrs. Castillo sees when she looks at him. Dementia—such a sad thing.

Her brother pulls to the curb. She spots where the red paint of the truck is already raked with scratches from mesquite and huizache and prickly pear. Texas pinstripes, their father calls them. The marks that say Pete's been out in the monte, some land like back home in Uvalde. She doesn't know where he would've found brush and mesquite out here on the coast or up in Conroe, where he says he's been for weeks. Perhaps he's lying to her again.

The truck smells of Febreze trying its damnedest to cover the weed smoke; Miller cans lie crumpled on the floor. Kristin tries to ignore them as she rolls down the windows and kisses him on the cheek.

"Nice pajamas," Pete says, nodding at her scrubs. He reaches out and fingers the silver lanyard and ID badge with her name and title. "I'm so proud of you. K. Caballero, Registered Nurse." Though he doesn't look at her as he shifts into drive, the softness in his voice tells her he means it. She basks in it for one moment—her big brother's pride.

"So where's this boyfriend?" he asks.

"He's not my boyfriend," she says, blowing out an embarrassed breath. "We're just dating. Kind of."

"Rudy something, right? What kind of name is Rudy for a Chinese guy?"

"He's Filipino, Pete, Jesus Christ."

"I'm kidding, kid. There was a Filipino dude in my unit. Jun. He was cool. So where's Rudy?"

"He's working, I think. He can meet us later at my place, if we still need help."

"We won't. You're in a second-floor apartment. How long could it take us to prep it for a hurricane? An hour or two? It's not like you can board your windows."

He eases onto the freeway, merges with evening traffic heading south. They begin the crawl through the Bay Area back to Galveston. He uses one hand to fiddle with his phone, then tosses it in her lap. "Take a look. You're going to be impressed."

She doubts it, but she looks at the photos on his phone anyway. They're of some ranch—Pete wants her to see the new job he's lined up for next month, the one he heard about from a buddy back home. He must have taken photos the whole drive down (*dangerous*, she thinks with some weary anger, *reckless*). South on 83, she sees, and doesn't need the phone to picture the highway she's known all her life, snaking through farmland past neat, even rows of cotton or cabbage or winter oats, depending on the season. Winding through ranchland, past Beefmaster and Santa Gertrudis steers and the occasional longhorn, until the hills thick with nopales and scrub brush settle into prairies and waving grass hip-high.

Just past La Pryor, before the turnoff to Eagle Pass and the border, a picture of a side road and a gate more rust than anything. Nailed to one of the witchy-looking mesquites, a hand-lettered sign: *El Dorado Ranch*. A caliche road ahead, pitted with holes, throwing up clouds of dust gone white in the September sun. And a video: Pete carries the phone through the brush, casting it down at his feet, picking his way as he goes, watching his step, and Kristin has to swallow hard. She does that, too: Even now on Galveston, hours away from the nearest prickly pear, she walks the way they both learned as kids running wild through the brush. Eyes trained on their feet for mesquite thorns, horse-cripplers, rattlers. Eyes always looking down.

The camera pans up: a cabin in a slight clearing, all but buried beneath weeds and gray-spined branches. Kristin sighs, seeing as decrepit and sorry a structure as she could imagine. Here, the thing he's going to fix up, pin the rest of his hopes to. "What do you think?" Video Pete asks, turning the camera toward his smile, then waving his hand at the cabin in a grand gesture. As if he hasn't already made up his mind. Beside her, Real Pete is tapping on the wheel along with Kenny Chesney. He does want her opinion—that's the thing. He wants her to tell him it's wonderful. That he has made the right choice taking this job, that more than the others he's left behind, this is the one for him; this is the right first step on the path to the man he wants to be. He's got that romantic cast to his face that she's come to recognize, to dread.

He catches her eye and smiles. "What do you think?"

They are children, Pete and Kristin, fourteen and eleven respectively, and their father is telling them another story about their name. They are sitting behind the register of their family's general store, and he is speaking loudly, in his historical voice, about how la familia Caballero can trace its roots to the days when Texas was Mexico. Before the border crossed them. Pete loves the stories—he calls them "the electric years," charged with danger and disease, lands wild and complicated. You could ride days without encountering another human, except maybe the Comanches, who roamed the South Texas plains taking scalps. ("They weren't so bad," he says. "In Galveston Bay, the Kronks ate oysters

and their own men." His little sister gapes, delighted. She
has a fascination with Galveston; though she's only visited
once, she imagines herself one day moving there.) Their
family had land back then, Dad continues. Acres of ranchland that was theirs from Spain long before the whites took
it, backed up by racist laws and the ever-loaded pistols of
the Rangers. Pete has known this a long time, but since she
is a girl, it will be many years before Kristin learns exactly
why her father spits when he says "los Rinches."

He tells them how, in the electric years, the name Caballero meant something. Still does, but now it's an antiquated
title, rarely used. *Horseman*, literally. In truth, *gentleman*. A
name given to nobility, men who sit tall and straight in the
saddle. Men with honor. "Eres un Caballero," Dad says,
over and over. "Act like it." He means Pete—his son, the
man—but his daughter hears the stories, too, and she will
fight for honor, try her damnedest to hold herself as high
as any man of Old Spain. They are children now, sitting at
the register, chins on their fists, eyes alight. Their years of
trying lie ahead of them. Succeeding only sometimes.

It is 2001, and Pete sits in his senior year homeroom, legs
sprawled, leaning back to toy with the long dark braids of
a smiling girl who is not his girlfriend. Kristin is a freshman, a few hallways over. No boys play with her hair; she
has cropped it short this year, and anyway she would have
punched any boy who tried. Her brother taught her how.
Pete drops the girl's braid when the principal comes on the
overhead, makes the announcement; halls away, Kristin
gasps as one with her class. Pete straightens in his seat
when his homeroom teacher wheels a TV into the room

and turns on CNN; Kristin's teacher does the same. In separate rooms Kristin and Pete watch for hours, the same looped clips of the planes hitting the towers, rising plumes of smoke, people caked by concrete pulverized into dust. Eventually Kristin turns away. Pete does not.

———

She remembers the box, then. Lists the contents she packed herself:

Leftover Halloween candy—heavy on the Twizzlers and peanut M&M's. Long-distance calling cards. DVDs of action movies starring Jason Statham and Vin Diesel on the covers, long-legged girls hovering behind them. Photos of Kristin in her sophomore year soccer and volleyball uniforms. Greeting cards with cartoon pictures of dogs and silly puns about Pete turning nineteen signed by her, Mom, and Dad. From his girlfriend at the time, envelopes stuffed with handwritten pages and a necklace she'd bought him during a vacation to Cancún. The necklace strung with blue and black beads, suspended about a silver charm of a dolphin—his favorite animal. Three copies of the *Uvalde Leader-News*. A poem Kristin wrote for English class called "What Do the Sand Dunes Say Over There?: A Sonnet." Too much postage on the package, but then again, they weren't sure what was enough ("Quién sabe with those trucks and IEDs," Dad says, making Mom cry). Two rosaries and a scapular, all blessed by the bishop, bought from Mom's last trip down to the Basilica in San Juan. A letter from their grandmother in the Valley: *Te amo mijo, ten cuidado, ten mucho cuidado.* Spare lenses for his new Oakleys.

Now: a different box, this one resting on her kitchen

counter. Two brand-new rolls of duct tape. Extra towels and washcloths swiped from Bay Pines. A case of bottled water. A printout of a FEMA webpage: *Hurricane Preparedness for Apartment Dwellers*. On her phone, a text from Rudy saying he got called in to work so not to wait on him; he'd check in with her later.

As they drove, she told Pete how she met Rudy at a bar with mutual friends—all nurses, the medical community a small, incestuous one. She didn't mention how she took him home that same night, admiring the spread of his narrow shoulders and his graceful hands. How they spent two dates comparing patients—he works intensive care at UTMB while she drives inland to Bay Pines.

"He's got a brother, too," she said. "Well, a cousin, but they grew up together."

Pete had grinned. "His cousin as cool as me?"

"As annoying as you. Like all brothers."

Near the end of Pete's first tour in Iraq, she starts taking driver's ed classes. By the time he comes home, she is good enough to drive them both up to the Frio. Kristin eases his truck out on 83 north, and when he buckles into the passenger seat with a thermos full of vodka between his knees, she pretends it doesn't bother her.

He lets her pick the radio station; they both sing along to Garth Brooks. Pete sips from his thermos as she navigates the winding roads. He laughs when she squeals at the sudden dips and rolls where the highway follows the foothills; he adjusts her grip on the wheel. "You're doing so great," he says with pride, and she feels more like a grown-up than ever before, flushed with her brother's delight. The brush and the live oaks zipping past in a green blur, summer sunshine beating down; he is humming.

As they approach the turnoff for Garner State Park, a possum in the distance ambles into the road—they can tell it from its scuttling walk. "Tlacuache!" Kristin shouts and, as Dad taught her, aims the truck for its wedge-shaped head, the black triangle flicks of its ears.

Pete has lost his smile. His voice is thready, quick. "Come on, kid, don't hit it," he says, shouting over the accelerating car. The tlacuache shuffles across the road directly ahead. "What's it doing? Nothing. Is it hurting anyone? No."

"They're pests." She's echoing her father. "Come on." Worse than scorpions around here, they've been taught. They burrow inside the walls of buildings, clatter around on roofs, spread disease, and eat cats. So Dad says. She steps on the gas. She aims. Then she looks at her brother.

He has closed his eyes tight, turned his face to the side window. He is biting his lips. He looks so stricken that she stares at him for too long, fear clutching her throat, and by the time she turns back to the road, the possum has scurried into the brush on the other side.

"Damn it," she mutters. Pete opens his eyes like a shot. He presses his nose to the window and watches the possum zoom past.

"Grow up, Kristin." His voice rings with a harshness she's never heard before. He spins the volume knob on the radio once more, Patty Loveless this time.

———

It's college that doesn't suit him, Pete says: "The teachers have it in for me." When he brings home his term paper from Intro to Business Concepts 1301 at the junior college, he sneers. "'Too confessional'? 'Off-topic'? It was all analysis! I fight for my country, but I can't express my opinions now?" He excels in philosophy classes. He talks for hours about social justice, criminal cases, theories in law and education that Kristin has never heard of. He fails every single practical application course, anything that relies on information he cannot argue or flirt into submission. He changes degree tracks from business to veterinary medicine. To physical therapy. To K–12 education. To law enforcement certification. Until one day he just doesn't enroll; he meanders through town in the passenger seat of his buddy's Jeep. The two of them spend their days circling the high school, going from H-E-B to Walmart, from Whataburger to the stretch of murky river where DPS troopers never patrol. To one friend's house to score weed, another's to smoke it.

Near the end of her first year in the nursing program, he visits people in San Marcos and stays two weeks. He returns bright-eyed, excitement sparking in his voice. A friend of a friend who was in the Army with him manages a kayak-rental business on the Guadalupe, he says. The guy needs a security guard for the warehouse—someone who has a background in retail and can do some light bookkeeping. It was decided, over what was likely several days' worth of Lone Star and sativa, that Pete is the man for the job.

"You've never worked retail," Dad says over dinner. "Pues, you don't even know how to keep books, do you?"

Mom eyes the beer Pete is popping open and, nodding at Kristin, taps three fingers against her cheek. His third since they sat down at the table.

"I'll learn. It's not that hard."

"What about school, mijo?" Mom purses her lips as he takes a long pull from the bottle.

"I can always go back. School's not going anywhere."

Dad grunts. He uses his fork to spear at them across the table. "N'hombre, your sister's going to be done with college before you. At this rate, she's more on track than you've ever been. What do you think of that?"

This gives him pause, her big brother—she can tell. Something in his face flickers, like the ghost of a thought he won't say out loud.

"That doesn't matter. She can do anything she wants," he says. He turns to look at her, but his eyes focus on her nose, her left ear. Anywhere but her eyes. "You know I always taught you how to take care of yourself."

No, you didn't. The words pulse in her throat, but the expression on his face—she knows it would be the tlacuache, again. So she says nothing. *Show respect. Treat him with honor.*

"None of this matters. Not right now. Don't you see, Dad?" He drums his hands against the bottle. "This is my *shot.* I can get into business from this way, get it all from the experience side instead of the education side. Work my way up. Security guard, salesman, then quién sabe?"

"Quién sabe," Dad echoes. He means it skeptically, but Pete is smiling, his sister's eclipse of him forgotten. He lifts the beer and his gaze reaches far away, to a future he is weaving for himself as they watch from the sidelines. The first stop: a warehouse full of kayaks and rafts and canoes, a caliche parking lot. A river.

———

2002. She is fourteen and foolish. She will get older but will not outgrow the foolishness.

It is like this: Her brother will ship out in days. Their

parents have thrown him a going-away party in Concan. His friends and his current girlfriend have attended. The mood: cheerful and false. The group is grilling burgers and hot dogs, passing cold Cokes and surreptitious beers to sip on. Pete is laughing, and they are revolving around him like planets, circling some six-foot, dark-haired sun they know is leaving. Desperate for warmth, they hover. They cling.

She is desperate, too, for the bright spot of her brother to stay fixed on her. She has planned a scary and stupid thing.

Step 1. Scramble atop the banks on the other side of the river, grip the swinging rope suspended from the ancient oak closest to the water, and call to him: "Watch this. Pete, watch me." He does not turn to look. Instead, he is whispering in his girlfriend's ear when his sister tightens both fists around the rope's knot and hurls herself through the air.

Step 2. Pretend to lose your grip halfway over the water. Flail your arms and legs and scream. Make this convincing. She does. She falls some ten feet to the spot where the water is shadowy. The flop stings the skin on her back, but it will be worth it. Be prepared.

Step 3. Once beneath the surface, blow out the air in your lungs—a steady stream of bubbles—until you sink to the bottom. Spot a big rock, big enough for your needs, and wiggle it into place on your chest. The sharp edges dig through her bathing suit, push into her tender skin. She ignores them, lets it weigh her down. This will be worth it, she reminds herself.

Step 4. Wait. Her lungs begin to burn. But he will help her. She reminds herself that he's a caballero, her brother, a gentleman. A few precious bubbles escape her lips so she clamps them tighter. Says this to herself: *Pete will save you. Any minute now.* She says it as her chest seizes, as her fingers scrabble at the rock, ready to heave it off. She squints up through the water at the wavering world.

Step 5. Wait.

Step 6. Wait.

———

"Okay." Pete drops the box inside her apartment, and she closes the door behind him. For a moment her brother stills, sweeps his eyes across the scene. One bedroom, one bath. Tiny living/dining room, kitchen, balcony with furniture. Framed photos of him, their parents and grandparents, on the wall.

He claps his hands and rubs them together. A service he can do, a difference he can make; she almost sees the purpose rise like steam off his skin.

"Let's get prepping," he says. "Take this roll and start taping an X inside all the bathroom and bedroom windows. I'll do out here and bring in whatever you've got on your balcony."

Twenty minutes later and she is finished, but the living room windows are bare. Her small patio set and three heavy ceramic planters still on the balcony, unmoved.

She finds him on the floor of her kitchenette, flipping through a back issue of the recent *Texas Monthly* issue with Concan on the cover. "It's beautiful, isn't it?" He waves it at her, beaming with pride. "We made the cover."

Kristin can't be mad; she saved the copy for him, after all. She lifts the duct tape from the floor and loops it around her wrist like a bracelet. She will do her own windows later. She knows how. She doesn't need his help these days, though he keeps offering, and she keeps accepting. A check-engine light, a window that needs resealing, a hurricane coming. Or maybe it's he who's accepting help, and she the one offering. *Be with me. Fix something for me.*

"It's not nearly that green anymore." She crouches to sit beside him on the floor and points to the glossy magazine cover. "The river."

"Yes, it is," he corrects her. "You just don't know where to go."

The nursing classes for the junior college's RN program last two years. Kristin hates statistics, has to take it twice, but otherwise she's aces. Mom takes pride in buying her the scrubs she needs during clinical rotations in the lab or on the med/surg floor or in the ICU; she picks patterns of puppies, fireworks, big calla lilies in the style of Diego Rivera. The Uvalde hospital has several openings, but she accepts a job at the nursing home for now. It's where she feels most needed—she cried during her rotation there, moved by how the men and women clutched her hands so tight when she murmured in her limited Spanish, how the conditioned air smelled sharply of powder and loose skin. She is still checking job listings near Galveston; it is a dream, she knows, but they went there once on vacation as kids, and she still likes the idea of going to the beach after a shift, of sand on her calves and humidity tangling her hair instead of this mesquite and springwater stretch of Texas that is all she's ever known. She dreams of going off on her own, as her brother did.

On the day of her pinning ceremony, her parents sit proudly, her father in a shirt and pants he's let her mother iron with starch for the occasion. But Pete's chair is empty.

His Army buddy who scrapes boats out in Corpus told him about a nonprofit that wants to clean up the Nueces River, and he headed out to meet them. Unlike Pete's last job, they don't need retail experience or a security background ("He says they won't try to pigeonhole me like that other place, they'll just let me be the *real* me"). Pete will return sixteen days from now, without the job but with a bottle of Crown as an apology gift. He will drink the whole thing.

CABALLERO, proclaims the stitching on his fatigues. The horseman, tall and straight in the saddle. In control.

What she can see now is that there is also something of the horse in him. Skittering, ready to bolt. And she doesn't know if it's Iraq, or if it's always been there.

Step 7 was this: She kept waiting, waiting for him. She stared up at the surface of the water where it quivered, where light pierced through in staggering spears. She waited until small things sparked in front of her eyes. Until she knew she couldn't wait for him anymore.

She heaved the rock off her chest and kicked, hard as she could, against the river bottom. Arrowed through the water, reaching up at the dark shapes hovering above. Her hand broke through.

Pete grabbed it. This was the first she had seen of him, that he was treading water beside the spot where she emerged, that he had been waiting there for her to rise.

She coughed out water and drew breath in long, wheezing pulls. Their parents were on the banks shouting. "I've got her," he called out to them, but she thought, *He didn't save me. He didn't.*

"Breathe. You stupid fucking idiot," he hissed. He called her stupid and dumbass and idiot over and over as they both swam back to land. Water streamed down his face. She thought it was just the river, but then she saw his eyes were red, that as he called her names his voice choked, that he was sobbing.

"So what do you think?"

"Of what?" It is two hours later, evening, and they are driving back over the causeway, the prep finally finished, her suitcase and supplies loaded into the back of the pin-striped truck. Headed north to Conroe, where Pete has been staying in a short-term efficiency while he works a construction job. Where they will ride out Hurricane Ike, barreling toward them, with another of his Army friends.

Kristin grimaces at the thought. She hates these men, the few of them she's met. Bolillos, all. The same upward tilt to their jaws, as if they're saluting in formation, the same cowboy-with-a-badge tone when they address her as "ma'am" even though she's years younger. The way they reject *Caballero* and its beauty—its echoes of an Old World that will outlast them all—because it asks too much of their gringo tongues, and so they call Pete "Cab" instead. But his friend has been working on the island, Pete says, a boat crew. A new islander—like her. He has heard and is heeding the same evacuation orders she is. Around them the freeway is clogged, Galveston emptying, bleeding out to the north. Not everyone is on the road, she knows, not even with a hurricane bearing down. She'll give this Schafer a chance.

Pete nods at the phone in his cup holder. "The cabin. Remember? You said you'd tell me what you thought. I start in two weeks."

"Oh, yeah." She has forgotten already, so she pulls up the video again. This time she studies the cabin closely. The wood exterior is weathered a sickly gray. Potholes riddle the road like so many moles on a complexion. Overgrown brush chokes the screen door and windows so they are barely visible, so thick, so hidden she would believe a curse is bent on keeping something within locked away. She tries not to curl her lip.

"Needs work," Kristin says with some disdain. From the corner of her eye, she sees Pete's face fall. "But it's not bad."

The lie is automatic—to reassure, to soothe. All these years and she can't stop lying to him. Her brother beams as if she's just gushed praises. She has to blink because when he smiles, he dazzles, such joy and delight in his teeth, his eyes, bright in the dark skin their father gave him. When he smiles, she still believes anything he says.

"It's really something, kid." He gestures in the air around him, building shapes with his hands as if they are standing in the monte, horse-cripplers all around, instead of on a coastal freeway outrunning a storm. He points right: the main lodge, the guest cabins, and the bunkhouses for the vaqueros. He tells her about the job—that he'll be repairing the corral and stables so the owner can house his quarter horses, that he'll be building a deer blind from scratch and installing salt licks and water troughs. Over there, not a strip mall with Deb's Nail Salon and a Pizza

Hut, but the sunflower patch he wants to quietly plant, to draw white-wings for the fall shooting. Over there, not a Pappadeaux Seafood but a garage to house all the four-wheelers the vaqueros want for herding cattle. Further still the gun lodge, where his military background and the fact that he is a man in Texas will lend him authority as he maintains the firearms purchased for hunters and plea-sure shooters. Kristin looks down at the video. Nothing anywhere, nothing to see except a cabin, a peeled-paint-and-scrub-brush shack where her brother will live and be fulfilled for a time, at least.

"That's the place," Pete says. "It's going to be perfect. That's where it's all going to happen." She can tell that he's looking at the twenty-two acres of thorns and rattlers out-side La Pryor, brush in need of clearing, work in need of doing. That light to his eyes like stargazing, like he's found a new, unnamed constellation that for now is his alone. And she turns in the direction of his gaze, trying to see it, too.

VOLVER

Magdalena

The thing you should know, about this story, is that it starts with daily Mass at Sacred Heart and una señal. A sign from the saints and spirits. I blame myself for missing it. Father Reynaldo's homily focused on how that June day was the feast of Saint Anthony de Padua, patron saint of lost things, and when Father started reciting the prayer, the one my mother taught me and that I taught you when you were small—*Tony, Tony, look around, something's lost and must be found*—I felt it. A tingle at the base of my skull, a surge in the channels of my veins. I heard something like a whisper from my mother, from the saint and the ones who have gone before me: *Pon attention, Magdalena, somewhere a lost thing is turning up.* So I did, and I would have been ready for it except a blue car cut me off on Broadway and 10th on my way home, and I pushed the brakes and screamed *Hijo de la chingada* out the window. I was distracted, yes, all the way back to Fish Village. I forgot about the tingle and the surge, the whispered warning. Until our little yellow house on Albacore came into view and Marcos, the son I had not seen or heard from in seven years, was sitting on our front steps.

He watched me pull into the driveway, park. Neither of us moved. I let the car run; through the windshield, we stared at each other. I don't fear strong emotions. Haven't I always taught you to permit their passage, allow them to course through controlled, that this strength is what makes us warriors? Haven't I taught you that much? But I bit my lip hard, gathering myself as I looked at him, my own prodigal son. Because my first thought was of you, and my first emotion was fear. Fear that you were still home where I had left you for Mass, snoring with your face down in the mattress and the pillows and colcha piled over you to keep out the early light. Fear that you had seen him out there and been frightened. Worse, fear that you had spoken to him, or let him in. A stranger he would be, no? You were five when he left, you were only twelve now, and you wouldn't know him, would you, your own father?

The fear was first, but there were other emotions, boiling together like brujería on my tongue: betrayal bitter, joy bright as a burst of lime, and love—sí, love—bright and bitter both. It shocked me, the strength of these feelings, how far away my control seemed to be. As a young woman, I was unafraid of losing control to the spinnings of fate. I kept my mind and power tight in my own hands; your grandfather never could beat that out of me, no, pero lo trató. Not in decades had I needed to rein myself in. But today I did.

The sun was hazy in the sky, the heat of the day beginning to churn. It rose from the ground through the car beneath me, seeping up from my low heels and pantsuit. I sat with my hands at ten and two, the Vicente Fernández

CD you gave me on my last birthday still playing through my speakers, though thankfully it was "Hermoso Cariño," full of delight and celebration, and not "Volver, Volver," because that really would have been too much.

When I finally emerged from the car, I was calmer. The feelings had traveled to those spaces around my lungs and heart, no longer in my throat and ready to bubble, double double, toil and trouble—you were reading Shakespeare in school that year, remember? Macbeth and his witches. You read those lines to me and we laughed and laughed. Eye of newt, toe of frog. Midnight hags, híjole. But their rhymes I liked. The power of words, as I have often told you. The power of women's words.

He sat in front of the screen door, knees bent on the step. I stood there on the sidewalk, looking down at him. For the first time in twenty-five years I was taller than him, mi hijo, and I drew strength from that small advantage. Down the street, a car honked; the ferry horn blew farther away. He tilted his head up to me.

He was thirty-nine but looked older, lines carved around his eyes and mouth. He was dark—he always had been; he took after me—but he wore a sweaty white work shirt with the sleeves rolled up so he looked even darker, sun-crisped at his forearms and in the Vs of his elbows. Blue jeans fraying and stained at the knees. His thick dark hair, mine también, was going white at the edges and in patches across his scalp.

I stared at him, wondering where my son had gone, who sat here before me.

Marcos, le dije. Just his name, not even a whole breath, but it came out broken.

Hi, Mama. When he spoke, it was almost a whisper, his

voice deeper, cracked, too, and at the sound of it I jerked away from him. I knew who this man was, ves, who he had become in the years away from me. Somewhere in that time, his face and voice had become his father's.

Before I could think, I had raised my hand.

I would have slapped him. I almost did. But I stopped before my palm hit his cheek. Someone kept me from it: the spirits, maybe, or Saint Anthony, or La Virgen, an infinitely better mother than me. No sé.

He hadn't flinched, Marcosito, just watched me with my own black eyes. I dropped my hand quickly, bit my lip again. I would not lose my control.

You—first, you. *You knocked?* I asked.

He nodded. *No one answered.*

Ah, yes. When I shook you to say I was going to church, you mumbled from beneath the blankets that you and Jess were meeting at his house to play video games. In the summer you two were always running off, you and Jesusmaría: walking across the neighborhood to the houses of Hector or Carlos or los otros amigos, or over to the park to play baseball, or across to the beach. Prowling the island like fearless cats. I loved that, your instinct to roam your own space, lay claim to this land. That will change someday, but that is another story, one of yours, and this one is mine and his.

The hands resting on his bent knees were large and rough, skin peeling across his knuckles, the pads of his fingers white with calluses. There were new scars on them, his hands, and on his cheek that I had nearly slapped. *How where when.* Mi hijo chulo, who had been such a striking boy. Everyone said he resembled me, like me he was always drawing looks with his sharp jaw and his smooth skin and

our long-lashed Karankawa eyes. His brows were thinner;
I used to run my thumbs over them to smooth them down,
the bushy caterpillars they had been when he was a boy. He
used to laugh at that. His eyes were lined and smaller now,
as if he had spent years squinting into the sun and didn't
know how to be in shadow. No spark, no life that I could
see. *Dónde.*

My hand on the strap of my purse was clenched, so I
lowered it to the ground, clasped my hand in the other and
tried to stop them trembling. I knew what the Lord would
have me do. *Forgive*, He would say, *ten misericordia.* But
I could not find the mercy. I wanted to demand, *Where
have you been?* Wanted to beat down on his shoulders and
into his chest with my small fists that were growing more
lined each day, another day without a word from my only
son. *Where have you been? Why did you go? What brought
you back now?* I wanted to scream, to strike. Women have
words, but we have hands también.

I sat down instead, my knees popping, on the step next
to him.

Marcos, I said again as I settled my bottom on the concrete. My voice steady this time. *What are you doing here?*

I was in town. I thought—I— He lifted his shoulders to
his ears nervously. Looked out at the street as he spoke. *I
wanted to see you.*

Again with the questions. They raced through my
mind, fluttered as if with bat wings behind my lips. *Where
when with who why why why.* You know I don't hesitate to
say what I want. I speak my piece. But right then, with
him, I didn't know where to start, and I was afraid. Afraid
I would spook him, and he would leave. Afraid you might
arrive at any minute and see us; afraid of what the wavering

woman-child you were, feisty, quicksilver, chiflada, would do. Hit him or embrace him: toil and trouble, los dos.

The wind was warm, comfortable as it ruffled the sleeves of my camisa. I smelled jasmine though they weren't in season—somewhere one must be growing in a cool, shaded space away from the summer sun. I didn't see a strange car parked nearby. He must have walked here, or someone dropped him off. Who must he be spending time with, life with? *Who who who.*

¿Por qué? I finally asked. *Why are you here?*

I told you. I wanted to see you.

Where have you been?

He sighed. *Working. Just—around. All over.*

Working, I said, and repeated it louder. *Working?*

Mama, please.

No. What control I had found I lost instantly. I slashed a hand in the air. *No 'Please, Mama.' Not now, not ever. You—you—*

Yet I couldn't say it. Seven years of nothing. No letter, no phone call, nada. Birthdays—his, mine, yours—and Easters and Christmases we spent without him. The empty spaces, in the gym at your volleyball games, in the hard chairs at school plays and honor ceremonies, beside us in Sacred Heart every week holding hands during the Padre Nuestro: spaces beside you and me and your mother where my son should have stood. And soon not even your mother, nada más you and me. I thought it all and my eyes filled with tears.

He glanced around then back at me. His look like cobwebs. It made my eyeballs feel sticky and cold. *Is she here? Carly?*

No. My anger was welcome this time, boiling up in my

throat to burn away that cold. That he would ask about you. That he would say your name. *No. She's not here. Ya se fue. You can't see her.* In my lap I was clenching my fists. *Seven years, Marcos. Seven years y nada.*

He puckered his lips and blew out a breath; I felt the cool air. *I know. I'm sorry.*

You know, I repeated. Betrayal thick and sour in my mouth. *You're sorry.*

He said nothing.

¿Y ahora? Are you back for good?

When he turned away from me, I could breathe again. He shook his head. *No, just for the day.*

Ah.

I'm sure my tone stung. I wanted it to, to pierce and lodge like a spina beneath his skin. He looked regretful, he did. But we know men, don't we, niña, the many ways they leave and lie. I had tried to raise my only son to be better, to put familia before desire. So many women do this, easy as breathing, but a man? A good man? Rare as snow on la isla. I tried to teach him to be dutiful, content in who we are and what we had and the many tides and storms still to challenge our warrior selves. But I saw the itch in his eyes when your mother put her head on his shoulder; when you lifted your baby arms to him to be held, I saw the road. A poor man after all. I knew I had failed long before he left.

I sighed. So tired in that moment. *Pues, tell me where you've been.*

Everywhere. He nodded out to the street, west to the bay, east al Golfo. *Working oil rigs, construction. All over. West Texas, even. The desert.*

The desert? I asked, and my voice with its excitement gave me away. He turned his face to me, and I saw cobwebs, sorrow, and an old-world knowing; recognition stabbed in me, so cold and sharp I shivered. *¿Dónde?*

El Paso. And Santa Fe, too.

The desert. You don't know, do you, that I once dreamed about it. How could you? I keep parts of me secret still. This longing lingers from when I was young. I have never been, never gone farther west than Del Rio on the border. Cesar had grown up for a time in New Mexico; he told me that on our first date, and I felt heat plump my lips, pool between my legs. Later I leaned my cheek on his naked chest and asked, *What's it like, the desert?* He stroked his fingers through my hair and said, *Red.* The desert was a rainbow only of red, *me dijo*, different shades like chiles or the brick buildings on the Strand, like blood both fresh and dried. Red slashing a wound across the blue sky, air so dry your skin cracked when you made a fist. Sharp edges every-where, plants with thorns, beasts with stingers and teeth. I sucked in my breath, hearing that, and I reached for him again in the dark. I longed for it, *la violencia de esa tierra*. *We'll go there someday, Nena*, me prometió. *You'll get to see something other than this island.* We never did—the first of many promises he would break to me.

A lifetime later, and it burns in my dreams still: the open space, rocks and mesas and sand that is not beach sand. An ocean of earth and sky. As a girl, I collected pic-tures of the desert, and each one drew a howl from my breast. A coyote, a wolf, when all along I had thought I car-ried a water creature within. We can have both, *sabes*—we carry many selves. I know that now. But I didn't then, and all I wanted was what I could not have. Ves, I understand that urge, the one you have, too, that you think I do not see. Yo sé.

He had been to the desert. He had lived some part of my life without me. The jealousy, the longing, small explosions in my heart. Pop, pop, pop.

Are you married? I asked him. *¿Tienes familia? ¿Niños?* That I would have to ask such a thing of my own son.

No. I— He hesitated a moment, and I sensed a story there. But then he pursed his lips and it was gone, another one I'd never hear. *No. It's just me.*

And are you happy, whatever you're doing? Did you find a happy life? Away from us.

I'm fine, Mama. My life is fine.

Fine no es felíz.

He smiled, almost the boy I remembered. *I know.*

Where are you living?

Beaumont. For now.

A car drove by; Mrs. Suayan honked and waved. I smiled and waved back, praying she wouldn't stop to talk, wouldn't ask who this was. But she drove on, gracias a Dios.

The smile was still on my face as I asked, *For now? So you will leave again.*

I have to. The work will move again in a few months. And then I don't know. Wherever I want, I guess.

Wherever you want, I repeated. *What about what your family wants? ¿Tu madre, tu hija?*

Is that what you want, Mama? For me to come home?

Marcos asked with his face turned down. He tapped a booted foot—they bore scars, too, and stains that I wondered were oil or blood or elements I didn't know, couldn't understand. In the silence Chente Fernández sang, in my own mind, and this time the song I hadn't wanted. *Come back, come back, come back.*

No, le dije. Simply, truly. Power in my words as I gave

them to him. *No, I don't want you to come home. Not anymore.* (This story is not a happy one, ves, and I am not the hero of it. I never said I would be.)

I couldn't tell if I had hurt him. His face didn't change, didn't slip. He nodded as if he had expected it.

Pero I want you to be happy, mijo. And if you want to come back, we—

I don't, Mama, he said. He took a long breath, and I wondered if he smelled the salt or hidden jasmine también, or if he smelled nothing except home, the home he had always known, and wished it were the scent of somewhere else. *I mean, I do. I miss you. I miss Carly. And her.* He slumped a little. *I miss her, too.*

I knew who he meant. *You miss us. A veces.*

A veces.

Pero not enough to be here. To stay with us, or to go be with her.

No.

No crying, Nena. Warriors, we. But my boy's words hurt; they pierced deep, you see. Yo, clavada. I clenched my teeth to keep back tears.

We sat there together, him blowing out air like it should be smoke, me watching him do it. Years he had been gone from us. Years when I held you and her—his child and his woman—as you cried for different reasons. I watched Maharlika drink herself away until she was nada, hollow inside, nothing left except her longing for the home where she belonged. And so she left.

If she had told me, had said anything at all to me, I would have let her know I understood that cruel power of love, how we burn up for it, become ashes of the people we once were. Yo lo sé. Though I know, too, the gift some of us have to rise. I rose. After your grandfather, every tear, every slap of his hand. I rose after he died; I remember Marcos, only twenty-two, weeping over his coffin while I gave a silent prayer of thanks to the ancestors for taking Cesar away, finalmente, so many years late.

Your mother rose by going home. I cursed her long ago, for making you cry, for leaving us both, but now I think differently. I see the ashes of what she was after Marcos, and I like to think she became a whole woman again back with her people. And you, niña mia. Didn't we rise together, after all that?

The sun slipped out from behind a cloud and pierced him, and that's when I saw it. How the light beamed through him. How he didn't reflect it or absorb it; he filtered it. I should have seen it, sabes. It fell into place as I stared at him and the light emanating from the dark body beside me—los señales. Saint Anthony, his arrival. Something lost. Like us riding the ferry to Bolivar and a scrim of salt forming on the car windows, cast up by the water, you trying to look through it. Or like a haze of smoke rising from a cauldron in a castle, and three brujas reaching through it to grasp hands. ¿Ves? Marcos was not you but the salt, not the witches but the smoke.

You're not here, are you. I said it simply. *Eres un espíritu.*

He turned to me. Those cold eyes again. *Mama,* he said, and shook his head sadly. *Still with this, I see.* He tried to smile, but his voice broke.

I have always wondered if the dead feel pain. I saw then how he seemed not only to feel it but to exist from it. It radiated from him like an aura, la tristeza.

You are, aren't you.

Ma—

Es verdad.

Ya, Mama. There were tears in his eyes. *Stop. I'm here, aren't I? Here with you now.*

Pues say what you came to say. I had to clear the way, open the channel for him to speak. I saw that now. I heard the ancestors, their whispers, guiding the way. *I'm listening,* I said.

He sighed. Clenched and unclenched his hands on the white knees of his jeans. So real, my boy, this man seemed. As if I could lean closer to feel warmth from his body, or smell the Vitalis in his hair like his father. Both men of mine reborn and redead before my eyes.

I'm sorry, Mama. Really, I am.

For leaving, you mean.

Yes. I had to. I—I had to. You won't understand.

Ah, no? I had to laugh. To think I had never felt the urge to leave, to run and keep running. Maybe he was the kind of spirit who only knew some things. *Ay, mijo. I understand. You had to get away. It's us, nuestra familia. It's in the sangre. Destined to stay yet always wanting to go. So, some of us do. Go. And some of us don't.*

I scratched my nails lightly on the concrete step. I looked into his eyes and wished it into him, what was in my mind. I hoped he'd see how I still wanted the desert; how I preserved it in a dark, secret corner of my soul. But I wanted the life I had here with you, on la isla de mi vida, more. And I had chosen you.

He turned his face away and sniffed. I lifted my hand to touch his cheek. I stopped again. Afraid my hand would pass through him, and just as afraid it wouldn't.

He pushed off the steps onto the sidewalk. When he moved, he made no sound, sabes. *I have to go. I'm sorry.*

He sounded as if he meant it. He faced me, straightened tall as I sat on the step. The sun glinted on his dark skin, caught the light off his hair. But I could see it, if I angled my eyes—*el humo y la sal*. He cast a shadow across me.

Bye, Mama. He didn't reach for me; he was afraid, too, I realized. We both knew there would be no more visits.

Que te vaya bien, mijo.

He took a few steps, then stopped. Se volvió.

You'll tell her I was here? That I was asking for her?

Sí, mijo, I lied. I don't know if he could sense the lie, the ghost of my son. I will never tell you this story, as good as it is, as true, because you will not believe me.

Right now, ves, you are angry. I watch you from my seat here by the window of my room. A hazy day, and here in League City, miles away from the water, I feel the hurricane blooming. If I squint, I see it, sparks like electric currents to the southeast. And there you are, in the parking lot, still sitting in Jesusmaría's truck. You run your hands through your hair and shout while his mouth moves, and I chuckle because he is surely trying to calm you down without saying *Calm down*—smart boy knows better than to say that to women like us. I sigh. I thought I had more time; the smell of smoke hasn't quite disappeared from the room. Esa Mrs. Reyes must have called you immediately and told you of the blessing fire. I tried but couldn't complete it. I will, though. I kept some palms hidden, though I will not tell you that, either.

You shake your head once more and climb out of the truck. Frustration and temper smoldering around you. Before you slam the truck door shut, I see the bags, the boxes, and close my eyes for a moment. So you are leaving after all, evacuating. Ah, niña. With both of us gone, who can say what is to come for la isla? You bring a battle with you; in a few moments, we will throw words that hurt at each other, as we have done so many times in your life, these tempers of ours colliding. But this one will end with you going, leaving me here, for the first time. Both of us gone. I think of the palm fronds tucked in my dresser, bundled in my pantyhose. You will stay safe, my girl. Despite another fight, despite another leaving. Maybe I cannot save Galveston, but I will keep you safe. Because you are the only one I have left, and I can.

You stride toward me, coming through the heat rising like a mirage from the asphalt, and I remember the ghost of your father that day years ago, walking away from me. I thought he would vanish—a shimmer in the light, or a slow fading. But he simply walked. Hands in his jean pockets, head turned down. No sound as he moved except the cars honking on Ferry. I watched him put one foot in front of the other, as you do now. I watched him walk down Albacore, past our house and those of the Alvarezes, the Jacksons, the Suayans, past the palm trees and the oleanders, the stray gatito you liked to feed sometimes, the corner where you skinned both knees racing Jesusmaría when you were ten. He walked all the way to where Albacore met Marine, and then he turned left in the bright white sunlight y ya se fue.

TELL ME A STORY

Carly

It takes longer than Carly expected for the guilt to get there. Perhaps it's the distraction of the city—the snarl of traffic, the rush of speed, how those two manage to come together in a uniquely Houston way. Speed, stop, speed up again. Go fast even in gridlock. If so, she is grateful for the delay, the headache of Houston driving. She has dodged and weaved for an hour, heading north on I-45, braking, cursing, merging. She is eighteen, experienced behind the wheel now; she hoped by late morning this rush hour traffic would dissipate, easing her escape. Dumb, she thinks now. Three years of driving, on the island and off, and still the city screws her.

She flexes her fingers on the wheel of her new Corolla. "New" to her, not to the world. A 1997 Corolla, five years old, but hers, all hers, thanks to the money she painstakingly saved from working at Whataburger part-time, from picking up side jobs after school or on her days off babysitting and helping Magdalena at the library. Its AC is on the fritz, and some of the black paint is peeling from its hood, but it is her chariot, her wild horse carrying her away. Together they pass the construction zones and chain restaurants of the Bay Area, watch the downtown exit ramps spinning out like whirlpools from the interstate, out and down—in the shadow of the city skyline, the Aquarium's electric-blue Ferris wheel. She drives through the stretch of intersecting overpasses north of Bush Intercontinental Airport, when Houston should be over, should be done. But still there is Spring and The Woodlands, still Conroe, the sprawl sprawling farther, endless. Taquerias, billboards, parking lots. It is nearly two hours before she and the Corolla emerge from Houston's last concreted, strip-malled gasp into—.

Trees. Tall trees, towering, skinny ones, shimmying thick green skirts high above her. Where there were just gyro shops and discount furniture stores, there are now trees lining the interstate like chorus girls. And grass, spread out to blanket the sides of the road. She cracks the windows, takes a deep, long breath of the wind whipping past. Warm air, tinged with asphalt and diesel. But no salt, no tang of the Gulf. This feels, smells, like the woods—or should she smell pine? Are there pine trees out here?

"Pretty," she says aloud, and with that tiny opening finally, finally, pours in the guilt. *What have you done, Carly Elena? Why?*

Going was her only thought that morning. Her hands on the steering wheel, her mind on the road, even as her grandmother moved around in the kitchen, as she spoke about her summer Thursday plans. Going.

"After Mass, I'll be with Ofelia, Patty is taking us to la Galleria to go shopping. And we will go to a celebration lunch, sabes."

Carly blinked and focused: Magdalena was smiling.

Her grandmother still on a high from retiring a week ago at the end of the school semester. She had said goodbye to the school library where she had worked nearly thirty years, was now launching toward the rest of her life—something new and unexpected, unformed, yet to be decided. A turning point. A crossroads.

Where she herself should be standing, Carly thought. Eighteen, Ball High diploma newly in hand. Summer, freedom. Shouldn't the world lie ahead of her, too? Shouldn't she be able to gaze ahead and glimpse another future? But she only saw Fish Village, the house on Albacore, caring for her grandmother, marrying Jess. Years and decades just like the years and decades behind her.

So much simmering. The restlessness, the longing to run from this known place, these people, toward the unknown. Have something for yourself. *Take* something for yourself.

"¿Niña? ¿Me escuchas?"

"Yes, Grandma." Carly forced a smile.

"What will you do today? See Jesusmaría?"

"No, he's at Mr. Pham's boat today, I think they're teaching him how to do shrimping. I'll see him later." She kissed Magdalena gently. "Have a good time. I'm going to go run some errands, go out for a bit."

Going, going, going. Her grandmother leaving; her boyfriend away. Like on that day years ago when she stole the car, whatever has long bubbled inside her has burst out; whatever tether keeps her bound has split apart. Like sparks snapping off a burning log, she saw flashes of her own life ahead: the changes happening at sea, building from a distance, well across the water, gathering strength to emerge into something tangible. An illness, a marriage, a storm. Someone leaving her; someone staying. And there she would be, Carly Castillo, standing on the shore, seeing the shape of whatever it was, and simply waiting for it to rumble closer.

She felt herself already adrift. She saw the road, herself throwing a change of clothes and money in a bag, the bag in the backseat. A note on the table. *I want to have something, Grandma, Jess. I love you, but I have to take something.*

"Ten cuidado, mi vida." Her grandmother's hand on her cheek, cool and dry.

"I will."

Gone.

She has enough gas to get to Dallas. Her Corolla contains nearly a full tank; her grandmother instilled the habit into her when she was fifteen and learning to drive. *Don't let the tank slip lower than a quarter because quién sabe when you'll be stranded, or stuck.* She knows to keep an empty gas container in the trunk, and always look for and remember the gas stations she passes so she can find them because *we don't wait for men to help us, niña, why would we, when we know so well how to take care of ourselves?*

The lilt of Magdalena's voice in her mind comes with a searing pain. *You've left her.* Carly shoves the whole mess of it away. Dallas, then. Just get to Dallas.

She has no plan. No steps to take, no final destination to aim for. She hasn't thought this through. *Take something for yourself.* She drives on.

She spins the volume knob hard to the right to turn up Sunny 99.1; it loses signal the farther she drives. She can only occasionally make out the croon of "Human Nature" amid the droning buzz of static. She sings along with Michael anyway. Soon she will lose it, lose all the Houston stations preset in her radio. She doesn't know any others.

———

A brown Honda heads north across the bay. In the back-seat a sleeping baby; in the front her mother dozes with her cheek on the seat belt strap. Her father dances his fingers on the wheel in time with the radio, some slow Michael Jackson song. This is a day trip, a quick dash into the city to buy some baby things, new scrubs for his wife. A few hours at the mall. But already he is thinking—he glances at the sleeping woman, in the rearview at the fat-cheeked infant—of the north, of going and never stopping. A car, a radio, a road. Singing along as loud as he pleases, no one to worry about waking up.

———

Carly hasn't planned to stop, but she changes her mind when she sees Sam.

His hand appears first. Blazing white like a sunbeam, it cuts a bright slash across the dark green of the trees. Large and curled, it thrusts itself forward, presenting his fingers to the freeway. As she drives on, the hand becomes a jacketed arm, snowy white. Below it, the tip of a boot and the line of a can stretching up. The boot becomes a leg, the arm becomes a shoulder and the border of a lapel, then a whole torso, and then the full statue comes into view, all at once like an apparition.

Carly leans forward to peer up at him through the wind-shield. The statue stands some seventy feet high, gripping a cane but not leaning on it. His head is high, and he looks past her, westward, beyond the trees, the mud-flapped eighteen-wheelers and lifted pickups and Corollas doing eighty on the interstate, to the rest of Texas.

Sam, she remembers. Sam Houston. Marking the gateway to Huntsville, to the university that bears his name. They learned about him in seventh grade. Texas history, Jess's favorite subject.

On impulse, she exits. She doesn't think. Murmurs to herself, "Today is about not thinking."

She follows the feeder road behind a thicket of trees. It winds, circles, until it comes to a hidden parking lot. There sits a small visitor's center with what looks like a gift shop, judging from the postcards and Texas-shaped magnets she can see in the window. Only one other car there, but no one in sight.

As she walks, Sam looms higher. The shadow he casts is long, and when she steps into it, she shivers at the drop in temperature. Finally she stands before him, craning her neck up.

Sam stands on a square platform of pink granite taller than her own head, its sheen catching the sunlight and casting it back even rosier. SAM HOUSTON, the etching reads beneath his feet, 1793–1863. She ticks the decades off on her fingers. Magdalena teases her about needing her hands to do simple math. Sam lived to seventy years old; older than her grandfather had been when he died, before she was born; older than her grandmother, strolling the crisp chill of the Galleria, listening to people chatter in Hindi and Greek and Korean, telling Mrs. de los Santos how she would look so good in that red camisa. *Enough.* Sam's legs are long, booted, encased in trim trousers. He wears a fancy-looking vest with a crosshatched pattern carved into the white. From this angle it appears quilted, as if to touch it would be to run your palm over something feathery. But it would be hard, wouldn't it. It must be. A man like Sam Houston would not be seen as soft. He has a handkerchief tied at the throat, an elaborate bow flaring beneath his chin. It seems like a formal thing. Jess, the history lover, would know. *No, no, no.* Over the vest, a long coat, open and pulled back on his left side by the hand hooked in his pocket. His thick hair waves down to his sideburns—*Wolverine-level mutton chops*, she thinks—and flares out from the sides of his face in wings. His eyes are level, his mouth a stern but thoughtful line. With his pocketed hand and cane, he looks as if he is surveying Texas, judging its purpose. Considering the possibilities.

"He was the president," she murmurs aloud. "When we were our own country. A general in the army during the rebellion. And—"

And nothing else.

A founding father of Texas, Ms. Morton called him. But Carly cannot remember anything more than that.

She searches, harder, quicker. She cannot find a shred of memory to tell her more about him. And she wants to. Her breath comes fast, almost in gasps. Panicking.

Why? She draws shallow breaths, presses her fist to her chest.

Sam is hers, too. She has collected stories from her grandmother, stories from a textbook. Filipinos, newly arriving like her mother, climbing off a plane or a boat, stepping onto a shore. Mexicans, who were here when it was not called Texas. Karankawas—or Comanches, the Kiowa or Tonkawa or any of the others—here before it had a name, or bore a name, no books or oral histories. The shaping of the state, the island, where she was born. The shaping of her.

Unfamiliar. She is here for something new, something unknown. Rode off in search of it. Funny, then, isn't it? This sudden, stabbing longing to hear Sam's story. Any story.

The child is panicking. On her knee a scrape, the skin peeled back to reveal jagged pink flesh, bits of gravel in the pink, blood already welling like the tears on her cheeks. *Mama.*

Enough, anak ko. Her mother's hand on her back, gentle, rubbing in small circles. *You're okay. Keep breathing.* She smooths a wet washcloth over the child's knee, shushing her when she cries out. *We have to clean it. I know it hurts. It will stop, I promise.* Cool dab of Neosporin, a Band-Aid. *You're okay. Keep breathing.*

It takes three rings, but he answers. "Hey, baby." The tears spill over at the sound of his voice. Of love? Regret? Need—she is afraid it is need. That she needs him and hasn't known it until now.

She lets the tears come, for once, though she swallows so he won't hear them. Speaks quickly before she can change her mind. "What do you remember about Sam Houston?"

Jess gives a grunt—something physical he is doing, on the boat, takes effort. She hears seagulls in the background, the grumble of some engine. "Mmph. There. What? Who?"

"Sam Houston. The general. Remember him?"

"Uh, yeah, sure. Why?"

"Just tell me, babe. Sam Houston. Tell me about him." *Tell me, Grandma.* "You're not busy, are you?"

"No, it's fine, we're sitting on the boat taking a break. Why do you—"

"Jess, *please*."

"Okay, okay." He pauses, and she knows he has the

frown on his brow that means he is thinking, rifling through the extensive Texas history catalog he keeps in his mind, where he cannot remember which of his sisters has a birthday in July and which in January but can recall that the Battle of Goliad took place October 9, 1835.

"He was the president of the republic of Texas. He was a general during the revolution and—"

"He was the one who beat Santa Anna. After the Alamo. I already know that. What else?"

"Okay, hang on." She hears the curiosity in his voice—*Why do you want to know about Sam Houston all of a sudden, you've never given a shit*—but he doesn't push. "He was from Virginia, but he came here when it was still Mexico. H-town was named after him. It was the capital of Texas for a while, before they changed it to Austin."

Her breathing slows, eases. "It was?"

"Yeah. It was the bigger city, but then they wanted something more central, maybe." She senses rather than hears his shrug. Another rumble of engine, male laughter in the distance. "He was a senator or a governor, I think? Maybe both? I can't remember exactly, but he was some kind of politician after we became a state."

Carly lowers herself to the grass, ignoring the damp, and sits. Stretches out her legs and looks up at Sam, and listens. Jess speaks in her ear, over the whine and whir of cars zipping by, heading north. Comforting. She leans backward until she is flat on her back. Closes her eyes. Grass beneath her hair, the roar of the road.

This. This is what she has always loved. Sitting quiet in her own bubble—but with people around, family, not strangers. Carving a pocket for herself in the noise and the movement. She falls asleep deepest when her grandmother murmurs or laughs in the other room, when she hears Jess breathing.

She listens to him. She doesn't want to think about the decision she is afraid she is making, the direction of her car turning in her mind with every rise and fall of his voice.

"What else?" she asks quietly.

"He voted against Texas seceding, during the Civil War."

"Outvoted, obviously."

"Duh." He chuckles. "But at least he opposed slavery."

She sighs. *Jess.* "Or else he just didn't want to leave the Union."

"Yeah, maybe." His voice bristles. Her reality checks, her questioning of the myths, never sit right with him. She shakes her head. He can be so romantic about the history of the state he loves, wanting the Texas story to be simple, straightforward, a gold-plated narrative. Carly knows the ugliness, what Magdalena never lets her forget. *They hurt us, beat us, killed us. They took our land, the home right out from under us.* But she questions that, too. Who are *they*? And *us*? A place like this can never be so simple. *They*: people who hurt and killed, and people hurt and killed. *Us*: the conquerors and conquered both.

She wonders about the fully formed future she is running from. If, in that version, she and Jess will keep balancing each other: one telling tall tales, one picking them apart. It doesn't sound so bad when she thinks of it that way. He would remember them all, keep them close. His stories, hers, where they diverge and where they wind together. He would pass them down, even if she wouldn't. He would tell them again and again.

"What else?"

"He lived with the Cherokee for a while. The Indians called him 'the Big Drunk.'"

"Stop it. That's not true."

"I swear." They are both laughing now, rising above the sounds of Huntsville, of the Gulf. They laugh together until Mr. Pham says something in the background, and Jess affirms. "Got it. I'll be right there."

"Go ahead," she says. A long sigh, the prick of tears again. "It's okay. I know you have to go."

"Yeah. Sorry." He pauses. "You're going to tell me later what this is about, right?"

"No real reason." She fingers a knob of grass, twists it into a coil. "I just went for a drive and started thinking."

"Mm-hm." He doesn't sound convinced. "I'll see you later, though?"

"Yeah, I'll be home." The weight, spilling out of her chest, settling into her bones. Gravity, where she had felt so light just an hour ago. She is going home. Sorrow in that knowledge, but a comfort, too. "Thanks, Jess."

"Anytime."

"I didn't know any of this stuff." She rises, swiping grass off her shorts and hair. "About Sam Houston. You must've read more books than me."

"We learned it together. You just don't remember."

———

A gray road, studded with vehicles, snakes through tall green trees. The sun rises higher in the sky. A black Corolla heads south, the girl at the wheel brushing away tears as she merges onto the freeway. A white man of white stone stands, staring west.

Six years pass, the girl and the Corolla gone. The white man unmoved. Blind to the scene behind him, how in the east, in the water far at his back, wind is swirling, gathering warmth and water, growing in pressure. Look, look. A storm is coming. A storm is here.

GOD OF WIND, STORM, FIRE

Ike

Ike is leaving. Just for breakfast, an egg sandwich that does not taste of plastic wrap and chemicals; he has told Catherine he will be right back. He steps through the sliding doors, out of the cool of the hospital, and the first thing he notices is the air—the way it cinches around him in a fist. The pressure a threat, a chord played wrong. When he was seven, his tío tried to teach him the accordion and Ike pressed every key he could reach at the same time. The discordant notes hung around him, hovered; that's the way the air does now. Everyone senses it, he can tell. The looks of the doctors and nurses, walking across the parking lot to start their morning shifts, patterned scrubs and crisp white coats and stethoscopes slung about their necks. Their mouths drawn, eyes squinting through the sunlit haze to find the source of the note, the energy. The source is the hurricane still miles away on the Gulf. Its name is Ike, too.

He felt it coming weeks ago, before the weather reports began, the constant radio announcements and TV updates cutting through his KHOU shows. Every islander worth his salt knows how to recognize the nuances of the air on skin, how the pressure seeps into the cavities of a body and aches. Storms are nothing new. He has lived through too many to count. Tropicals, depressions, hurricanes; names like Danielle, Josephine, Alicia, Jerry. But this one felt different from the beginning—he thinks he always knew, down in the pit of his belly, the moment it formed far out of the Gulf and, weeks later, when it crossed Cuba and pivoted toward Galveston. When he told Catherine as much, she laughed at him. She doesn't believe in things like this, elemental things without explanation, but then again she grew up white and atheist in Denton County, so he supposes she wouldn't. When the newscasters said the storm had formed enough to be named Ike, even Catherine had to pause and squeeze his arm affectionately. I suppose the storm really is yours, she said, coughing as she had been for days. Or maybe I am the storm, he added. He meant it, though when she blinked at him he wiggled his brows to make her think he did not. The next morning her coughing was so bad he finally drove her to the John Sealy emergency room. She was admitted for pneumonia; he has been there, at her side, for three days.

Ike likes the idea of himself as a hurricane. At seventy-four, he knows he has not been remotely formidable in decades. He was a tall man in his twenties, narrow-waisted, powerful in the chest and arms. But in the forty-odd years since he traded the pitcher's mound for the driver's seat of a Trailways bus, the top of him has deflated while the bottom of him has plumped. He walks out of the hospital into the humid air and feels himself stooping, the upper part of his spine bowed, his shoulders shrinking inward where once he had to turn sideways to fit through doors. Catherine keeps a photo of him from his softball days tucked into her vanity mirror at home—the corners curl around his serious stare, the sharp line of his jaw. His jaw has not been sharp in many years. In the photo his Toros de Monterrey cap is on, but beneath it his hair is thick and crow black—that, too, no longer so.

Someone calls his name; he sees Catherine's night shift nurse emerging from the sliding doors. He has long, shaggy dark hair, with the tilted eyes and broad face of the Filipinos Ike now recognizes, having spent so long in Fish Village. They are like fleas here. No, he thinks as the nurse approaches. That is rude. He never liked it when white men called him spic, wetback, beaner. They do so less these days because of his age, but he remembers the scald of anger in his young throat, the crunch of his knuckles against a cheek-bone or a gut. And yet—there really are so many Filipinos here, in this corner of the island, working in the hospitals and clinics, handing out lottery tickets at the gas stations, reading the prayers of the faithful at Sacred Heart. So many.

He nods at the nurse—*Rudy*, the ID dangling from his lanyard reads—and tries to listen.

They believe the hurricane will make landfall tomor-row morning, Rudy is saying. They predict the storm will be very destructive. The hospital has been ordered to evac-uate all patients, including Mrs. Alvarez. She will be sent to another hospital: Parkland, up in Dallas. The day nurses will begin preparing her for transport this morning. Mr. Alvarez, Rudy asks in that singsong accent, do you have an evacuation plan?

He does not. He is seventy-four, after all. His family is long dead, his friends gone. Catherine is everything he has. When he says this to Rudy, the nurse shakes his head. The mayor has issued a mandatory evacuation order for island-ers, but the hospital can only transport patients, not family. Ike will have to make other arrangements. There are public buses from the city that will take people inland; Rudy can look into that for him. He could even drop him off at a bus, Rudy says—he may be heading that way, too.

Ike considers this, standing in the hospital parking lot, the September sun throwing weak light but still enough warmth to draw sweat. Yes, he could go. He has been retired from Trailways and Greyhound for fifteen years, but he finds comfort in the thought of a long-distance bus: the scratchy vinyl cushions, the murmurs of passengers and the current of the air-conditioning, the rumbling cadence of the tires. A trip to Dallas or Austin or San Antonio after he has been island-bound for so long. But the romance of the road is for a younger Ike, a firmer body, sturdier bones. He is too old to sit for eight hours in a bus seat, only to sleep on a cot in some school gym. He thinks of his and Catherine's small house on Albacore Avenue, where they have ridden out every storm for three decades. He casts his mind to the knot of wind and rain that bears his name out on the Gulf, on the water that shivers with heat. He wants to see it roll in. He feels he ought to, somehow. Ike thanks Rudy politely and says he will make his own evacuation arrangements.

Ike walks along the Seawall to watch the storm surge. He has already been to the Walmart off 69th; the shelves were mostly picked clean, but he scrounged up canned salmon and two jugs of water. He was in his truck heading back up the boulevard when he spotted the first waves.

He stopped and stared. After a lifetime in Galveston, he understands the dangers of the surge that is the hurricane's harbinger, water thrust forward by the force of the storm winds—but these waves are unlike anything he has known. They engulf the beach sands and hurl against the concrete of the Seawall with such muscularity they seem to climb the air, leaping high over the seventeen-foot barrier. Ike was so mesmerized he pulled over, parked, climbed out. Joined several other islanders doing the same: a woman in jogging pants and a University of Houston shirt; a couple with a Labrador yanking on its leash and whining; a man and his teenage son struggling down the steps for a better (stupider) look. The wind whips at them, pushing Ike with such force that he staggers.

The bright midday sky shimmers like a glass dome, white-gray clouds stretched thin, curving above and around him. When he was driving down Seawall looking at that sky, Ike felt the pressure of the trapped, and for a blinding instant he wanted to step on the gas, or rip the shirt from his chest, fling rocks at the invisible glass, roar. The instinct startled him. It has been years since he felt anything stronger than mild annoyance.

The waves—crashing into the wall with a noise like thunder, one after another, sending sheets of foamy brown water high above him to splatter in his hair—calm him somehow. Ike sees his rage, so familiar to him as a younger man, echoed there. They rip, fling, roar at his whim.

Thinking like this is foolish. Catherine would laugh, as she already did, as she has so many times in their marriage. His wife of fifty-two years, who is being given a nebulizer treatment in the back of an ambulance headed to Dallas, has the brain of a pragmatist. When they met in a Houston bar in their twenties, she was a math teacher and he was playing softball for Monterrey, driving from Texas to Mexico each week, only to drive back across the border on his team bus to play against American teams. Catherine chuckled at his rituals—when he pressed his face into his glove for ten seconds each morning, tapped both sides of the door-jamb before leaving for a game, touched his fingers to first the brim of his cap, then his silver crucifix, then his tongue before every pitch. Silly baby, she would say. But because he knew they made a difference, she laid out his uniform in the pattern he liked and poured his coffee into the same brown mug each game day. How she came to love Ike, with his ballplayer superstitions, the child of Mexican immigrants who breathed curanderismo and Catholicism, he would never understand. They were married in the Denton court-house; Catherine would sooner swallow dirt than be wed in a church.

As she was being prepared for transport, she lifted his hand to her cheek. Where will you go? she asked, voice raspy from the infection. He could not tell her, I'll hunker down, querida, and I swear I'll be fine, this storm is mine and it will not hurt me. Could not put into words what he felt in the marrow of him. So he lied to his wife of fifty-two years, who was breathing with the narrow wedge of an oxygen tube in her nose, and said he was boarding a bus to Austin. It was not the first time he had lied to her.

Ike blinks through the boom and churning spray of another wave, the barks of the Labrador. He was still that wide-shouldered pitcher, known for his riser, when he first cheated on his wife. He wore the Monterrey cap low over his eyes and swung his arm underhand—the superior way, he often thinks now, watching overhand pitchers on TV with a sneer—and coaxed the ball to start low, low, before arcing up and above a batter's swing. He seduced women in the same way. Shadowed eyes, careful hands, first slow, then a fast rising. He considered it another ritual, one for away games, and when a woman smiled at him from the stands or bought him a drink at the hotel bar, he honored it with equal fervency. Younger Ike thought nothing of reaching for someone else, then someone else after that, one after another, so much energy churning to get out, pounding at the walls. He gave up softball in Year 5 of their marriage, and he gave up his rituals—all but this one. Year 6: a woman leaning over a pool table, watching him through the smoke of the bar. Year 9: a passenger on his southbound route who invited him to dinner when the bus pulled into Victoria. Years 13, 15, 19, 20, 22, 28, 36, 40, 44—single nights, weekend flings. Only one ever became something more—Year 22. Nena. But that was different, and long ago.

Ozone and salt sting his nostrils. He wonders if Catherine knew then, knows now. At times he recalls a tightness around her mouth after he returned from a multiday route, or a lingering over his collar when she hugged him and inhaled. Year 22 she must have seen the way his gaze flicked to the house across the street, but she never said a word. Ike has carried his guilt, felt it prickle in his throat when they attended weddings in Sacred Heart or St. Mary's and followed along with the vows: Love and honor. Be true to you. Catherine beside him with her arm in his and her fingers gently tapping his palm. He has wanted forgiveness for years 1 through 44 but has been unwilling to face the inevitable fight. He has felt old and tired for so long. If he still bore the battle spirit of youth, he would have asked her decades ago.

Spray droplets spatter across his hair and eyes. He looks at the waves thundering into the Seawall and knows that this storm understands. His storm.

———

Ike is hammering the first square of plywood into place when the surge reaches Albacore Avenue. He knew it was coming. He felt the same flutter on the back of his neck that he did on the mound when he spun the ball, hurling his arm in just the right way. His fingertips tingled beneath their nail beds. Come, water, he thought, and it slithered in.

He squints behind his prescription glasses and watches the brown liquid trickle over the weed-bedraggled lawns on the north side. The surge. Ike still hundreds of miles away and its pressure so strong it raises the level of Galveston Bay, pushes the water toward the island from the bayside. The Seawall along the south edge guards them from the ocean, but not their own bay. A sneak attack, like the military formations his father watched on old movies, studied in history books. While they were watching the Seawall, the storm slunk past and approached them from behind.

The wind has strengthened, too. It whips around him and races through the high, thick-leaved palms, the mismatched houses of Albacore Avenue, over the brown bay water steadily creeping onto the street.

Since it is already here, Ike takes his time boarding the windows. He loves this house, its one story and two bedrooms, its faded blue siding and white trim, even the pink oleander trees planted in the front. They came with the house. When they moved here in Year 12, Catherine pointed to them and told him a story she'd heard, about a troop of Boy Scouts camping on Galveston who unwittingly plucked branches off an oleander tree and stripped them clean, then spiked their hot dogs and marshmallows for roasting. The next day their scoutmaster found them dead—every, Catherine said with solemn pauses, single, one.

That story's nada, Ike responded with a laugh. An urban legend. Though it's true that oleanders really are poisonous.

They had it confirmed the next day. They were unloading boxes when Mrs. Castillo first crossed Albacore Avenue. She walked over to where he stood beside the open tailgate of his Chevy. She took in a quick dart of her eyes the dark brown of his skin, the Aztec-warrior nose, just as he did her. When she spoke, it was in Spanish she knew he could answer.

Bienvenido, she said. Ike wiped cardboard fluff off his jeans and took her outstretched hand, her grip firm and strong. Magdalena Castillo.

Mucho gusto. Her husband was watching from the window across the street, Catherine from the doorway behind Ike.

Mrs. Castillo gestured to the rosy blossoms, the slender branches of the tree in the yard. If you handle the oleanders, wash your hands good, she said. El veneno, tú sabes, and bad spirits.

Sí, claro, he responded. She was in her late twenties, younger than him, but he recognized in her a deep respect for the old ways; he knew that if he told her of his former game-day rituals she would nod solemnly. Mrs. Castillo was short, stocky, black hair falling loose around her face and down to her wide hips. Pointed chin and high cheekbones that made her look young; black eyes that made her look ancient. Ike felt a tingling in his fingertips, beneath his nail beds. Touch, touch, let the locks slip through his hands like rain. Years from this moment, Ike will fist his hands in that hair, say her name, the shortened version of it that not even her own husband called her anymore: Nena. But in Year 12 he stepped back, proud of his control, and smiled at her.

He drives the last nail home, and the plywood stays in place over the windows. He moves slowly, carefully down the stepladder. His softened, fragile body and its limits frustrate him. Across the street lies the pale yellow house where Mrs. Castillo—as he has tried to call her in his private thoughts, afraid of the power her nickname holds over him—lives with her grown granddaughter, the husband peering from the window long dead. They must have evacuated, too: the windows are boarded, and only one car sits in the drive. He listens for the coming rain and hears it whistling, snatched up in the wind. The surge has grown. Inches of water slink atop the street.

———

Ike is waiting. Candle flames quiver in the darkness and he feels as though he is in a séance. He has never been in one, though, so he does not know what he would actually do. He switched off the power hours ago, and he glances at the leather wristwatch that was his father's to see it is 10:28 p.m. That glass dome of the sky darkened swiftly after the rain came, only a few hours after he headed inside and locked up. In the wavering candlelight he wrapped furniture legs in plastic, moved boxes of Catherine's jewelry and family photos and bank statements to upper shelves, lifted potted plants off the floor to the counters, stuffed towels beneath the front and back doors. All the while dazzled by the wailing of the wind, the way the house moans and leans into it.

In the guest room, he is stretched out on the lower portion of the bunk bed that was given to them in Year 9. The bed is made of oak, sturdy and shining. Catherine's brother in Houston gifted it to them after her third miscarriage, when the sight of the crib Ike had assembled made her wail—not unlike the wind now, shrill and dark, a frenzied sound.

He wonders what a séance is like. He flicks the lighter—though he has not smoked since Year 39, he still carries it—and touches it to the unlit candlewick beside two others on the dresser. If he knew more about séances, he might try to summon the heart of the hurricane. Speak, Ike to Ike. He flushes a little at the thought. He is sure he is being ridiculous, and if Catherine could hear his thoughts from Parkland Hospital in downtown Dallas, she would laugh at him. How mystical you've become in your old age, she would tease. And though she wouldn't say it, he would hear in the air between them: How Mexican. How Galveston. Perhaps he is, this Ike. Perhaps he regards the handful of years he has left like seashells in his hand, wanting to hold them gently and turn them over, marvel at their beauty and cruel unknowability. Grief, bitterness, romance, all around him. Catherine would scoff, but he is no longer afraid to feel wonder.

The hurricane draws nearer; it must be close to landfall. He thinks a more reckless version of himself, that angry, strong-armed man he once was, would have thrown open the doors and stood in the storm. Screamed into it. He could have used this storm in Year 9. In those days after the last miscarriage, when he spent every morning pushing the tear-and-mucus tangle of hair out of Catherine's face, coaxing her to sit up in bed and swallow food the way he coaxed softballs and women into motion. They had named the first—Arturo, after Ike's father, who wept into his bottle of Tecate when they told him the name—and thought nothing would match that wild sorrow when it died. Ike had not named the next two, not even to himself; when he eyed Catherine's expanding belly, he forced his mind against a blank wall. To name it would be to end it. Look what happened last time. For the third pregnancy, Ike created his own gestures of protection. He placed a trinity of kisses around Catherine's navel every morning, slipped a drop of holy water from the Basilica of Our Lady of San Juan del Valle into her orange juice. When the woman from the bar invited him to her hotel room, he should have said no; he had slept with others during the last two pregnancies. Yet he could not say no, he never had been able to say no, and besides, he did take care to make love to her only in positions Catherine disliked; in this way, he reasoned, he kept his wife and child separate, whole, untouched in his heart. Create a ritual, respect it, and all will be well. He had believed that. Years away from a field and he was a ballplayer still.

When the third one died, too, the devastation arrowed deep, coursing through his every vein. But Catherine was worse. He took unpaid leave from Trailways and held her to his chest and shoulder and lap for hours, days. After she emerged from the worst of it, she borrowed books on physiology and biology from the library and pored over sections about infertility. She stayed late at work or at the coffee shop on Broadway she liked; several times he saw her simply sitting in her car in the driveway, the engine idling, staring out the windshield at their garage door. At home he felt like scraping the heel of his hand against the walls or smashing his foot through the nightstands—he had a throttling urge to make something bleed. So he went out and stayed out. Signed on for the longest routes Trailways would give him, spent nights in strange women's beds, or swallowing well whiskey in smoky bars, or shifting gears on dark interstates, passengers snoring behind him, the blinking lights of some distant town his only companions.

He and Catherine kissed, held each other in the day. But at night she rammed her fist into his shoulder or kneed him hard in the thigh, shoved him away so he nearly toppled off the bed. Every time, she had been sound asleep. He did not mention this in the daylight, nor did he ask her why. He didn't defend himself by revealing to her how he had tried, how he had not named the last two, how he had honored every superstition he could think of or invent, how for months after he dreamed he was lifting a crying child to his chest, a different child every night. She knew, in the depths of her she knew, and blamed him. As he did himself. The rituals had not failed him—he had failed the rituals. His own weakness. Her anger aimed outward in the dark; his aimed inward.

They settled back into equilibrium, their comfortable life. The years helped. Day passed into month into year into decade, and they worked, lived, loved. They reached an ease together, moving separately in their own spheres and rejoining in the evenings, on the weekends, and, after Year 43, in retirement. They have been happy since. Their jagged edges worn smooth, been smooth so long he cannot recall the last time their tempers flared. But he remembers Year 9 now, fingering the wood of the bed frame. Her fury and grief, his impotent rage. What the two of them could have done with a hurricane like Ike.

He smells the water before he sees it, a scent of copper and salt, both natural and unnatural, and his eyes fly open in the flickering dark. Water seeps beneath the door of the guest room, a trickle, no rushing sounds or splashes. A steady creeping. Hurricane Ike has entered the house. When he swings his feet to the floor, the rug squelches.

———

Ike is on the top bunk, listening to the whistling wind outside and the soft slosh of water inside when he hears something he shouldn't. A high, keening yowl beneath the wind. It sounds very close. Rain hammers against the windowpanes, but Ike stretches his already-limited hearing. There it is again: a yowl, pitched in panic. A cat. Coming from the front yard. His father's watch reads 12:51 a.m.

Ike doesn't hesitate to reach for his shoes, lying neatly on the bunk's attached shelf. Idiot, Catherine would say to him—he can hear her voice as clearly as if she sat next to him, watching him pull on the sneakers and lace them tightly. That is a *hurricane* out there, hon. Stay inside. Stay safe. Ike taps a kiss to his finger and touches the mattress where in his mind's eye she is sitting; then he tugs on the windbreaker lying beside him. He climbs slowly down the bunk ladder and descends into water midway up his calves.

The shock of it—water inside the house, where it does *not belong*—sings up Ike's legs. *Wrong*, the wrongness of his submerged feet when he should be dry and feel floor beneath him. Though the water is warm, he begins to shiver. Gingerly, he moves through the inches of wrong water, making his way to the front door. Except for the lapping against the walls and furniture and the splashing sounds his legs make, the house is silent. He toes the now-useless towels aside from the door and grunts as he pulls it through the water to open. Then he opens the screen door.

Catherine, he thinks in that heartbeat before it hits him.

Rain screams into his eyes, thrown in sharp pellets. He gasps, tugs the hood of his windbreaker over his head to protect his glasses, but drops still beat like bullets. The screech of the wind is immense, and the world is water. Albacore Avenue sits beneath at least two feet of rain-churned liquid. The cottonwoods and live oaks in his neighbors' yards whip back and forth; the palm trees are bent over nearly double, so far he is amazed they haven't snapped. Branches and debris spear the air, flying without pattern. He wavers, fighting for balance, and moves down the driveway to the street, hands cupping his eyes, blocking the worst of the storm. Ike has arrived finally and all of Galveston is witness.

Ike the storm muscles through ocean and atmosphere, onto the narrow strip of sand-seawall-asphalt-wood-tree-gravel-earth, the only thing between it and the continent. Ike was a cluster at first, small points of loose, scattered weather systems before the heat came—the warmth cast down from the sun and rising from the salt water, tendrils reaching through and weaving the storms together, stoking them like embers. They bloomed into Ike. Ike has roiled and whirled, charged and swirled across the ocean, hurling cyclones, stinging rain. Ike whispers and bellows. Draw near, people, webs of paved roads and buildings and bridges, all icons of men's hubris. Draw near to Ike, who breathes them in and exhales them in pieces. Stilts beneath houses on the beach splinter, snap.

Buildings crumple into the water. Boats spin, take flight, crash in streets and cars. Sparks catch and fire ignites, but the water of Ike is too strong, the wind too ferocious, to be stilled or even slowed by fire. People run, huddle, cry out, drown. In control and reckless, restless, Ike is cruelty and compassion both: tear down to raise up again in the image of what was and will be—all wind, all water. Ike surges across the island and plunges through a tangle of homes at the east end where a man stands in the street with his hands raised high. To him, Ike is silence that lasts forever; Ike is a single voice forged from so many keening sounds that take the shape of Ike's own name. Ike is howling, howling. From the throat of the funnel at its heart, Ike opens, holds in its mouth the man with its name. The man staggers in the water and lowers his arms to clutch himself.

This is how it had been, Ike the man thinks absurdly, in Year 22. The year of Nena, and the year Catherine left. They fought every day, bitterly. Dirty dishes left on the coffee table, his truck parked askew in the driveway, her overwatering of the sábila on the front porch—everything flinted their tempers, burst into flame. She was tired and irritable, and he was cheating, but more than that he was thinking of leaving.

Ike squints in the wailing wind. He pulls his jacket tighter around himself. He had pulled the shawl tight around Catherine, too, when she stood by her car that chilly day in Year 22. She caught cold so easily. With his hands on her shoulders, her face crumbled briefly, but she slipped behind the wheel—parked right here, where he stood—and drove to her amiga's place in Texas City without another word. This was a sign, he believed then, watching her turn left from Albacore onto Ferry and vanish. He had been mentally packing his own bag for weeks. He told Nena so that night. Es una señal, he murmured into her hair where it was draped across his face, still long and thick and mostly black despite their middling age. We can be together. Vámonos, mi amor, let's go let's go let's just go.

Nena pressed her fingers to his mouth and shook her head. Her ancient eyes cool and firm. I will not leave, she said. Tenemos ahorita, no más. Lo sabes. And he did know. Like her, he understood the pattern of their lives, the shape of the path God or the gods or her Karankawa ancestors had laid out before them. Her restless bartender son and indifferent husband across the street, his lonely wife somewhere on the mainland—they would return to them, honor the bonds fastening them tight. But this was not nothing. These months with her had been special to him. When he murmured so, she nodded. And to me, she said, before sliding her thigh over and rising above him in the dark of his bedroom.

There—the yowling. Keening pitifully from the oleanders to his right. Clutching at the branches there, angry and wild-eyed and drenched, is a striped gray cat. He recognizes the cat of the woman who lives two homes down, an indoor-outdoor pet. Once, it approached them in their yard and he bent to stroke it, but Catherine, who is allergic, hissed and kicked at it until the cat ran. Now, before he can register his actions, he is moving, pushing toward the oleanders. When he reaches out, the cat leaps on him frantically; its claws rip into his skin, his sodden windbreaker, and it clambers up his back to his shoulders, where he uses one hand to force it in place, wincing and swearing. Easy, cat, damn it, cat. Its howls like sobs and pleas at once, make it stop, make it stop. And it does, for just a moment: The wind quiets fractionally; the rain slaps with a bit less bite. I made it so, Ike thinks. Shh, he whispers to the cat and the storm both.

The cat struggles and yowls all the way back to the house, and only quiets once he sets it on the kitchen counter and begins drying it with a dishtowel. With its fur spiked and damp, not sopping, he sees it has white paws and a metallic tag on its collar: Winifred. Winifred, he says aloud. Shh, Winifred. Want some salmon? The water steadily licking at his legs, his jeans soaked through. By the time he wrangles the can open and scoops the salmon chunks onto a plate, Winifred is yelping eagerly and the water reaches his knees.

In their little galley kitchen, the sounds of the hurricane amplify; they must be in a tunnel as a train rushes through it—or at least Ike imagines so, as he has never been on a train or in a train tunnel. He has heard something like this sound before. Only once, Winifred, he says aloud. Year 7. He was driving his bus on a stretch of I-27 outside Lubbock when the dispatcher came through about a tornado spotting near them. Ike pulled beneath the next overpass, as close to the curved wall as he could, so close he could have leaned through the driver's side window and licked the concrete had he wanted to. The passengers ducked down beneath the seats, huddled together; a few wept, a baby cried, some held hands and prayed.

We never saw the tornado touch down, Winifred, but the wind was enough. The *wind*. He remembers the way it barreled past them, around them, through the half-moon tunnel beneath the overpass; started first as a low grumble, then a roar, built to a high-pitched whine. Nothing like it, Ike thought then, a young man still but beginning to soften from two years in the driver's seat. There could be nothing like this sound anywhere in nature, he told Catherine when he made it back to Galveston the next day and she hugged him, kissed him frantically. That night, she told him she was pregnant, and for the first time in their marriage, Ike felt fear. He has felt fear many times since. He feels fear now, stopping his heart like long fingers reaching in.

I'm afraid, he says, but Winifred just buries her nose in the salmon and keeps eating.

IN THE EYE

Yvonne, Mercedes

"Shit, fuck, shit."

"Yvonne, you sound like such a lady when you talk like that."

"Leave it, Mama."

Yvonne is praying or, more accurately, trying to. She can't exactly recall the words to the Memorare. She reaches for them, but they dance out of her memory as if she hasn't spent the last twenty-three years saying it over and over, as if every Sunday of hurricane season she doesn't recite it from memory along with the rest of the Sacred Heart congregation. The Hail Mary, the Our Father, the Apostles' Creed—those she can say in her sleep, in English or fumbling Spanish, feeling the pinch of her mother's fingers on her inner arm when she or Jess or any of her sisters don't enunciate clearly. But the Memorare is the one she needs to say, for all this to be over, for them to be safe. Yvonne has been a poor Catholic in the few years since she married and had her baby, but she is sure of this.

She could ask her mother for the words—Eva is sitting beside her in bed on the second floor of Yvonne's Pompano Avenue house, worrying rosary beads and murmuring. But Yvonne hesitates. She has not asked her mother for help since she was fifteen, and she sure as hell doesn't want to start now. If her little sisters were awake, she would ask them, though when she last checked they were snoring in the guest room double bed, a pile of blankets and gangly tanned limbs and Sarita's stuffed elephant, which she sleeps with every night despite just starting high school.

"So many hurricane seasons—we pray the Memorare, and we've always been okay," she leans to her left and whispers to her cousin.

Mercedes nods. It isn't that she doesn't believe Yvonne; it's that she knows better. Prayers, Christian or otherwise, Catholic or otherwise—they are feelings, at their heart. They are just requests made of the gods. They fall on deaf ears.

They have been sitting, the four of them, in Yvonne's upstairs bedroom, for hours now. They moved when the water started trickling in, the surge reaching long brown tongues beneath towel-lined doors and up through the floorboards. Fearful, she bundled Aaron in his baby blankets and carried him up the stairs, followed by Mercedes, guiding Yvonne's mother carefully. When she last went down to peek at the damage, Yvonne saw the water had risen several feet, submerged the lower level. Oily brown water in her beautiful house, the one she and Russell bought last year after she found out she was pregnant. While she was sobbing, talking about how she'd have to quit nursing school, he had laughed and said, *Let's get married, yeah?* Outside the eternal crashing of rain and wind, as if something were colliding over and over, endlessly.

The sound has lulled the baby into sleep; Eva pats his back, humming, two rosaries twined around her wrists and fingers. Mercedes sits on the floor, cross-legged, calm somehow—*how can that be*, Yvonne wonders. *Girl from the Valley, girl from both sides of the border. What does she know of hurricanes?*

Yvonne is more afraid than ever, which she hates. She despises looking weak, and she knows she must right now, to her older cousin, to her mother with her eternally judging eyes. She is married to a lawyer, damn it, one who was calling every five minutes from his business trip to Killeen to hear her voice until the towers went down. A good man, a white man. She is a nurse—an LVN, sure, but she completed nursing school while pregnant, landed a job in a cushy family practice clinic that even Carly is jealous of. She is the mother of a sweet, pink-cheeked boy who will be nothing like any of their fathers. She has made something of herself.

And yet, despite all that, she needs the prayer. Yvonne grasps for the words, snatching at what she does recall—*Remember O Most Gracious Virgin Mary never known anyone left unaided confidence I fly unto thee my mother before thee I*—but they shred apart in her memory and on her tongue. As she reaches for another word—*intercession intercession*—she hears the change in the storm. Mercedes straightens; she hears it, too.

Mercedes reaches up to where Aaron is sleeping, lays her palm flat against his small back. "Listen, Papa," she murmurs, soothing her favorite nephew in his sleep, but he does not hear. *Dream, then*, she thinks. *Dream of this storm that visited you, that showed you its strength as you slept.* Despite what Yvonne thinks, she is familiar with hurricanes.

Brownsville and Matamoros are at the tip of Texas, curling toward the Gulf. She remembered to board up the windows of the duplex apartment on Tuna she rents from Yvonne and Russell, to unplug the appliances and run the sinks and bathtub full of fresh water, to move as much as possible to higher ground. To take herself to higher ground, too—although there is no higher ground on this island, she has learned in the years she has been here, so she settled for the mental and emotional higher ground of family. The family she has cobbled together in Galveston, after leaving the others behind.

Aaron gives a little jerk, then continues to snore softly. Beneath her hand, his back rises and falls, rises, falls. She closes her eyes; she remembers when Celia was this small, when she could tuck the whole form of her sister against her chest and inhale the powder-milk-skin smell rising from her hair. Now Celia is fourteen, starting high school, playing volleyball and dating a girl from Edcouch-Elsa. Her texts to Mercedes are full of exclamation points and smiley faces, far cries from the fists beating on her shoulders three years ago, the ragged tears she wept when Mercedes told her—told them all—that she was moving away. When she showed them pictures of Galveston, Celia had sobbed and screamed, but their mother sat perfectly still. *Mi vida*, she said simply, with a smile that trembled and faltered when she turned to Mercedes. *I understand.* And she did, Mercedes knew suddenly, blinking back tears of shame because she hadn't thought it earlier. Who else but her mother would understand the electric thrill and the terrible dread of knowing you must leave? She has not had a visit from them in a year; the checkpoints on the Valley highways make her mother nervous, even when she drives with Tío Carl, who looks most like a bolillo. So she resorts to phone calls and texts to tell them about living first with Tía Eva and the girls, then renting space in the duplex Russell owns. Landing the job at the Sand Crab, with its view of the bay and the *Elissa*, making friends. Getting to know her cousins, to be part of their lives here, to build one for herself. She has not yet told them of the application Yvonne gave her for a college on the mainland with a program in social work and a page on the website reading *Undocumented students welcome*. She has not yet returned Luis's last text from months ago: *I miss you*.

Mercedes stills her body and the words in her mind so she can hear the rain. Listen. It is weaker than before; it strikes the roof and the boarded windows and the ground around them with a lesser ferocity than before. The wind—still strong but calmer, too, no longer a scream so shrill it stabs her ears. Her skin detects it: a resettling, a lightening. She holds her breath, as the hurricane does, and realizes.

"This is the eye," she says. Her watch reads 2:09 a.m.

Yvonne thinks, *Intercession intercession intercession*.

———————

The snap yanks Mercedes violently out of sleep. Yvonne hears it, too. An enormous splitting sound, like an iceberg shedding chunks in the nature show she and Russell watched months ago; *calving*, Russell said it was called, and kissed her when Yvonne, whose great-grandfather had been a cattle rancher outside Monterrey, said that was ridiculous. Other than on TV she has never seen an iceberg.

The splitting sound, from a distance outside, reverberates and slowly dissipates into rain. Then comes a roaring of wind that is not storm wind; too far away, harsher, guttural in Yvonne's ears. It doesn't take long for her to smell smoke. The black, choking scent snakes into her nose.

She meets Mercedes's eyes across the king-size bed, in the dark. They are wide and frightened.

Fire. Mercedes's breath stutters in panic; she wills herself to calm. Where? She blinks at her watch: 4:11 a.m. As she rises, Tía Eva and Aaron shift in sleep, mumble. She turns back to her cousin.

"We need to know where it's coming from," Yvonne whispers, and Mercedes nods. They need to know. *If we're in danger. And if we have to go—somewhere. Where? Somewhere.*

"You stay. I'll go check."

"No." Yvonne was already pulling on her waterlogged shoes. "We'll both go." Shit, shit, if she could just recall the words. *O Most Gracious Virgin Mary*, or was it *Most Blessed*?

Mercedes's hand rests tight on her shoulder as they make their way downstairs. Yvonne grimaces at the last dry step; then her cousin squeezes lightly, and she steps down. The water is warm, and a shock—to be so wet, so submerged, inside her house—but she keeps going, feels Mercedes behind her. When Yvonne's feet touch the ground floor, she is in water above her waist.

"Fuck," Mercedes whispers.

In the dim light of Yvonne's flashlight, the water appears colorless, dark and menacing, as if they are wading through a bayou instead of a home. They move into the living room. The water around Mercedes is stagnant and reeks of garbage, slicked with rainbows of oil that catch the flashlight's beam. They pass the couch, kitchen chairs, television stand, three-level bookshelf of Russell's John Grisham hardcovers and Yvonne's Nora Roberts paperbacks, all almost fully underwater. Yvonne pushes her legs through the water, bumping them against debris: books or knickknacks or pillows, she cannot see. Flotsam from her own home. She shivers, thinking of the many storms she remembers here in Galveston, how none had this level of surge—this high water, this lasting. Ike is different; it has turned their own bay against them.

At the front door Mercedes passes her their windbreakers. Yvonne's has a hood, which she zips up. Mercedes makes do with piling her hair up beneath the Vaqueros ball cap and pulling it down over her face.

"Ready?"

"Ready."

Yvonne takes a deep breath and slowly, through the water, pulls open the front door.

Mercedes's first thought: *Everything is brighter.* This is a lie—it is the middle of the night, hours away from dawn—but it feels true. The rain falling without its cruel edge, the wind died down to a mere breeze. If not for the water lapping at her ribs, this could be four a.m. on any given night. The utter stillness is eerie, foreboding.

"Come on," Yvonne whispers. "We don't have long." Eyes only last a few hours and are fickle; a lifetime as an islander has taught her so. Sweat gathers on her brow from the humidity, but she shivers as they wade carefully down the driveway; she uses her elbows to bat bobbing soda bottles and palm fronds and sodden scraps of cardboard out of their path. At some point, Mercedes links arms with her. They push through the water together like conjoined twins.

"Anything?"

"Nothing." No sign of fire anywhere, though they can smell it on the air. Yvonne looks back at the house and scans it frantically. Flames, tongues, smoke—nothing. Relief floods into her stomach. "Let's see if it's nearby."

They are in the middle of Pompano before Mercedes grips her arm, points. "There." The cause of the iceberg crack and the smoke smell: a house down at the east end of the street is on fire.

"Putamadre," Mercedes swears, sucking in her breath. She has never seen a building aflame before. Its walls are alight, its roof breathing black plumes of smoke.

"It could have been an appliance still running," Yvonne says, staring at the columns of smoke. "It just needs a spark. A curtain, some wood." She has forgotten that her cousin already knows this. She is thinking of her mother, asleep upstairs with her hand on her grandson's back, and of the last tropical storm they weathered together before Yvonne moved out of the house on Dolphin. *Unplug everything, mija. Make sure there are no sparks, nothing nearby that could catch.* "In a storm everything becomes a wick."

Strange, she told her mother that time, hunkering down with the wind screaming outside and the girls playing a video game, screaming inside—they hadn't lost power then—how so much water can lead to fire. It should be unnatural, shouldn't it? *It's the electricity,* Eva replied in her steady motherly tone of explanation, the one Yvonne hated even as she heard herself use it to scold Jess or the girls, to correct Russell. She imagined blue water—another lie, Galveston water and storm water never blue—and red fire circling each other, boxers in a ring. *One should win the fight,* she said at the time with a shrug. It doesn't seem right that both can simply exist. Eva shook her head; when

Sarita ran over in tears from something one of the girls said, their mother held her close and cuddled her. She had never done that with Yvonne; had barely looked at Jess since he moved into his apartment and started working at the marina. But Yvonne saw her sister nestle in, close her eyes in comfort against her mother. And she longed for that, too, just for a moment.

The rain is picking up. Mercedes hears an urgency in its falling, the quickening pattern. She moves closer to the house, down the street.

"Where are you going?" Yvonne hisses. "Get back here."

Mercedes has to see it. She keeps going, moving as carefully as she can. One yard, then two. Past one house, then another. Yvonne following behind, wading and cursing.

Once, Mercedes stumbles in a pothole; the water engulfs her up to her shoulders. She fumbles and steps out, resolving to shuffle her feet beneath the water—as Luis taught her, years ago, on trips to the white sand and blue water of South Padre. *Shuffle your feet rather than lifting them in steps, M, and you won't come down on a stingray.* He liked watching her practice, the underwater drag of her feet making her hips move awkwardly above the surface. She saw him watching and laughed.

I miss you, he had written, and some days—like today—she knows her response would be *I miss you too*. Mercedes walks forward, eyes fixed on the scorching house. Luis would never have let her do this. She slides her foot forward another step. He would tell her to turn back. She lifts her chin and takes another.

Her cousin looks enraptured, and Yvonne understands why—the burning house is magnificent, horrific, holy. A pillar of flame. The wind strengthens, buffeting their faces, churning the water around them into tiny waves, but the women creep closer. The flames sway but do not diminish. At last, Yvonne recognizes the home as the green two-story with the giant old palm tree adorning the front yard. In the eye of the storm, the tree stands forty feet tall, arcing in an elegant comma curve. Its wide, fanning leaves move gently and then frantically, as the wind rises, high above her head.

"That poor tree," Mercedes says, and squeezes her eyes shut, a tang of salt filling her mouth. It could be the rain, but she imagines it is the tree. Imagines—madly—that she is the tree. She forces herself not to choke, wills the tree to do the same. A palm tree can survive some salt water but surely not five feet of it, not days of submerged roots. Surely nothing could swallow so much and breathe. Still, she thinks, *Breathe*.

"Prima, let's go. Come on." Yvonne reaches for her arm. The wind roils around them, the lightness they admired minutes earlier evaporating. Mercedes fights to keep her balance in the water. Flames roar into the sky, brilliant, eager tongues of orange and yellow thrusting upward. Even from this distance, houses away, her cheeks and the tip of her nose flush with the heat. Rain streams down, too much for the island to handle but useless for the house, and the tree. The tree will catch in a moment. She knows this. It has to. *In a storm everything becomes a wick.* Mercedes tastes the salt water on the tree's root tongues, but Yvonne sees the tree catching fire, can picture it before it happens. Flickering in front of her eyes are broad-fingered leaves striking as if by a match—flaring into life—crown of flames atop the lean trunk—skirted with water—snarl of roots drowning.

"It's crazy, isn't it?" Yvonne hears herself whisper. "How fast something can be destroyed."

"I know." Mercedes hugs herself. They stand in the rain for long moments, amid the dirty surge water pooling in the street, watching fire consume a house in the eye of a hurricane.

Yvonne doesn't know where the words come from, but she suddenly says, "It's taking it all back. Taking it all down. Like none of this is supposed to be here." She laughs, hysterically. "We put boards on windows and stuff towels beneath doors and think that will keep us safe. As if any of that shit matters or makes the slightest difference. Crazy, right? Stupid of us?"

Mercedes squints through the rain at her cousin. She understands. This house, the palm tree someone uprooted and planted in the lawn. Yvonne's house and Tía Eva's house and Mercedes's house; Pompano and Tuna and Fish Village; the stilt-legged homes on Bolivar and Crystal Beach; the brick buildings on the Strand and the cruise ships at Harborside and the towers of the Bishop's Palace; all of Galveston, a city built atop the ruins of another city demolished once before, by another hurricane. Jess told her that. He's always telling her Galveston history. He wants her to feel like she belongs here.

"But it does, sometimes," she says. "Make a difference. Maybe one window doesn't break, or one house doesn't catch on fire. You know? Some things will make it, prima." The fire crackles, gives a brief belch that makes her tremble. "Some things survive."

They look up into the dark sky with its eerie gray light.

"Aaron," Mercedes says, and Yvonne registers her son's name like the word that breaks a trance. She glances around with her eyes sharp again.

"Let's go."

They stumble as they turn in the water, the rain and the wind that has built up again, shoving them, back, back. Yvonne pushes through, Mercedes's arm in hers, and they shuffle back to the house. It takes a long time, longer than before, when the eye was still upon them. The word comes again: *intercession*.

And then: *unaided*.

Yvonne laughs, earning a wary look from Mercedes. "I remember," she says. "I remember." She snatches the rest of the line in her mind so suddenly and so clearly that she sees the wooden pews of Sacred Heart, the white-robed priest before her instead of this nightmarish version of Pompano. *Remember, O most gracious Virgin Mary, that never was it known that anyone who fled to thy protection, implored thy help, or sought thine intercession was left unaided.* No other line comes to her at that moment, but she only needs this one. She repeats it under her breath, clasping Mercedes tight as they climb the driveway, wade to the door, shove it open, and force it closed behind them.

Upstairs they peel off their sodden clothes and pull on dry shorts and two of Russell's San Antonio Spurs T-shirts. Mercedes climbs into the bed on Tía Eva's side. Her aunt is still sleeping, but when Mercedes moves closer, she shifts to accommodate her. She lifts her arm to drape it over Mercedes, to rub her hand lightly across her back. Mercedes thinks of Luis, again, his hand on her back; she smells her mother in Tía Eva's skin. She smiles. *I stood in the eye*, she will tell them, someday. *I stared down a hurricane. What else do you think I can do?*

Yvonne wraps her arms around Aaron and pulls him closer. *Russell*, she thinks. *Jess. Carly. Be safe, be safe.* Aaron breathes against her chest, sighs in his sleep. The house shudders, trembles, and Yvonne listens to the rain splintering against the windows. *Remember, O most gracious Virgin Mary.* She shifts the words of that one line, rearranges them. *Never was it known that anyone was left unaided. We did not flee*, she thinks; *we never do. We implore thy help. Remember. Intercede.*

NUESTRA

Carly

Rain slams against the glass panes of Hector's house, peppered with hail, maybe. Carly cannot tell. Beneath the sheets of the pullout couch, Jess slips his hand under the T-shirt of his she wears, but she is not in the mood and tells him so. The power has been out for hours, so why get sweaty? He heaves a dramatic sigh but lets her curl in. She rests her cheek on his chest, in the curve of his collarbone where her ear fits perfect as a seashell. She knows neither of them will sleep. He twirls her hair around his finger, and she listens to the drumming of his heart and the hail.

"Maybe it will weaken over Cuba," he said—was it just a few days ago? And she had told him, "We won't be that lucky." She couldn't pinpoint how she knew it, but she knew. She watched the news in the early hours of darkness during her night shift, coffee growing cold in her mug. The storm drew strength from the warmth of the Gulf waters, the weatherman said. Ike once again claiming Cat 2 status, curling steadily toward Galveston.

So it began. Jess called Hector, living with his wife and baby in Sealy. Hector told him yes, don't be stupid, they should get their asses there pronto quick once the storm prep is done. His parents and his grandmother were already there, but they could have the pullout in the living room, just bring extra sheets and supplies. "This one looks bad," Hector said, whistling. When she saw Jess's mouth taking the shape of another Ike-Turner-better-not-beat-the-living-shit-outta-us joke, Carly leaned in and kissed him so he would shut up. Later, after he spoke to his mother, learned she and the girls were hunkering down at Yvonne's two-story house—"It will be fine, Jesusmaría, for God's sake, don't worry so much"— Carly kissed him again, this time to soothe.

It was all-hands-on-deck at UTMB once the evacuation order came down. Overnight she moved machinery, handled IV tubes and caths, loaded the babies from NICU into evac choppers and ambulances bound for Austin and San Antonio and Dallas. She wasn't assigned to emergency crew, so she could leave with Jess instead of having to sleep at the hospital. Evacuation ate up her whole shift, but Jess knew what needed to be done. By the time she made it home, he had hammered boards over the windows, emptied out the refrigerator and freezer, and unplugged all the electronics. She took a quick shower as he packed; she hadn't slept in eighteen hours, but she was running on adrenaline. While he loaded up his truck, she threw clothes and toiletries into her duffel, then remembered her nursing diploma.

She knew where Magdalena kept the waterproof lockbox; dust bunnies made Carly sneeze as she maneuvered it out from under her grandmother's bed. She carried it and her duffel out to the truck where Jess was waiting. He locked up, and she traced the sign of the cross into the lintel by the front door. Jess saw, placed his palm against the screen door for a beat longer.

As they began the crawl north on the causeway, surrounded by other evacuees, her cell phone rang.

"Hello?"

"Miss Castillo?"

"Yes."

"This is Evelina Reyes, at Bay Pines Care."

Carly listened for a few moments. When she hung up, turned to Jess, her eyes were snapping. "We have to go to League City." It would slow them down, stopping, but it had to be done. "She tried to burn the fucking thing down."

———

She stopped first at the manager's office. It took nearly half an hour to listen, to argue, to insist and plead with bleached-blond, stern-eyed Evelina Reyes that her grandmother wasn't a threat. Yes, it was terrible that she tried to start a fire in the piano room; no, she couldn't understand how it happened, her grandmother was always so gentle, so timid. Yes, she was aware of the zero-tolerance policy for offenses, but was trying to light a candle atop the baby grand really an offense? What palm fronds? No, she had no idea where Magdalena could have obtained those. Where was the day nurse Magdalena liked, Kristin? She could explain the old woman wasn't a threat. But Kristin had evacuated and would not be back at work for days.

In the end, Mrs. Reyes agreed one more chance could be given—the small patch of burning palms had been put out quickly, the fronds themselves hardly singed, and Magdalena had not been belligerent. Actually, she had seemed calm, watching quietly as the orderlies smothered the fire, explained to her why that was not allowed, and led her back to her room. Carly knew that was the medication, the steadier demeanor, the longer spells of gentleness between bouts of confusion and irritation.

No more chances would be given from here on out, Mrs. Reyes warned. Carly shook the woman's hand and thanked her profusely. Inwardly, she seethed.

Magdalena was watching a novela in her room when Carly walked in. A man was shouting; a woman was crying. That was nothing new. The woman stiffened and, with a look of righteous fury, slapped the man. He stared. She lifted her chin. Commercial break.

"Grandma."

Magdalena turned with a smile. "Niña." She reached up for her hand, tugged her down for a kiss, but Carly snatched her hand away.

"I heard what you tried to do. Are you kidding me with this shit?"

Her grandmother's mouth fell open, and her eyes sparked—not with irrational rage from the dementia, but with normal anger, like they used to when Carly came home after curfew or back-talked as a teenager. Now Carly was the grown one, looming tall, frustration spreading like a rash over her cheeks, her throat.

"Do you know how long I had to beg them to let you stay here? They want to kick you out!"

"I did it for protection," Magdalena said, jaw set. "I did it for all of us. Now we will be safe."

"Burning palms won't work. Chanting made-up words won't, either. This is a real storm coming and you can't stop it."

"Lo hice por tí."

"You don't need to do anything for me—I can take care of myself. Besides." Carly leaned forward, locked her hands onto the arms of Magdalena's chair. Enough. Enough now. "I don't believe in this shit, Grandma. You. Are. Not. A. Karankawa. They're gone. They've been gone a long time. We don't come from them, you and me. We're just us."

Magdalena turned sideways, and Carly—smarting with guilt—opened her mouth to apologize. But her grandmother whipped back. Her face, like that of the novela actress, bore the sheen of righteous indignation. The tears in her eyes reflected it, cast it back like an echo.

"You know better," she snapped. "We fight, as they did. You used to believe what I told you, even when *she* didn't." Carly flinched at the mention of her mother, and Magdalena steamrolled past. "If I tell you we come from fighters, es verdad. Because *we* say it is."

"I don't come from fighters, Grandma. I come from runners." Her grandmother's face rippled; her whole frame shuddered. Still, the words were out; Carly was tired of holding them inside. Let them come. "Your son, your daughter-in-law. They're my blood, too. More than some long-gone people, more even than you. They left us both and never looked back."

Magdalena said nothing in response. Carly thought of the oyster shells lined along their TV stand, the ones Magdalena collected, how they gave off a hollow gleam without the oyster, all the life scraped out of them. Her grandmother looked like that now—emptied, scooped clean.

"You can't will things to be different, Grandma. I came to tell you Jess and I are on our way to Sealy. We're evacuating—this storm is going to be bad, and we're not going to stay. We boarded up the house, we took care of everything. You'll be safe here."

She expected more fury, more indignation, but her grandmother pressed her lips together and turned her face toward the mirror with its BOI bumper sticker. She gazed at the green palm tree.

"We'll come back once they reopen the roads." *I'm sorry*, Carly thought.

Magdalena nodded distractedly.

"Grandma?"

"Just go, Carly Elena." She sounded so sad.

It took more than an hour with the traffic, and though Jess tried to say calming things, she ignored him and opened the lockbox.

She found her diploma and the birth certificates—her grandmother's and her own—and a photo of a very young Magdalena holding Marcos as a baby. There was one more, one she had never seen. Carly inhaled, slowly. She lifted the wedding photograph.

Marcos Castillo was young, about her own age. He angled his head in the curious way of posed photos, smiling just enough to show the upper row of teeth. His hair was cropped short. He had her grandfather's bones, his heavy eyebrows, but the laugh lines beside his eyes were her grandmother's. Carly's, too. She recognized nothing else in him, this handsome man whose leaving was the first of the losses that measure her life, like channel markers indicating deep water.

It was the woman beside him who earned Carly's careful looks. A younger, crisper version of the woman in her memories, Maharlika Velasquez Castillo had thick dark hair that waved appealingly around her wide face. The curls were styled—Carly knew her mother's hair had been Pocahontas-straight. Her fingertips fluttered with the sudden memory of movement, of slipping softly down that waterfall of black where there are no bends in sight.

Here, her mother who rarely smiled was beaming. She leaned her right ear toward Marcos's shoulder. His hand rested lightly, fingers bent possessively, around her waist. They looked innocent, bright with promise. They could have been her and Jess; the thought, which should have been sweet, filled Carly with dread. In less than a decade from this photo's taking, both these people were elsewhere, out of each other's life.

Her mother looked happy, tilting her body and her mind already to her husband. Was there something in there that showed how she would implode after he left? How she would shrink to a point and keep collapsing until she became a spore of what had once been a person, with no room for a daughter or a mother-in-law, nothing except the urge to seek out another shell, another reef, start over again?

Carly replaced the picture, remembering bitterly that she had left once, too, though she had come back. That she promised her grandmother she would stay this time, ride out the storm no matter what, yet instead was running. *No better than you*, she thought to the photo. *No more loyal*.

———

They both sense it, the moment Ike barrels into Sealy. The wind, which has been a steady whistle, suddenly crescendos to a shrill pitch. Carly winces. Jess freezes.

"Bad one," she says, and feels him nod. Tighten his arms around her.

"Wonder if Alicia sounded like this," he says. Neither of them was alive for the '83 hurricane, but islanders still talk about it. The entire city lost power; roofs of whole buildings sheared off; dozens of tornados sprouted from the big wind.

They fall quiet again, silenced by the storm, awed and troubled into stillness so they hardly move or even breathe. Carly thinks: Galveston is lying out there, in that. Her house, her car, her hospital. Coworkers, neighbors. Jess's mom and sisters and cousin. A sign of pride for islanders, hunkering down whatever the weather, plowing through.

But this. She swallows hard as the roof rattles. They are in Sealy, a hundred miles inland. Galveston could not have expected *this*. The cracked, tipping headstones and mausoleums of Old City Cemetery, the elegant towers of the Hotel Galvez, the marina with the *Cig*, the lot off Ferry Road where she had broken her collarbone playing football, the stretch of beach by the jetties where Magdalena liked to walk barefoot. Beneath all this ferocity the island huddles together and bends down, maybe breaking, and Carly miles away, and her grandmother, too. Alone, away, just as she wanted. Tears spring to her eyes, but she wills them back. She left; this is the cost.

"Maybe letting her light a fire wouldn't have hurt," she says, immediately blushing with embarrassment. Jess strokes a hand down her back.

"Maybe not."

The seething sounds of the wind work their way into

her fitful dreams, become her grandmother around a bon-
fire on the beach, her face lifted to the sky. She wears a
wedding veil. She is screaming.

———————

They do not open the causeway, not for days. The ferries
stay shut for even longer than that; only helicopters and
rescue vehicles can reach Bolivar, picking up survivors,
the remnants of people who didn't, or couldn't, leave. In
Hector's living room they gather to watch the news reports.
When aerial footage shows boats, fragments of boats, ran-
dom scraps of wood tossed across a barren and churned-up
stretch of beach, Carly gasps. Tall lengths of timber stick
up from the sand—stilt legs that once held up houses. All
empty now.

"Jesus," Jess says softly.

Mrs. de los Santos—the old one—makes the sign of
the cross and begins to murmur. Beside her, Hector's wife
slips her hand into his. His mother is weeping softly.

"Our house?" Carly asks aloud. She hears the wildness,
the raw scrape of worry, in her voice. "Fish Village?"

Mrs. de los Santos bites her lip. Hector sighs. Beneath
her hand Jess's leg is bouncing with anxiety. She knows
they are thinking as one: their friends, neighbors. With
their mind's eyes from high above, they skim the streets like
seagulls. On Bonita, the de los Santos bungalow with the
herb garden in the back where his grandmother works daily.
On Marlin, the cottage owned by Carlos Saldivar's parents,
with the roses Luz pruned before they moved away, before
they divorced months ago and Carlos came home. Down the
street, the three-bedroom with the porch swing where Mr.
Pham and his wife like to drink salty dogs when he isn't on

the bay. On Barracuda, Ram Jackson, who played football with Jess and asked Carly to prom, in the lavender two-story where he fosters stray dogs with the Filipino lab tech or the Black PE teacher or whoever his boyfriend is these days. On Pompano, the ranch house with the wide porch where Jess's mother and three youngest sisters still live. On Tuna, the duplex owned by Yvonne and her husband, which Mercedes rents for cheap, lining the front steps with potted succulents and geraniums that she keeps overwatering.

They watch the news footage for two more days, hoping for a glimpse of Ferry Road or UTMB or their corner of the island, but the images focus on the historic Victorians on Broadway and the shattered stilt houses on Crystal Beach. Once they show shrimping and pleasure boats tossed onto the street like bath toys—Jess sucks in a sharp breath, and Carly twines her fingers into his. Ball High, missing chunks of roof. Sacred Heart, flooded. Nothing of Fish Village or their people.

"We won't know until we go," Jess says.

The phone in Carly's pocket buzzes, startling them. Somehow she knows who it is even before looking at the caller ID.

———

She set a fire during the hurricane. A small one, but real this time. She let the palm fronds dry completely, then tore them into small strips and shaped them into a pile in her bathroom, setting them alight with the lighter she'd stolen from a resident who smokes. Jess points out her genius; she even ringed the fire with small, smooth rocks taken from the gardens in the courtyard so it wouldn't spread. When the smoke alarm in her room started blaring, the nurses and manager had found Magdalena in her nightgown, her hands in the air, cupping the smoke as if she could lift it to her mouth and drink. Her eyes were red and streaming, but she couldn't stop laughing. Neither could Mrs. de los Santos, Hector's grandmother—she hooted and clapped, hearing about her friend.

They cannot make it down to League City for another day, until the city clears the tree branches and debris. Carly speaks in clipped tones to Mrs. Reyes and the skeleton staff as she apologizes, signs the discharge papers. But Magdalena has a smug smile on her face, and Jess doesn't bother to hide his grin. Only Carly sits, icy with shame. She stays silent as they drive away from Bay Pines, her grandmother a disgraced former resident.

The causeway is still closed, so they head west, back to Sealy and their friends. Jess explains that they have no news of the house yet, that when he spoke to Yvonne he found out about the surge. "It was flooded, too, I'm sure," he says. "We'll have to be ready for some damage when we go back."

"Don't worry, Jesusmaría. I cast the protection blessing, remember? Our house is still there," she says, with such confidence and cheer in her voice that Carly looks back, startled, before remembering she is angry and turning around in a huff. "Our island is strong. I protected her. She bent but did not break." She gives a short laugh. "Isla de malhado."

Jess frowns a question at Carly in the passenger seat. "Malhado?"

"Misfortune. Doom." It is the first time she has spoken the whole way, and she has to clear her throat.

"Never heard it."

"That's what Cabeza de Vaca called Galveston when he shipwrecked here. Isla de malhado."

"Oh, yeah." He looks at her again, grinning. "You remembered something I didn't."

She is pleased, but turns to the window so he can't see her smile. "Don't get used to it."

"La isla mia," Magdalena says. She reaches forward and scratches the back of Carly's head lightly with her fingers. "Nuestra."

Carly considers pulling her head away, but she is tired of worrying, tired of anger. The smile feels good. The touch of her grandmother feels good. She lets Magdalena's fingertips weave through her hair and watches Houston spread out from I-45 in every direction. She remembers the sorrow she felt in Sealy, how alone, even with Jess there. *Grandma is slipping away*, Carly thinks. Soon she will be the one to leave for good—never to be left behind again.

And then there will be Galveston. And Carly, too. She is rooted here, fused fast like an oyster seed to its shell, that shell to its reef. The idea doesn't make her gut twist or lightning dart through her blood anymore. Some alchemy, maybe, like Jess talks about. She has bent beneath it, but not broken. Though she has lost nothing, she feels an ache—something she cannot name pulling away from her. But the sun through the windshield warms her skin. She smells Jess's deodorant, smoke from her grandmother's hair. Carly closes her eyes and drifts.

She is eight, and she's heard the word *malhado* for the first time. Even with her Spanish—which is fluent, not broken into chunks of *excuse me* and *no thank you* and *motherfucker* like Jess's—she doesn't recognize it. But she knows it means something bad because of the way her grandmother says it. She hardly moves her lips; the word darts through her teeth like a forked tongue.

Carly doesn't know what she's done wrong. All she has asked is, "Do you ever hear from my mom and dad?"

Magdalena straightens where she's facing the stove; her shoulders lower and set as if beneath plate armor. "Nunca," she says, her voice firm but not unkind. "I don't, and I don't think we ever will." She looks at Carly over her shoulder. "Llenos de malhado, esos. You be glad they're gone."

Tears prick the top of Carly's nose. Magdalena turns fully to face her. "Don't you cry," she says. "No tears. Would the Karankawas shed tears over this?"

She knows the drill and shakes her head.

"Would they cry like sad little chickens over every hard thing?"

"No."

"*No.* Who were they, our people?"

In the living room, the window AC rumbles to a stop; instantly the air becomes heavy, losing the cool of the conditioning, swelling again with the weight of the Gulf. Her grandmother seems to swell with it, too.

"They were warriors."

"Claro." She takes Carly's chin in her hand, shakes it gently. "So are we."

REBUILDING

Jess

He needs new gloves. Jess makes a mental note to buy a pair the next time he's at Home Depot, which will probably be in a few hours given the way he keeps running back and forth for more supplies. Sledgehammer, drywall hook, demo fork. Tools he does not have, has never thought to buy. But now he is busy, not just with the Albacore house but with so many others in Fish Village—what feels like an endless stream of demolition, days spent with the crew breaking down all that Ike damaged. Rey got him the work, and he's been doing it full-time since the boats are out of commission and the fishing season, it seems, is at a standstill. Like most of life in these weeks, these months post-Ike.

The rebuild is coming. Jess drives down Broadway, trying not to look at the brown-leaved trees. They will be replaced, he tells himself, though the sight makes him want to cry. He turns into Fish Village, passes the piles of debris still lining the corners and some lawns: soaked and rotting trash, scrap wood, stained sofas, useless refrigerators, water-logged TVs. Demo has begun for many homes, including theirs on Albacore and his mother's on Dolphin. Industrial dumpsters sit in the driveways, jagged chunks of lumber and drywall extending upward like broken teeth. Soon it will all be rebuilt. He wants that part the most, longs to see the gleam of new wood and clean drywall, replaced shingles, green grass. Be patient, he thinks. Soon.

He turns onto Albacore. As he approaches the Castillo house, he slows to a crawl. Shifts to park, stops. Stares through the windshield.

The man on the concrete steps rises to his full height—a few inches under six feet. Jess doesn't remember that. In his mind, the man was taller. Jess takes a deep breath to slow his pounding heart. As he turns off the ignition and steps out of the truck, he realizes he now towers over his father.

He has lost weight. Jess remembers a burly man, but the Orlando Rivera before him is leaner, rangy. Shaved head. Old work boots, fraying jeans, a blue shirt rolled to the elbows. Tattoos climb up his forearms; Jess spots the Mexican flag and the Virgen de Guadalupe, thorned roses in the shape of his mother's name. Those he remembers.

"Mijo," Lando says. His voice is raspy, that higher pitch that always—he's not sure why—surprises Jess. He hasn't spoken to him on the phone in months, not since well before Ike, though they have exchanged letters in the years since he was released. He was living in Port Arthur, Jess thinks, tries to scan his memory rapidly. Beaumont? An oil refinery somewhere. Lando lifts his arms, lowers them, clasps them together before tucking them into his jeans pockets. As if he is not sure how they work and he is learning.

"Dad." Jess's voice, he is proud, doesn't break or waver. He steps closer, shaken and trying not to seem so. "What are you doing here?"

"Your mom told me where you would be. Said you're helping fix everything around here."

"Yeah, I am." Dad. Dad is here. "I thought—I thought you weren't in town. You were out east."

"I was," Lando says. His hands rise again, fall again. "She told me what you all were going through. So I figured I'd come down here."

"Why?"

"Thought you could use some help."

He smiles a little. Tentative, hopeful. They both stand, stare, take each other's measure. After a minute, Jess smiles back.

EAST ANYWHERE

Pierre

He bends his knees to lower the tray of drinks from his shoulder to the tabletop. Not smoothly enough: Lone Star spills from the glasses, sloshes down. Pierre grimaces. He shakes his head and apologizes, but Table 10 smiles, tells him not to worry. Nice people, this group of three, so he jokes with them, deepens the lilt of his accent as he confesses that he has only had a few weeks to master the technique. They laugh, though it is a lie. Pierre lacks upper-body strength; he always has.

This kind of thing would come so naturally to Rudy. The two of them had run around every day back home, barefoot despite the debris and the jagged palm bark strewn about the beaches of Lumangbayan. Whenever Rudy spotted a girl, he would drop and count push-ups to make her giggle, to make the pubescent muscles on his arms look ropy in the light, while Pierre stood and kicked sand at the chickens that roamed the beach. But Pierre's hands are careful, graceful—superior to even Rudy's mother, Tita Grace,

Pierre's aunt who is like a mother to him, the midwife whose stitches are better than the village doctor's. When Tita Grace wanted fresh buko juice, Pierre's were the hands she trusted with the coconut and the machete, saying her son would slice off his fingers and then they would have to sew them back on.

Pierre uses his hands in this new job, distributing bottles of beer and ladling salsa into small cups, mixing margaritas and tequila sunrises in the Sand Crab, this bar and grill off Pier 21 in Galveston. He does not split coconuts anymore. Does Rudy still do push-ups to impress girls? He has no way of knowing. The worry for his cousin hums steadily under the skin; like a chronic illness, it has flare-ups.

Table 10 is ready to order. Pierre scribbles down their meal requests, trying not to squint as he translates the Texas drawls—into unaccented English, mostly, and occasionally even further into Tagalog. He tucks the pencil and notepad into the pocket of his jeans, promising that their shrimp nachos and jalapeño poppers will be out soon. The jukebox chooses that moment to launch into "Jessie's Girl." One of them asks over the wailing, "What's your name again?"

Pierre is ready. He has been thinking about a name since the three of them walked in, sunburned even though it is April, their shoes caked with sand from walking along the beach, a few of the rare visitors brave enough to stroll Galveston seven months after The Storm—*day-trippers*, he thinks, *from Houston, most likely*. Who aren't put off by the debris that still drifts in the bay, the construction trucks and repair crews that line the Gulf beach, the Seawall, the Strand—the tourist areas—thick as fleas. He likes that he can recognize them after only a few months here himself.

Their eyes had been sharp as he first approached their

table, then friendly, with the too-bright smiles that said they were trying hard not to say something insensitive. He felt their gazes land purposefully on his face, away from the shape of his eyes, his black, coarse hair that sticks out like feathers, his skin shades and shades browner than their darkest tan. This week he has been leaning toward the exotic—Federico, Isaiah—but today he thinks all-American. Joey, Christian, Kyle. Something to make them comfortable. Help them negotiate the alienness of him.

"Kyle," says Pierre, and he hefts the empty tray onto his shoulder.

———

He asked Tita Grace only once why his mother named him Pierre. He was seven; his mother had been dead for six years. At the question Tita Grace didn't turn from where she stood over the stove, using both hands to toss a mountain of rice noodles. (She always made enough pancit for a crowd.) She said Pierre had been the name of a Catholic missionary in their village when the sisters were young. The missionary was very tall and had yellow hair. They'd never seen yellow hair before, and he knelt down so they could touch it. He was the most beautiful man Pierre's mother had ever seen.

"Where does my name come from, Inay?" Rudy asked.

"My ninong," Tita Grace said tartly.

Though it was still too hot Pierre bit into a lumpia roll and burned his tongue for his awkwardness, his desperation. He knew Rudy would ask the question despite knowing better. As if by filling his own mouth Pierre could stop Rudy from opening his.

But Rudy could never resist. "Why didn't you name me

after Tatay?" he asked, belligerence casting a dark edge to his voice.

In the silence that ensued, Pierre felt the air freeze; he saw it in the shape of Tita Grace's back, a bow in her shoulders that made him sad. It had only been a year since Tito Eusebio had run off, but Pierre had noticed the way his aunt's mouth twisted in anger when they spoke of him. She would be happy if Tito Eusebio's memory stayed locked outside the walls of the house.

"He didn't like his own name," Tita Grace said after a very long, furious session of noodle tossing. Her back projected so much anger Pierre wanted to cry. "Rudy, you are blessed you are not named after him."

"Lucky, you mean," Rudy muttered, here at last lowering his voice so she couldn't hear. His mother—so devout a Catholic she was just a wayward husband and two small boys away from being a nun at some iron-ruled convent—hated that word. "Not lucky, *blessed*," she would say whenever someone used it. Both boys thought it was stupid. Tito Eusebio used to hate it, too; Pierre remembered suddenly.

To cut through the tension, Pierre leaned over with a grin and whispered, "Pinsan, you're a ninong like Godfather Marlon Brando!" Rudy nearly spit out his food laughing. At the stove, the line of Tita Grace's back eased.

For the rest of the week, Rudy insisted that the barrio boys call him Godfather. They did it, too. People listened to Rudy almost always. His plans—to stand in one spot and see who could throw a stone closest to the stray cats at the end of the alley, or who could run the fastest in the low surf, where the sand was wet and flimsy beneath their feet—were followed without question by the other boys.

Pierre was the only one who could put him in his place, and that was because they were closer than brothers. Tita Grace had been the one to deliver Pierre, during a particularly bad storm, and two months later she had delivered herself of Rudy, with the help of Pierre's mother.

The boys were inseparable, as opposite as sea and land. Pierre let Tita Grace cut his hair short; Rudy's was always falling into his eyes. Rudy was taller and broader; Pierre was wiry as a palm trunk. Rudy could scurry up trees and run across the dry sand of the beach as if rocket-propelled; Pierre bore scars all over his body—scabbed across his knees and elbows, carved in the palms of his hands—where he had tried and failed to keep up. When he lost a race or faced a task, Rudy plopped on the sand, complained, threatened to quit. Pierre ignored the scars and kept collecting them because he never stopped trying. In the quality of persistence, at least, Rudy was the one trying to keep up with him. As adults, they had both graduated at the top of their nursing class in Manila, but Rudy was the first to receive his placement at a hospital in the States. The two read his letter together in the bedroom they shared when back on Mindoro.

"Galbeztown?" Rudy looked at Pierre with bewilderment. "Where is that?"

"Galveston. It says Texas."

"*Texas?* They'll probably make me wear a cowboy hat."

"And boots," Pierre added. "And a gun!" They both laughed because Rudy was pretending his mother wasn't in the next room weeping; that instead of clutching at his face and begging, "Don't leave, Rudy, don't go," she had been happy about his placement in America.

"Are you scared?" Pierre asked, unable to stop himself.

Rudy bit his lips, then shrugged. "Anywhere is going to be better than this. And if it's east, even better."

Pierre smiled. It was a joke they had shared in school, the scorn for the American textbooks that regarded Asia as *the East*. "Which way do *they* travel to get here?" Rudy had sneered. "Which way do *we* go to cross the ocean?" East Anywhere—their answer for every question about where they would travel, where they would move at the slightest opportunity.

Pierre moved to Manila—north—while Rudy went east. Rudy wrote in his first letter home that he loved the place. That Galveston had a beach similar to the beaches of the northern islands—brown sand, murky water, trash, seaweed—yet the brand of trash, the shape and elasticity of the seaweed, was different. That people flocked to the sand to sunbathe, the jetties crowded with fishermen. That the buildings all had air-conditioning, and in the hospital, where he worked in ICU, the air was not only cold but clean, often too much so, lemon-scented chemicals stinging the fragile insides of his nose. That there was a sizable Filipino population clustered together in a neighborhood called Fish Village (mere blocks away from the hospital, obviously), and he had been told that in January they even celebrated Santo Niño. That he had two roommates from the islands, Lorenzo and Reg; they spoke Tagalog in the apartment off Ferry Road, but Rudy's English was the best. That he had been offered drugs but no guns yet. That Texas girls were beautiful. That he missed them both.

He sent three more letters after that, called once a month for the next five months. He booked his flight to come back starting in the American Thanksgiving, he promised, and made his mother ecstatic. The last call, in late August, was the first time he mentioned the name Ike.

Pierre sat in the quiet darkness of the kitchen with the phone in his hand; it was three a.m. in Lumangbayan, where he was spending the weekend visiting Tita Grace. Her door was closed, so she was either asleep or looking at the old pictures of Eusebio that she had saved and thought Pierre didn't know about.

"Bagyo?" Pierre asked, his voice quiet.

He knew Rudy was shaking his head over the line, smiling an American-citizen smile. He responded in exaggerated English. "Here in the States, we say 'hurricane,' bro."

Pierre places the empty tray on top of the stack near the kitchen, punches Table 10's order into the computer as Mercedes strides through the doors. He didn't know she was working that night, and he waves at her.

"Oye, primo." She stretches to give him a fist bump. When he started at the Sand Crab eight weeks ago, Mercedes was his first friend. She volunteered to train him, and she had not batted an eye when he introduced himself as Pierre looking like the antithesis of a Frenchman—short, dark, unkempt. People thought her name was French, too, she said with a grin, but she was Mexican, from a place called Matamoros and another place called Brownsville.

"We mojados have to stick together," she told him as she pulled her masses of dark hair off her neck with a baseball cap that read *Vaqueros*. Pierre had never heard that word. Later, at the apartment, he asked Lorenzo and Reg what it meant, and they said *wetback*, a term—Reg said with an arrogant curl to his mouth—for "the aliens who swim across the river." Pierre thought the word odd, mean even, but the way Mercedes said it, with that big smile, almost made it make sense. The tie between them, the migration that linked them. Between her once-great river and his miles of blue salt, they both had crossed water to get here.

Mercedes ties her waist apron. Pierre refills the water and sweet tea pitchers while she does. "So, what name are you using tonight?" she asks.

She, along with the rest of the staff, know his ritual. They think it is funny. When he runs out of ideas, they delight in compiling a list of options. "Lawrence!" "Cesar!" "Fabio!"

He tells her and she grins. "Kyle sounds like a quarterback. Or a rich lawyer's son."

He laughs.

"Look out, *Kyle*." She nods her head to indicate something behind him. "People waiting at the bar."

"I'm not at the bar today."

"We're doubling up, Jules just said. He can't hire extra help until the tourists come back, which isn't . . ." She trails off. Pierre knows what she isn't saying: *Until the city gets back on its feet.*

He nods, wipes his hands, and heads to the bar without complaint.

He is lucky to have this job as it is. Jules has a don't-ask-don't-tell policy for undocumented workers. Mercedes claims it is because Jules's parents were undocumented themselves and he has a soft spot for immigrants looking for work. INS has cracked down a few times, but somehow Jules always slips, quicksilver-smooth, out of real charges.

Pierre only has this job because of Jules, who is friends

with Lorenzo, Rudy's roommate. Lorenzo, who sat in their apartment living room patting Pierre on the back while he cried, while he wondered aloud how he was going to stay here with no Rudy, no work visa. Lorenzo, who had an answer: his friend Jules is a manager at a bar and grill.

Jules understood Pierre's reluctance to use his name at work. "It doesn't fit," he agreed in a Texas drawl, a lithe Vietnamese man whose own name was a new one to Pierre, one he thought only women could have. "Nah, you just don't look like a Pierre, you know?"

"What do I look like, then?

Jules shrugged. "You look like you."

Pierre poured himself another Jack and Coke. He, Jules, and Lorenzo were drinking at the bar that day, not working. It was March, the six-month anniversary of Rudy's disappearance. Pierre was getting very, very drunk.

———

Rudy didn't have a cell phone, and Tita Grace didn't own a TV, so Pierre called in sick to work and stayed on Mindoro. Every day that September week he escorted his aunt the half mile through the neighborhood to sit in the church rectory and watch the news footage from the States. It was all anyone over there could talk about. The slow stain of silver across the weather maps was massive at first, but it shrank as it approached the strip of island where Rudy lived. Still, reporters cautioned about the swell of water pushed forth by the winds, and once the storm finally hit, that was the word spoken with force. *Surge.* The surge was devastating.

They sat together when the aftermath footage finally rolled.

Pierre honestly didn't think the damage seemed worse than any bagyo here. Houses buried in sand, knocked into piles of scrap wood as if an invisible fist had smashed down. Trees toppled. Furniture submerged, swollen with salt water and splitting in the heat. Men on army trucks distributed food to barefoot, weary-eyed people. This all could have been Mindoro two summers ago, or Luzon just last year.

The Galveston citizens who had evacuated began to trickle back. Pierre and Tita Grace watched them on the news, carrying ice chests, pickup trucks piled high with cans of food and cleaning supplies and containers of gasoline. Rudy had said in his last call that he would evacuate, so they waited a week. Then two.

As soon as the phone lines were restored, Pierre called Rudy's apartment twice a day, every day. He didn't get through until Lorenzo finally stole away for a nap between shifts. (The hospital had slashed their staff down to a graveyard crew.) Tita Grace held the phone between her head and Pierre's, angling it so they could both hear the tinny voice speaking Tagalog. Lorenzo said he and Reg had stayed at the hospital, but Rudy was nonessential personnel, so he'd evacuated. They arrived at the apartment after the storm to find minimal damage, Rudy's bed neatly made, his toothbrush in the bathroom, his suitcase gone, and the closet empty of even the wire hangers. "He was planning on going back to the Phils in a few months anyway, so we thought he went home," Lorenzo said. "We haven't seen him."

Tita Grace crumpled like a coat slipping off a peg, all at once, folding as she hit the ground. She still held the phone in one hand, so Pierre took it from her and raised it to his ear. Lorenzo was talking, his voice becoming panicked. "We thought he went home, po. Po, he went home, didn't he?"

———————

Table 10 has moved on to tequila shots. Pierre slices limes behind the bar counter where he is now splitting his duties, and when the woman speaks, he almost doesn't turn because the name she says isn't Kyle, or Pierre, but Rudy.

His hands, his breathing, his expression freeze; he feels them harden in place. He whirls around. She says it again—"Rudy?"—and he is looking, wild-eyed, into the equally wild face of a dark-haired girl he has never seen before.

Her smile fades. "You're not Rudy." Her voice sounds dense, weighed down by sadness.

"I'm his cousin," he says, and she blinks.

"Oh. *Oh*. You're Pierre?"

Hearing his own name is another jolt. "You know Rudy?"

"He told me about you. I didn't know you worked here. That you *were* here. I thought just—you look like him from the side, and the way you move your hands. I'm sorry. I'm sorry—I just thought—"

Questions swarm his mind. On the other side of the room, Table 10 is waiting for their shots. Lime juice seeps into cracks in his cuticles. He ignores it as he stares at her. "How do you know Rudy?"

"We were dating—kind of." Splotches of red begin to crawl over her light nose and cheeks; her eyes well with tears. He can't tell what color they are. "I don't know."

"Have you heard from him?"

"No."

"Do you know where he is?"

She shakes her head.

"When's the last time you saw him? What happened to him? Where would he go?"

"I don't *know*." She raises her chin. His hand darts out, snatches hers in a tight grip.

"Tell me what you do know." He must sound crazy, must be scaring her. His voice is ragged, the words pouring fast as water from a faucet, but he can't stop. She has the answers. She knows things he does not, and it has been seven months without the slightest sign of Rudy. "Tell me. I came all this way and I can't find my cousin."

"I don't think I know any more than you do." She glares. "Let go of my hand." No longer teary, no longer panicked.

He releases her. "Sorry."

She has straight dark hair cut short as a man's, a fringe of bangs that nearly hide those big eyes. Brown, he can tell now. "I don't know where he is. Do you?"

"No. And I've been looking for him for months."

"So have I. Well." She pauses. "Mostly. I've mostly given up now."

His stomach clenches. She does know something.

"When does your shift end?" she asks.

"Eleven."

She nods and gathers her purse. "I'm Kristin. I'll come back then."

———

Pierre has heard her name before.

After he hung up with Lorenzo and soothed his aunt ("He wouldn't leave," she kept saying, "he wouldn't leave us, would he?"), they agreed that he should head out as soon as he could get a tourist visa. He would go back to Manila, start the process. Tita Grace gripped his hand as he walked onto the ferry to Luzon. When he took his hand away, he found her rosary pressed into it. "He would not," she said again, eyes clouded. "Find him."

In November, Lorenzo picked him up at the Houston airport and drove him back to their apartment on the island, navigating streets mostly cleaned, a few piles of trash and scrap wood still in places on the sidewalks. Pierre's eyes were red and crusted from the twenty-two-hour trip, and he didn't glance around, take it in—his first time in the US. Rudy's apartment was thick with the scent of chicken adobo. A rice cooker steamed gently on the kitchen table. The Filipino flag hung above the TV. He could have been home, in the living room of any of his friends in Manila. After he ate, Reg and Lorenzo showed him his cousin's room. He set his bag on the dresser and looked at the fragments of life Rudy had left behind: a half-full Ozarka bottle; dog-eared copies of *Texas Monthly* and *Rolling Stone* swiped from hospital waiting rooms. In the living room some framed pictures of his—amid the snapshots of the two of them, of his mother, of Mindoro, were others: Rudy and his roommates in the apartment, Rudy struggling with a surfboard in the brown waves, mid-laugh.

"None of Kristin, though," Lorenzo said idly from the door, and Pierre turned. "Who?"

Kristin was a girl Rudy had been seeing. She lived in an apartment on Whiting Avenue. Sometimes she spent the night. She was dark-haired and Mexican, they thought, an RN at an upscale nursing home in League City. They had

no idea where to find her. Pierre filed the name—Kristin—
but he didn't have the energy to start searching for her, too.

His tourist visa had only been approved for fifty days,
so he wasted no time on jet lag or culture shock. He spoke
to Rudy's coworkers in the ICU; walked across the UTMB
campus with his picture in hand; knocked on doors from
Coral to Mackeral and every corner of Fish Village. Nothing. He broadened the search to other pockets of Galveston, teaching himself the phrase *¿Ha visto este hombre?* and
struggling with Texas or Spanish or Vietnamese or Black
accents. He used Rudy's room as a home base, sleeping
there at night and walking around by day, forcing his body
to adjust to the time difference.

He was one of many searching for the lost. Ike had
displaced dozens—mostly low-income, he learned, non-
white. So many immigrants. He noticed this when he
walked into the police station with a flyer he had made of
Rudy and the desk sergeant pointed him toward the lobby's
bulletin board, awash in *Missing* posters. Beneath images
of two Black men and an elderly white woman, he pinned
Rudy's face. Whenever he remembered it had been two
months since the storm, nearly three, he fought to keep
from weeping.

Even though he told her he was hopeful, Tita Grace
cried on the phone. So to please her, Pierre made his way
to the crenellated towers of Sacred Heart Catholic Church.
He found it easily; amid the dead palms and dark-bricked
buildings of Broadway, it glowed pearl white like a beacon.
The floor was bare, stripped. The kneelers and some of the
pews were gone, waterlogged, he assumed, and metal folding chairs had been arranged in rows. It still smelled of

salt water, the air heavy as he stepped inside. He pinned another flyer—*RUDOLFO "RUDY" PIÑEDA LAST SEEN SEPTEMBER 15TH IF ANY NEWS PLEASE CALL REWARD!!!*—on the board next to the holy water, lit a candle beneath the statue of the Virgin Mary, and watched the flame flicker as he silently said the Chaplet of Divine Mercy.

He was halfway through the second decade before he noticed the sign asking for a two-dollar donation per candle. His wallet was empty.

Pierre bolted out into the watery sunlight, clutching his rosary, tears throwing a haze over the street. He should have blown out the candle; instead he had stolen from the Church. Look what Rudy had made him do.

The village said Rudy was a good boy but a bad influence on Pierre. Of the two of them, Rudy was the troublemaker, snatching wallets from tourists—rare in Lumangbayan—or losing hours at the neighborhood cockfights. This was all before he went to nursing school, but people kept whispering that Rudy seemed directed that way, a train on a track, his long-gone father the conductor and Pierre the caboose, poor baby, poor pinsan. Doomed to bring up the rear.

Pierre found himself following Rudy even in Galveston, even after he had vanished. He traced his steps, wandered across the neighborhoods he frequented, stopped in his favorite haunts. Walking in his path, he seemed to hear Rudy urge him to be reckless, to break rules, as he had when they were boys. First the church, the two-dollar candle. The second when he violated the terms of his tourist visa.

He was fast asleep when he became illegal—facedown

on Rudy's bed—and when he remembered his visa had expired and he had not booked a return flight to Manila, he wasn't quite sure what to do. Should he feel different? Heavier, somehow, beneath the weight of criminality? He searched the corners of his chest and gut for a feeling, something dark and jagged that might be guilt. It was there, but smaller than he expected, so tiny he could tuck it away and ignore it when speaking to Tita Grace or passing a policeman on Broadway. He was here illegally. Breaking the rules. What would Rudy say?

He fried eggs and Spam with rice for Reg, Lorenzo, and himself. "I got an extension," Pierre said later that day when Tita Grace called, frantic. "Don't worry."

"Don't lie to me," she said, and over the miles and ocean of distance her voice felt like a slap. "Not you."

———

Kristin is waiting for him in the parking lot, sitting on the hood of a Toyota with peeling gray paint, when his shift ends. Mercedes walks out with him, lingers as she sizes up Kristin.

"Want me to wait with you, P?" she asks. "Give you a ride home?"

He looks at her, the shadows in her eyes beneath the Vaqueros baseball cap. Between work and babysitting her nephew and coaching her little cousin's softball team and only just now starting to take phone calls from her ex, she hasn't been sleeping well. He squeezes her shoulder, grateful.

"No, it's okay. I'll see you later."

"Yeah, all right." She is still giving Kristin the eye. "Let me know how it goes."

Kristin pulls a cigarette out of the pack she holds and offers it to Pierre. He shakes his head, taking a seat on the hood beside her. "I shouldn't smoke," she says around the cigarette as she lights it. "I'm a nurse, I should know better, I know."

He agrees silently but says nothing. She breathes in, then begins.

"The last time I saw Rudy was a few days before the hurricane. We'd gone back to his apartment, and I thought I was staying over. I planned to." She looks uncomfortable, biting her lip.

"Were you and Rudy together?"

"Sort of. I met him at a bar. I'm new to the island, just moved here last year. I work at a nursing home in League City, but I live out here. I like it out here. I have friends at UTMB, so we hang out at the bars nearby. I met Rudy in July. We started dating. I wasn't dating anyone else. I don't know if he was—I guess he could've been."

Pierre takes a deep breath. The night air is cool but balmy, not sticky the way it is back home. There it engulfs him, throttles him. Here it whispers salt over his skin, snuggles close. He has started to prefer it.

Kristin goes on. "So, we're seeing each other. I thought it was going well. We talked a lot—how we were both new here, how we liked Galveston. I told him that my home-town is close to the river area of Texas. He said he'd never been to a freshwater river before. He told me about the Philippines, your island, his mom. You. It sounded really nice," she says in a gentler tone, as if she can see Pierre's throat working, hear him holding back tears. "Different. I told him no one in my family had ever traveled out of the country before—my brother was in Iraq for a while, but . . ." She waves in a vague gesture, trailing smoke.

"A few nights before the hurricane, he finally got a night off. I came over. We talked about the storm, about plans to evacuate. He didn't have a car—you know. He said he'd figure it out, and he had to work the following night. I offered to pick him up that afternoon when I was getting out early. I said I could bring him to Conroe with me and my brother." She draws from her cigarette. "We talked a little, and he got weird. That's when I decided to go."

"What do you mean?" Pierre is baffled. "How did he get weird?"

"I don't know. I've tried to figure it out, but I can't. He was talking about how he had a plane ticket to visit you and his mom back in the Philippines, and he was excited to visit, but he liked Texas. He said he was happy here, just here."

She tosses the butt of her cigarette and pulls the pack out to light another. "He seemed like he was in a good mood, so—I told him I liked him. Like, really liked him. Told him I was . . . you know . . ." She blows smoke through her nostrils like a dragon and lowers her eyes.

Pierre wants to shake her. He clenches his hands. "What? You were what?

"That I was happy," Kristin says, regret in her voice. And steel—Pierre can hear it. "I felt lucky that we found each other. He didn't say anything for a minute. He looked . . . weird. And he said, 'Not lucky. We're blessed.'"

Pierre closes his eyes against a sharp sting in his gut. Knowledge, swift and sure: Rudy is alive. Alive. Thank God. Thank God thank God thank *God damn it*, he thinks, a vicious note he didn't know he could summon. Rudy is alive, but now he knows what Rudy has done. That Rudy has run.

Kristin is still talking. "He got quiet. I kept waiting for him to say something else—like how he felt the same? But he didn't. It was awkward. I felt awkward." She sighs and takes a long drag. "I got out of bed and got dressed. I told him I'd call him after he got off work the next night, and he smiled and said okay. I kissed him and I left."

She waits for Pierre to ask something else, but he doesn't need to. He can see it exactly as it must have happened. Kristin pressing her cheek against Rudy's as she says goodbye; Rudy flinching slightly, moving back, eyes already shuttering against her smile. Pierre knows it went this way because he and Rudy have seen it before. The last morning Tito Eusebio left for work, he patted both boys on the heads, but when Tita Grace leaned in to kiss him, he drew back. He said he loved them all with a mouth-smile that didn't reach higher, and he put his hat on his head and turned to walk up the lane into town.

"I'm sorry" is all Pierre could think to say, gritting his teeth against the fury and the bitterness and the loss. Old habits again. Apologizing for Rudy. Cleaning up the mess he left.

"He's not coming back, is he." Kristin's voice sounds flat, the sadness leached out of it.

Pierre shakes his head. "I don't think so."

"Do you—" She pauses, screws her face up, pushes on. "Do you know where he might have gone?"

Weeks ago, he might have answered, *Anywhere. Let's keep looking together.* But now he is illegal, breaking his own rules, without Rudy in sight. So who could possibly say?

He reaches over and takes a cigarette from the pack between them. Kristin blinks, then fumbles to light it for him. Her gaze when she peers up at him through her bangs is wary. Pierre likes that, likes the way she seems cautious of him for reasons he doesn't deserve, things Rudy and not he has done. As if Rudy were the sun and he the reflecting moon, honed harder, sharper in the cast-off glow.

The smoke is pungent, hot; when he breathes it out, he feels the rumblings of fire at the base of his throat. He wants to cough but forces himself to take another drag. Another. He and Kristin watch the sparse traffic move slowly down toward the causeway. When he leans over and places his hand on her cheek, it seems like he is watching himself from a distance, the way he watched Rudy; when she tilts her face up to kiss him, he feels as Rudy must have, hands triumphant in the air after winning a race.

It was easy for Rudy to leave. Less easy for Pierre to kiss Tita Grace goodbye, empty his savings for a plane ticket, stand in line for hours waiting for his visa processing, fanning himself in the hot, oppressive air of the government building with the application papers bearing his job status, his hospital pay stubs, his birth certificate. Cross not just a bay but an ocean and a continent. Less easy to make a life here, cobble it together from the rubble of a hurricane in a new world, than to return home to an old life fully formed. Rudy ran, but Pierre will stay. He has always been the stronger of the two, seeing things Rudy could not. *Here*, he thinks, inhaling Galveston salt, Kristin's shampoo, *here you can be anyone you want.*

LUCKY GIRL

Maharlika

When I look back on this night years from now—long after Inay is gone, long after I have broken apart the life she left me and rearranged it—I will not remember much. What month, how many hours on the water, how the night ended, all of that erased. And maybe I forced myself to forget; I have been known to do that. *Maharlika the runner*, they probably say on two continents, *Maharlika the abandoner*. Sige, I don't deny it. Forgetting has been a friend; she has pulled me forward when everyone would have me turn around, crawl back. They breathe my name thinking it means *nobility*, forgetting it means *warrior*—one thing I will never lose. Some things, like my name, I cannot forget; other memories will strike quick as heat lightning the rest of my years. I rinse rice in San Teodoro, the milky water swirling, and feel cold air from the Galveston casino boat's vents, Inay beside me pulling her sweater close (though not the color of the sweater). I pluck a ghost-white hair from my temple—one of the few battles I do quit—and picture Inay's debit card where her driver's license should be, in the clear pocket of her wallet, first thing in sight. *In case I get lucky, anak ko, in case I need cash fast*—and though I will lose the sound of my mother's voice, I'll keep the way the stained tooth on her dentures winked when she laughed, how she rubbed her skinny fingers together in the sign for money. I used to think, *So American*, ignoring my own dentures and thin fingers, the work visa that proclaimed me an American, too, or a version of one. Who could know that forgetting, denying—the skills I already had—would be the most American things about me.

On that night, *this* night, before the vents of cold air and before she opens her wallet and laughs, I stand at the port of Galveston with my mother beside me. Her hand firm around my elbow, we walk through the parking lot on Harborside, gravel crunching beneath our tennis shoes, the ramp before us. *Anak*, Inay asks, *anong tingin mo?* and gestures at our destination, the *Lone Star* casino boat.

What I say: *Very nice, po.* What I think: *Ang cheap naman.* The three-level boat is tall, already busy. A rooftop deck with twinkling lights; people move across, drinks in hand. Light spills out of the windows on the lower levels, and a band I can't see is playing an ABBA cover. Inay loves ABBA; she told me three years ago the surgeons were listening to "Take a Chance on Me" in the operating room during her oophorectomy. (I reminded her the tumors came back months later, spots on her liver, but she still listens to "Waterloo" each morning in the shower.) Rust like old blood stains the boat's portholes, and the gold-buttoned uniforms fit the workers poorly. *Perla*, Inay says. But I think, if the *Lone Star* is a pearl, it is fake, like the ones kids back home sell at tourist beaches—*This very real, ma'am, this a beautiful local pearl, touch it feel it lovely so lovely*—the rest of us laughing when someone pays too much.

We step aboard into voices, the band music, alarm-bell rings of slot machines that are ready and waiting, but we are still in Texas and not allowed to play until the *Lone Star* leaves the state boundary. Cigarette smoke curls on the air. Familiar, all familiar, ang mga tunog, ang mga amoy. That year we visit Coushatta, Shreveport, Eagle Pass, even travel as far west as Ruidoso. In Coushatta, Inay earns four bonus spins on a leprechaun machine and wins $300 ten minutes after we arrive. In Shreveport, she holds my hand while we play nickel machines beside each other, and when she says, *Bet the maximum on this one, Maharlika, I can feel it*, I win $205. In Ruidoso, we watch horse races, the first for us both. While I scream at the thundering hooves, dazzled by the streaks of color whipping past, Inay screams because she picked a black horse with braids woven into its hair she thought were beautiful, and we take home $1,177.49.

Makinig ka. This is what I forget: How that year we take so many bus trips the Trailways driver in Galveston learns us by sight, helping Inay up and down the stairs carefully every time, calling her señorita and me mijita. How my mother's cheekbone digs heavily on my shoulder on the long rides, how chemo affects her taste buds so she no longer hates bagoong but craves it, scoops the pungent shrimp paste onto any fruit I can find. And this is what I remember: Her slipping me the winnings after each trip, the teeth marks imprinted on my lips where I bite down to keep from crying when she does, because we both know she is dying and this is the only inheritance she believes in—what she has passed down to me since I was eight and she left me with her sisters so she could go to America, to earn money for me even though I wanted nothing but her. How she said in one letter that she found a $50 bill under a chair and used it on a machine in Oklahoma and won $800, and when I told Tita Bel I thought Inay was very masuwerte, I did not understand why Tita cried at the word for lucky; I did not know yet the chair had been in the waiting room of a radiology unit where Inay had also found a lump in her breast.

The boat lurches, and a voice over the intercom announces we have begun our journey, and it will not be long before we are in federal waters. Inay wants to look at the machines first, so I move alone, curling around the empty tables, remembering to smile when someone looks at me because my skin and nose and eyes mark me as an immigrant, and Inay taught me in America an unsmiling immigrant is a dangerous one.

I turn a corner and spot the bar, catch the eye of the bartender. What I will remember: that his hair is too long, falls into his eyes; that he looks my age and just as unhappy. What I will forget: almost everything else.

Like how as I approach he puts on a wide smile that fits the planes of his face badly—a face brown as mine, though he is probably Mexican—and behind that false smile I see myself hiding. How he pours me a rum and Coke as the band starts "You're So Vain" and I sing along under my breath, and when I admit I love this one, he says *Me, too* with a smaller, dimmer, genuine smile. His voice is light and rumbling with the accent Ate Beeb and the other Sacred Heart ladies hate but I think sounds beautiful, a purr like a car engine, a rhythm like the sobbing ballads Tito Boyet plays back home. He waits a full five minutes before he asks where I am from; he says he has Filipino neighbors and knows the Tagalog words *patay* (dead) and *beer* (beer). He tries to pronounce my name, but it comes out *Ma-hair-lika*, and when he tells me his, I snap *Like the president?* before I can stop myself. (Our own names—that should have been a sign, di ba?) He looks confused, so I say *Never mind* and *It's nice to meet you, Marcos*, transform into a smiling immigrant once again.

Marcos pours drinks as we talk. His attention and the rum heat my cheeks, make me brave, stir a desire in me to tell him true things. I talk about Inay and her chemo. He tells me his father is dead and his mother is complicated. He is from Galveston. I say, *I live here, too*, and his eyes light in a way that warms me even more. I explain our gambling trip; he asks how I've been doing.

Can I tell you a secret? I stretch over the bar; he leans in to hear my whisper. *I have won almost $1,800. I'm trying to get $3,000.*

He whistles softly. *Why $3,000? Ticket to Vegas?*

A ticket home.

He opens his mouth, but an announcement sounds overhead: *Welcome to federal waters. The tables and machines are open for business.* People cheer and clap; beyond them, through the open windows, Galveston has disappeared in the twilight haze. I look at the gray waves, trying to spot the boundary that must exist somewhere, the invisible line drawn by Texas and America separating the waters. No buoys, no markers; no passports or green cards or visas. Paano—how would we know we had crossed a border? That we had left something behind and arrived elsewhere?

Inay will appear soon; it is only a matter of time. So I rise, say goodbye. Thank him. *Maybe I'll see you around.* His eyes, his smile, hold mine. *Buena suerte.* I do not know yet that he will be my luck and my jinx. We will be each other's.

My mother waits by the snack bar, scratching beneath her wig. The last treatment was stronger than ever, and she lost her hair, her eyebrows, and eighteen pounds. I waited two weeks before booking us a night on this casino boat in our own city, just down the road from the apartment we share in Fish Village. The last stop in our trip.

She sees me and waves. *Tara na,* she says as I draw close.

Opo. She takes my hand and I let her guide me into the crowd. We weave past blackjack and poker tables, around blocks of slot machines. People win and lose, shout and cheer and curse, and my mother's face is glowing; she is alive with all of this. And I should be, too. Part of me wants to lean into her, laugh loudly, swear to love all I have been offered, susubukan ko, susubukan ko.

Play with me, anak? she asks.

Kahit anong gusto mo. And it is true. Whatever she wants, I will give, I will take, for as long as we have. After she is gone, I will go home.

We find two King's Treasure machines empty, side by side. This game is her favorite; she loves the kings and queens and rascal jesters who cover their mouths and giggle when you lose money. Inay feeds one of her own twenties into mine. She winks as we both play.

It doesn't take her long to lose the twenty. She digs into her wallet, slips out the debit card from the front pocket. Rises.

Bad machine. She pats me on the shoulder. *I will be back. This is fun, di ba?*

Opo. I watch her narrow, frail shoulders easing into

the crowd. So many nights as a child on Mindoro I slept with a creased photo of her on my pillow, praying, *Please, Diyos, bring her back.* But Inay stayed in America, and I did not see her again until the day I landed at Intercontinental Airport and she was at the gate with plastic-wrapped lilies, crying too hard to say my name. Now when she looks at me, she imagines all I did to be with her: applying for a visa, packing my things, and leaving behind my life to fly twenty-two hours to a new place, new people who ask *What are you?* She thinks I will settle here, as she did. That our stories will be the same.

Señorita, mira, miraló. The old man on the other side of me, black cowboy hat on his head, is gesturing to my screen. My little king has jumped down from his tower and is dancing around a tree with jesters, a yellow-haired maiden. I spun the bonus round and did not even notice it.

Oh. I smile and nod. I have to touch the screen and choose which of the four tower windows I want to open. Behind one of them is the jackpot—two hundred times the amount I bet. I only get one choice.

I turn to the old man. *¿Quieres?* I ask, and gesture. Choose, please. Choose the one that will send me home.

He shakes his head. *Ay, no. No tengo suerte.*

So I place my fingertip against the screen, against the tower window that is closest to him, where he hovers so close to my machine that his breath fogs a corner. Somewhere a white man rolls a seven and his table whoops; somewhere my mother draws American bills from a machine, foreign cells hurtling within her. Marcos the bartender refills a gin and tonic and awaits the *Lone Star*'s journey back to Galveston. The jester does a cartwheel and jumps to the window I have selected. The veils part.

Why I recall any of this now, hindi ko alam. I am standing with my bare feet in the Puerto Galera sand. I listen to the chatter of people and I breathe in the storm brewing, the humming energy of the air. An army of charcoal clouds across the water march closer; I pull my shawl tight against the rising wind. Perhaps Carly is a warrior, too. She must be grown now. The ship is long gone, but I imagine her riding the *Lone Star* and marveling as I did at the way people can sway and rock together, between water that belongs to Texas and water that belongs to no one, or to us all. I picture a storm bearing down and her stepping out from shelter to watch it come.

GALVESTON: A GLOSSARY & GUIDE FOR THE UNINITIATED TRAVELER

Bishop's Palace, the

Once there was a Roman Catholic bishop—(*Editor's note: If you think that's the right place to begin, you are wrong. Start again.*) Once there was a Civil War colonel. Once there was a woman who married the Civil War colonel. The colonel's wife casts her gaze about her, staring at the island where they will live, a snaky strip of land hugging the crescent curve of eastern **Texas**. She takes in the salt and stink of the ocean, the sun that beats down so heavily it feels like liquid, like rain soaking through her parasol and into the pleated fabric of her blouse. This is nothing like Virginia, where the colonel is from. She wants Virginia. She squints at the empty lot on the outskirts of town and tries to see what the colonel and the architect beside him are describing with such enthusiasm. She is a painter—she should see promise. She sees only an empty lot.

"It will be of its time," the architect says, waving his hands about in the damp air. A mosquito whines into the ear of the colonel's wife. There are no mosquitoes in her imagined part of Virginia. "Cast-iron galleries. I'll incorporate the Tudor arches that are popular now with geometric forms to add structure. Sharp roofs, long chimneys."

"Steel," the colonel adds. "Stone."

"Sir, of course. Your home will weather the strongest storms (*see:* **hurricane**) the ocean offers. Sienna marble columns flanking the entrance hall. Mahogany from Santo Domingo for the stairwell and a fireplace in the front parlor." The architect is from Ireland, but his voice is a rumbling canyon, like the ones out West the colonel's wife has always wanted to paint. She cradles it in her ear, turns it over like a seashell. There are seashells here. She has seen them.

The colonel's wife wants stained glass. If the **Texas** sun is to be a part of her future, she wants it stripped—filtered at the very least—of its current brutality. Broken down into manageable, pretty pieces, shafts of sunbeams dyed crimson, cerulean, purple cool and dark as a bruise. The colonel shrugs and turns away, but the architect smiles at her. Says, "Of course, of course."

The colonel's wife will wait five years before the house is finished. Her husband will cofound a major railroad slicing through the region. He will serve on the state legislature. The architect will design dozens of churches, buildings, and houses for this stretch of Galveston; marry a local woman and make love to the colonel's wife on a settee in her parlor while the colonel and her children are away. When she kisses him, she will taste salt and dust; he will leave damp streaks from his fingers on her wrists and eyelids and thighs. He will install the stained glass she wanted in the sitting room windows, the front and rear parlors, even flanking the octagonal mahogany stairwell. She will think of him each time she sees them, each time she paints in her third-floor studio, each time she looks up at the skylight he sketched for her. It will not be long before she hates them—and him—but that is another story.

Years from now, there will be a bishop named Byrne living here, donating his title and ownership to the structure itself like a gift, like something to be proud of, until the house seems utterly his and the names of the colonel and his wife and the architect are forgotten. A Catholic church will sprout next door like a white **oleander** amid the mud of the thoroughfare. The Gresham House/Bishop's Palace will come through the **hurricane** of 1900 virtually unscathed. The windows will not.

BOI

Acronym: "born on the island." Designates who belongs and who doesn't, who has staked their claim here and who has not, who is an islander by blood and who is a tourist in all but address.

May not be used to refer to Vinh Pham, no matter how much he wishes it, no matter that he has been here since he was eleven and played varsity tennis and junior varsity offensive tackle for Ball High and married an islander and had two children born at John Sealy and fishes the bay for shrimp and oysters and lives in a Fish Village bungalow with a porch swing and a four-foot-high watermark of where the surge from Ike rolled in. No matter all that. Vinh Pham's birth certificate reads Hải Phòng and marks him eternally as a transplant. This does not stop his wife from buying him a white ball cap with *BOI* emblazoned in green letters, the *I* shaped like a palm tree. Vinh wears it every day he goes out on the bay, until the white is no longer white, smeared instead by years of sweat and salt and grease and mud.

On September 13, the sweat-salt-grease-mud cap is snatched off the pilot's bench of *La Cigüeña* by 110-mile-per-hour winds and hurled nearly a mile away into the Gulf. The same winds yank at *La Cigüeña*, but the double lashings and extra ropes applied by the strong hands of the two youngest men on Vinh's crew hold it fast to the fixed dock. So the winds and the surge take the dock, ripping it up in pieces, casting ragged planks of wood like broken teeth across the marina. On September 15, Vinh walks from Fish Village down Harborside and finds his shrimper, *Miss Saigon*, thrust halfway up the dock and listing on its side, the barnacles scabbing its flat bottom drying in the sun. But the *Cig* sits tight, strewn with debris and spilled diesel, bobbing gently on the water.

Six years later, when Vinh sells the *Cig*, the new owner will slap a green bumper sticker with the same BOI logo on the back window of the pilot house. "Because we've earned it," the owner will say, and Vinh will smile and remember how the two of them worked their hands bloody scraping off debris in the days after Ike, patching holes, running new lines through both boats. How the first day they got *Miss Saigon* out and hauled up the dredge they found tree branches, a Louisiana license plate, a mangled beach chair, two mud-clumped long-sleeved men's shirts, and no oysters. How the bay reeked of salt water—too much salt, too much surge—for months, and the only work for immigrant fishermen left behind was loading garbage from the parking lot scrap heaps. How they thought the delicate balance was drowned, but Vinh knew the bay would come back, the oysters and shrimp would come back, the island would come back. "Yes, Jess," Vinh will say to the new owner, smoothing his hand over the palm tree *I*.

Broadway

Main thoroughfare. Halves Galveston city down the middle, like the seam of a zipper. Becomes the causeway over the bay, and on the mainland Interstate 45.

Look closely. Can you see the tread scored into the layered asphalt? There: Those are the tire marks of a Greyhound bus on a steamy day in September 2008 carrying evacuees, those who heeded the **hurricane** warning (*Editor's note: See definition 4*). The tread sinks heavily, bearing the weight of the people and their possessions, backpacks and suitcases and garbage bags stuffed with T-shirts, underwear, waterproof ponchos, framed wedding photos, baby toys, heirloom jewelry. In the left window seat, fourth row from the back, beside a woman holding a crying child, Rudy Piñeda watches the **live oaks** lining the avenue hurry past. He holds in his lap a bus ticket to San Antonio and a backpack containing a week's worth of clothes, his work visa, the credit card he opened after receiving his first UTMB paycheck, two cans of Spam, and an issue of *Texas Monthly* with the photo of a tire swing suspended over a green river and the words *Concan: The Cancún of Texas* on the cover. He holds in his mind a cousin he loves and a woman he likes just fine, the one who first told him about this place he is headed, and that green river unfurling between tall trees. A place to be alone, to be anew.

Another tread, if you lean in closer. This one: headed

north as well, tracing back and forth, scar tissue burned into the gray. (*Editor's note: Belongs to a young* **BOI** *who is a sometimes-devoted granddaughter; an abandoned daughter with issues; a pretty-OK girlfriend; and a future mother of two, though she will not know that until three years after she has sold the Corolla.*) The tread is lighter going north, heading to the causeway and the mainland. This is speed; the car is rushing excitedly on its way. On the southbound stretch, the tread slows, clings, drags. Does not want to return home.

Look again. See another set of tire marks. Southbound this time, heavy beneath a Toyota Tacoma loaded down with suitcases of men's clothing, boxes of track awards and Ball High yearbooks, of realtor-license documents and photo albums of a wedding in Concan, at a chapel where the groom's family drove seven hours from Galveston and the bride's parents drove fifteen minutes from Uvalde, where the bride wore her mother's lace dress—altered, updated with coral ribbon and a sassy short veil—and in one photo she beams between the groom and her mother, unaware of the decade to come when she will lose them both. (*Editor's note: The albums and the boxes and the truck belong to the groom, a young* **BOI** *who lived on Marlin, took district titles in the hundred-meter dash and the relay where he ran anchor, once called a dear friend a chink and regrets it every day, and later met a girl at a party on a river who dazzled him before she broke him, is still dazzling him with her capacity to break.*) See tread marks of a truck that never thought it would be back on this ribbon of road but picks up speed like a horse that feels the familiar, that scents home.

Recognize the marks buried in the asphalt, seeping in the heat: those who have wanted to go and keep going, and those who have wanted only to return, to stay. Many stay forever (*see:* **Cline, Isaac M.**).

Cline, Isaac M.

(1861–1955) Chief meteorologist, US Weather Bureau, Galveston office. A Tennessee native, Isaac transplanted to the island in 1889 and helped found the **Texas** branch of the bureau. No storm, he believed, could do serious damage to Galveston—simply look at the unique geography of the Gulf, its inlets and its valleys, the mud muck at the bottom; look at the way the wind circles in patterns, waxing and waning like cycles of the moon. Predictable. Measurable. Such as he wrote in an 1891 editorial in the daily newspaper: *The opinion held by some who are unacquainted with the actual conditions of things, that Galveston will at some time be seriously damaged by some such disturbance, is simply an absurd delusion.* He paused in his writing of this, searching for stronger words, ones he could pressure into conveying the severity of his stance. *Absurd,* yes. *Impossible*—ah. Better. Isaac lifted the pen once more. *It would be impossible for any cyclone to create a storm wave which could materially injure the city.*

He remembers little of what came before the storm. But he always remembers what came after. The vitriol from his brother and fellow meteorologist (*You could have stopped it, you should have seen it coming, Isaac*), and the publications one after another after another (*The deadliest weapon of a* **hurricane** *is the surge, the wind-driven tide, and it is this tide in which we gather our most important warning signals*), and the grief—for his wife, for his unborn child swept away in the salt water—a wave edged with glass that slices, keeps slicing.

Now, decades since his own death, Isaac wanders. Like a splinter shard that has come off in the skin, coaxed the tissue of its host to grow and seethe around it, he is part of this place; he is here to stay. Instant by instant he opens his eyes and finds himself somewhere else—sprawled on the roof of the **Bishop's Palace**, broiling like a shrimp under the August sun—the next moment tangled up in fishing wire off the jetties in the bay—the next strapped into a bumper car beside a screaming teenager on Pleasure Pier—the next facedown in horseshit on the Strand, left behind by one of the horses pulling an old-time carriage during the Dickens festival. His mouth blistering in the heat, or his skin plumped by humidity, or perhaps it is sweat rolling down his back, or ice gathering in the spaces behind his knees. Always changing, the next and the next and the next. If he believed in a heaven or hell, Isaac would wonder which this is.

Elissa, the

Sailing ship. Three-masted, iron-hulled. Constructed in 1877 in Aberdeen, Scotland, by a boatbuilder who loves the *Aeneid,* whose eyes sting with tears when Queen Dido of Carthage appears on the page. She fled from Tyre to Africa, founded a city, her tragedy taking shape as inevitably as the hull appearing in the iron arc before him. Her Phoenician name Elissa.

Pete Caballero read the *Aeneid* in high school, but it was assigned the month he enlisted so he does not remember this, and when he looks at the *Elissa*'s nameplate, he thinks instead of the girl he sat behind in homeroom with that name. She was the drum major, with long hair in braids that, if he smiled charmingly enough, she would let him play with. He does not mention this to Adam Schafer, standing beside him on the pier, though he could. They talk about most everything and nothing at all, as only men who have shared dust and blood and bullets can. Men of honor, Pete thinks.

As Schafer leans in closer to admire the *Elissa*, Pete remembers Elissa, how she pronounced it *Eh-lee-sa*, which is how Pete says it now, peering against the bright sun casting sparks into his eyes.

Schafer shakes his head. "It's *Uh-liss-a*," he corrects him. "The guy I worked with last year, out on the boat? That's how he said it's supposed to be said. And he would know—he was big on Galveston history."

They stand for a moment, the two of them, looking at the ship bobbing lightly in the water. She—Pete thinks of it as a *she*, of course—has a long white frame, rose-tinted wood gleaming richly in the afternoon sun, her prow like a swordfish's spear casting a long, thin shadow across the water. There is a light breeze, and her nineteen sails flutter half-heartedly, but Pete imagines them in full sail, plumped out and pure white. *Elissa* flying across the Gulf, dolphins leaping to guide her way, the rocking red deck beneath his feet.

In a few minutes the men will part, as swiftly as the idea to meet up in Galveston came together (a series of texts the day before, about the timing of Pete's arrival and Schafer's two-hour drive from Beaumont, meeting for burgers and beers at a place called the Sand Crab). When he leaves, Pete will head to the apartment on Whiting where his sister and her boyfriend live. He will leave his things in the living room corner she has fixed up as a second bedroom for him, complete with a privacy screen Pierre dug out of a Texas City thrift store. Kristin will secure him a job at her nursing home driving the shuttle bus, ferrying patients to their doctors' appointments. "Stable," she will say, "simple." And Pete will do it, for a time—sleep on his sister's couch and store his boxers, socks, and pot in the cloth bins she has purchased for him, drive the shuttle bus and flirt with wheelchair-bound old women, down Crown and Cokes with Pierre at bars on the Seawall.

Schafer will return to the refinery in Beaumont, working beside men with blistered hands, and one in particular who used to be a wildcatter near Devine and says there's still potential out there, that the brambled, thorny sweep of South **Texas** is an untapped oasis for a man with vision. In six weeks Schafer will call Pete and say there is room for one more in their truck, and Pete will consider for only a heartbeat, loading up his things that night while his sister watches, dry-eyed, while he pictures himself squinting up at an oil derrick or riding fence on a dappled Appaloosa.

But for now, Pete likes the look of this island—the way the **oleander** trees shimmy their blossoms in the salt wind, the pink and green and teal homes on the alphabet avenues, the Victorian buildings that lean and tip beneath the weight of history. And the *Elissa*. He sees its appeal to the people who over centuries have been drawn to it like a song, people like Schafer, his sister, and her Filipino boyfriend. Pete sees the tragedy, the potential, and the promise of Galveston. He likes to think he's the only one who can.

hurricane

1. An extremely large, powerful, and destructive weather occurrence with strong winds that occurs especially in the western part of the Atlantic Ocean.
2. On Galveston, interchangeable with "storm."
3. *Storm:*
   a. The Great Storm: Hurricane that struck Galveston on September 8, 1900. Estimated winds of 145 miles per hour, making it a Category 4 occurrence. Loss of life estimated at roughly eight thousand, or up to ten thousand. Deadliest hurricane in US history.
   b. Ike: Hurricane that struck Galveston on September 13, 2008. Estimated winds of 110 miles per hour, making it a Category 2 occurrence. Loss of life estimated at 103. Responsible for largest search and rescue operation in **Texas** history.
4. A weather occurrence with the potential to seriously damage, cause harm or even death. A storm one should not take lightly. Island residents in its path should heed warnings, prepare homes, and head for the causeway. Island residents should evacuate to well within mainland. (*Editor's note: This is a false definition.*)
5. Part of island life. Board up.

Karankawas, the

Carancahuas, Carancaquas, Capoques, Kohanis, Kopanes. Dog-lovers, dog-raisers, keepers of coyotes and foxes. Eaters of fish, shellfish, and turtles; not-eaters of human flesh, or perhaps only in ritual. Nomads, migrants, navigators of the shifting seasons between the barrier islands and the **Texas** mainland.

Mercedes turns more pages. She should be studying—she has a psychology exam in two days, and this is her only day off from the Crab—but since Jess dropped off the library book on the Karankawas she hasn't been able to put it down. He found it while he was doing research for Señora Castillo, for the scrapbook Carly is helping her compile. (La señora called it a family history when Mercedes asked her about it the other day; Carly rolled her eyes when she did.)

"You'll like it," Jess said that morning, leaning out of his truck to hand it to her—he and Carly had a meeting with the insurance adjustors—and he was right.

Hunters, fishers, gatherers, she learns. Crafters of baaks, portable wigwams, baskets and pottery lined with the asphaltum tar coughed up on Gulf beaches. Shapers of red cedar bows. Bearers of tattoos, Spanish moss skirts, deer-skin breechclouts, cane shards through their lips and nipples, shark- and alligator-greased shoulders. Smoke signalers. Family units. Movers, leavers.

Karankawa Kadla, she reads in one part. *Mixed descendants.*

The illustration shows the Karankawas standing on a beach that could be the one just down the road from her. She is strong, tall like them, skin brown as theirs. She has come alive in water, too, sleek as an eel. Carly would sigh, but Mercedes smiles at the idea. Perhaps this is what Señora Castillo holds on to, why she clings to what she has always believed about her family. To belong here, Mercedes thinks: What a thing that would be.

live oak, Southern

Quercus virginiana. Evergreen (*Editor's note: This is questionable*) tree of the family Fagaceae, native to the southeastern US. Grows wild across Galveston. Survives in a maritime climate. Outlasts wind-borne salt spray. And yet not immune to **hurricane** surge. This last pointed out by Genevieve Macaraeg to her cat, Winifred, December 2008, as she drives them down **Broadway** on her way to the vet: "Hay nako, Winnie, look at those trees."

The cat seems unconcerned; Beeb wonders if she is ill, although Mr. Alvarez swore she wasn't the day he brought her back to the house, when Beeb hugged him and wept with joy and he looked uncomfortable but patted her shoulder kindly. He was on his way to pick up his wife now that the roads were clear. Winifred licks her paws daintily, so Beeb looks at the trees for them both. The trunks are the same as before: thick and dark, the bark rising in ridges that would scrape soothingly against her hands. "But the roots, Winnie." They have swallowed fifteen feet of salt water, and nothing can survive that. Though Winifred inside her cat carrier cannot possibly do so, Beeb points through the windshield, "Look up, Winnie," see death by drowning in the branches, once heavy with green leaves, now stiff and brown and brittle.

oleander

Nerium oleander. Evergreen shrub or small tree of the family Apocynaceae, the dogbanes. Toxic in all its parts, but Eva Rivera knows this, has warned her grandson Aaron since he was tiny. "Go wash your hands now," she says to

Aaron, who stands a few feet away running his fingers over the fuchsia blooms. He is six now; she is watching him while Russell works and Yvonne naps, swollen with her second. "What do I always say about these flowers?" He is still a child and requires teaching. As all men do.

"They're poisonous, Grandma," Aaron says dutifully.

"And in Spanish? ¿Cómo se dice *poisonous*?"

"Ven—venso."

"Venenoso. Good."

Aaron dashes inside to wash his hands—she hopes—and Eva eyes the brown snails on the walls, the palm trees all around. A cruel world her grandson has found himself in, with plants that look beautiful but can kill, men who smile as they lie, children who leave you again and again. But she has to teach him. She has hopes for Aaron, and for the sibling on the way. For the ones Jesusmaría and Carly may have, now that she is finally wearing his ring. Eva has no Sight, not like old Señora Castillo does, but she wishes she did. She would like to know if the baby is a boy. She prays it is, for then his life—like Aaron's—will be an easy one. A simple blossom like an iris or a bluebonnet, unsnarled by vines, untainted by the veneno of gift or exceptionality or womanhood.

Seawall, the

"This is where we first met, you and I." Magdalena murmurs it, lifts her hands high as she does. "Remember, Cesar? Remember how beautiful I was, how handsome you were in your swimming trunks?"

Her long-dead husband hovers ahead: a blurry blaze like the shimmer of heat above asphalt. She never thought she could see the dead. All her life her Sight came mostly in feelings, prickles across her palms or deep in the corridors of her ears. But one day, as she approached Sacred Heart for daily Mass, she looked over at the **Bishop's Palace** and spotted a man on its roof. He was clinging to the near-vertical slant of the uppermost turret, splayed across as if he had been thrown down from a height, though he was four stories up. He wore an old-fashioned dark suit, a shock of crisp white at the collar, a wide-brimmed hat, and no shoes. Though he was far away, he looked straight at her and Magdalena at him, feeling him vibrate through her like the plucked string of a guitarrón. She sensed not wildness or fear in his gaze but a weary resolution, a satisfaction. By the time she drew his name out from the vibrations—Isaac—he was gone. She has never seen him again but has seen others. Cesar, many times. Her son, just once.

Now she and the shivering blaze of Cesar turn together to look at the Seawall. The wall constructed in 1904 to protect the island from future **hurricanes** (*Editor's note: "Never again," they are wailing, they are chanting as they pour concrete and crushed gravel over the pilings for the wall, as they pump in a slurry of sand and water and grit and raise the level of the entire city more than sixteen feet; "never again," they say, "never never never again"*), pero both she and Cesar know that it will not serve. The wall rising seventeen feet high but not high enough for the rush of salt water that is to come. How soon, quién sabe. Months? Years?

"Can you tell me, Cesar? Can you hear anything from that side?"

No answer, of course, because Cesar is dead and his voice silenced forever, his hair and beard littered with gravel from crushed oyster shells. He didn't want this in life. Como él quería, they buried him just up the road in the 65th Street cemetery, in a tasteful oak coffin with ivory pillows, his favorite cowboy boots and a navy suit she and Marcos bought secondhand. Even Ike had attended the funeral, looking at her with quiet eyes from across the top of his wife's hair. Catherine admired the cowboy boots, commented on them, her gaze steady on Magdalena's, knowing. She knew about Magdalena and her husband, had known all along. And now Cesar does, too. At times when he appears to Magdalena, his eyes burn into her, but of course he does not speak, can no longer insist that she is loca, bruja, has invented this history for herself from nothing, that she is nothing more than a Galveston woman with a long, muddled bloodline of tejano y mexicano y conquistador e indio y quién sabe. As if her father had lied to her, and his father before him. In this life, she held her hands over her ears when he screamed, "None of this is real." He screams it now, through his gaze; he echoes what Carly says at times, when she is home between her shifts and staying at Jesusmaría's apartment, in the quiet moments when Magdalena speaks to her of blood, of a native history she carries. "None of that is real, Grandma."

Yet Cesar stands before her now, bearing the marks of her own power. When he first appeared a week after his death, she told him firmly, "You do not speak. Do not say a word to me. I am here, one of the last **Karankawas**. And I have taken your voice." Cesar's spirit obeys. In death he is more docile than in life, when he insisted upon her loyalty with the back of his hand. Ya no. She is the one with his loyalty now. His palms and fingers that used to crack across her lip or wrap around her throat, his mouth that opened for shots of tequila and bourbon or to call her bitch, whore, maldita bruja—they lie quiet, sealed. His once-booming voice is silent while hers throbs with power. Would this be possible in her real life? And if not, which life would any of them choose? She knows for herself, and she has chosen.

Their granddaughter is walking on the wall, heading as she always does for the **statue**. Cesar turns toward her and nods, and Magdalena knows he, too, sees the images flickering behind her eyelids, a future unspooling like gold thread and arranging before her: Carly driving over the causeway, Carly coming back. She will learn. She will accept the fate of her blood, like the island will accept its own, a truth Magdalena knows and always has: to be swallowed up by the sea. Algún día. Not yet.

state of Texas

State in the southern US, bordering Louisiana, Arkansas, Oklahoma, New Mexico, Mexico, and the Gulf of Mexico; spans 268,597 square miles, second-largest state in both area and population.

~~State of~~ Republic of Texas, declared on March 2, 1836; individually governed entity whose independence is to be protected and defended ferociously even generations after its annexation into the United States.

~~Republic of~~ Tejas; Spanish adoption and pluralization of Caddo word *táysha* meaning *friend*.

Home to 28.9 million people, including 5 million immigrants.

~~Home.~~

~~Immigrants.~~

See also:
 "Lone Star."
 Six flags (history, not theme park).
 Alamo, Goliad, San Jacinto (Battles of).
 Austin, Stephen F.; Houston, Sam; Crockett, Davy.
 Oil.
 Slavery.
 Football.
 Rebellion; revolution; oppression; independence.
 Canyons, plateaus, tumbleweed-strewn mesas stretch-
   ing into the setting sun. El Paso mountains. Lub-
   bock dust.
 Long fingers of concrete scraping the sky, freeways
   knotting and unknotting, exhaust and potholed
   asphalt and streaked rubber from countless cars.
   Houston strip malls. Dallas gallerias.
 Austin (*see:* other).
 Piney woods, close clusters of elm and ash stand-
   ing like sentinels. Rivers green or brown, still and
   stagnant or fast-flowing, tumbling over rocks,
   rushing cold. Lined farmland, corn, winter oats,
   wheat, cabbage, sweet onion. Unlined ranchland,
   mesquite-thick, thorned, cactused. ~~Ocean Sea~~
   Gulf. Water: fresh, salt, none.
 Mexico; America; other.
 None of the above.
 All of the above.

statue, "Place of Remembrance"

Memorial for the eight thousand dead during the hurricane of September 8, 1900, dedicated in a September 2000

ceremony to commemorate the centennial. Cast by a local sculptor (*Editor's note: Don't worry, don't worry, **BOI***). On their walks along **the Seawall**, Carly makes it a point to stop at the statue, no matter how loudly Jess sighs or how much her grandmother rolls her eyes. Jess parks his truck (Magdalena prefers the lift, the height, over Carly's Corolla) in front of the statue. Magdalena climbs down and descends **the Seawall** steps—carefully—to the beach and the Gulf. Jess escorts her and then wanders off for a raspa from the stand, dreaming already of the tiger's blood syrup and the shaved ice. Carly prefers pickle juice, which he hates, but he'll bring her some anyway. He's like that, Jess is.

It is 2006. The tourists not scared off by **hurricane** season, not spooked by last year's Katrina or Rita, pulse along the brown-sand beach or beneath bright umbrellas. Seagulls wheel high above, calling out. Carly tells the tourists by the ones who toss chips into the air to attract more, more, more. Above her, the sun beats down so heavy it feels like liquid, like a rainstorm soaking through her bathing suit and cut-offs. She breathes in the salt and stink of the ocean.

From this high on the wall, she can see Magdalena wading into the surf. Foam about her ankles. She is lifting her face to the sun and moving her mouth, and Carly wonders if she is thinking of the **Karankawas** who once roamed this place. Magdalena raises her hands in praise, or in seeking.

Carly stops in front of the statue, ten feet tall, the metal now oxidized to a pale, muddy green. Why she loves it so much, is so moved by it, she couldn't say. Three bronze figures—a woman, a man, and a child, pressed together for warmth, all three naked from the waist up. The man is staring at the sky, chin raised high, one arm stretched up with the hand turned as if cupping rainwater. Some call it a powerful pose, though Carly doesn't think so; he looks angry, his upturned palm empty and demanding.

She prefers the woman, cradling her child close to her breast, her chin against its curly hair. Her hands are tender, long fingers soft where they rest on the child's bare back. Some say she is resigned to her fate, but Carly looks at the high forehead and the lines of her brow and sees a quiet, iron pride. Like she has made a choice for herself, for them all, and she will see it through. The woman's gaze Carly follows until she is casting her own along with it, down to the pink sandstone in which she and the three green figures are submerged, sandstone that cuts them off at the waist like water rising, rising, still rising.

ACKNOWLEDGMENTS

What an impossible thing: To thank all the people in your life who have made a book—a career—possible. And what a gift, to have so many.

The places I love and have written here: Uvalde and Concan and Southwest Texas, Brownsville and the Rio Grande Valley, and especially Galveston and Fish Village. I have taken some liberties with geography and history, as the locals may spot, but I have worked hard to stay true to the soul of them. Thank you to the land that inspires me and to all the people, present and past, who have shaped these places and stories. Thanks to the writers of Texas, who write our diverse, challenging, complex home into being. And to the Chicanx and Filipinx writers, the women in particular: Thank you for paving the way.

My incredible editor, Ruby Rose Lee, who saw all along the best version this book could be and refused to rest until it was there. Thank you for your sharp eyes, your humor, your patience, and for loving these characters as much as I do. Thanks to Catryn Silbersack, Laura Flavin, Maia Sacca-Schaeffer, to Lynn Buckley and Elizabeth Lennie for the gorgeous cover, and to the whole team at Holt for treating the book with care and enthusiasm and turning my dream into a reality.

Alex Glass, agent extraordinaire. You made this all happen! Thank you for being the first to believe in me and my work, for fiercely championing this book from the beginning, for making me cry over ceviche, and for your constant advocacy.

My writing teachers, many of whom I am lucky to call friends. Above all, Miro Penkov. Thank you for your insight and your instincts, for answering my inane questions—you know I have more—and for the tireless support on this journey. Thank you to Ian McGuire, Javier Rodriguez, John Tait, Corey Marks, and Jill Talbot. Elizabeth McCracken, who saw some of these stories in their roughest forms and polished them, and who helped me find my voice in fiction. Oscar Cásares, for being the best example of writing our roots, our people, and our corners of Texas for the outside world. Steve Harrigan, Jim Magnuson, Cristina García, Peter LaSalle. Elizabeth Harris, the first to tell me I should keep writing. Mrs. Collier, who handed me *The House on Mango Street* in freshman English. Mr. Hernandez, who told me in fourth or fifth or eighth grade that he loved my stories. Mrs. Cockerill, for inspiring me to move forward, dream big.

My friends, brilliant people and writers who have made me a better person and writer. Thank you to the dynamic duo of Dana De Greff and Sally Treanor. Virginia Wood, for so much encouragement. Ross Wilcox, Spencer Hyde, and Peter Clinton/Clint Peters, who remind me to hustle as only a white male writer can. Bryn Agnew, Charlie Riccardelli, Ruby Al-Qasem, Kate Gollahon, Allyson Jones, Conor Burke, Jeff Pickell, Natalie Foster, Katherine Schneider, Shannon Couey, Andrew Ross, Cole Jeffrey, Christa Reaves, Mandy

Hughes, and all my friends in the UNT trenches. Sebastian Páramo, for endless support of the DFW writing community and for giving me the title of this book. Claire Beeson, for being the best damn reader, book clubber, and hype crew around. Alexis Loyd, who believed back in Houston that this could happen. The faculty and staff at UNT and UT-Austin, and my many classmates and students.

David Vance, Jackie Cuevas, Sonia Saldívar-Hull, Norma Cantú, and my colleagues and friends at UTSA. Thank you for having faith in me, for sharing words of wisdom, and for sending mountains of support as I completed this book during a pandemic. Thank you to my wonderful students here in San Antonio.

The journals that first published early versions of these stories—*Copper Nickel*, *Huizache*, *TriQuarterly*, *Puerto del Sol*, and *CutBank*—and their editors. Thank you for giving my work such good homes.

The bad-ass cohort of the 2019 Bread Loaf Environmental Writers Conference. Thank you to the inestimable Claire Vaye Watkins and our whole fiction workshop. Special thanks to the amazing Kate McQuade, who pointed me to Alex and helped me navigate this whole process!

The San Ysidro Ranch Writer's Residency and Alston and Holly Beinhorn. Thank you for giving me time and beautiful space (and that coyote soundtrack) to revise and recharge so close to home.

My extended circle of friend-family. Elissa Luevano Martinez, Rocio Cruz, and Pam and Kristen Mendel, for the love and encouragement. The Lutton clan, my tíos in the Do-Nothing Club, my titas from Houston. Thank you to my stepmother, Ester, who has the best taste in books

(I hope you like this one). My loved ones in Galveston and Houston, Brownsville, and back home in Uvalde who have carried me with them all these years.

Kevin "Mr." Yanowski, librarian to the stars. Thank you for coffee and friendship and fierce belief, and for allowing me to take full advantage of the Yahouski Couch Residency whenever I'm in Denton.

Amanda Yanowski. For being The Person at every turn, through every change, big or small. First and best writer and reader, first and best friend. Thank you, thank you, thank you.

My family, the Garzas and the Riveras. What can I say? Gracias and salamat to my grandparents, tías and tíos, titas and titos, who raised me to be proud of my heritages and the places and stories that run in my blood. To my cousins, my ride or die: Thank you for inspiring much of this book (and checking my Tagalog—thanks, Kim Gian!). To my nieces and nephews, for keeping us all young.

Finally:

My father, Steve. Thank you for giving me books and telling me stories, teaching me to love them—and baseball, and the Valley—and for still being the foremost expert on all things South Texas. My sister, Lindsay. Thank you for making me laugh, for crying with me and making sure my hair is OK on Zooms and having my back at every step, especially the strange and scary ones we have climbed together. And my mother, Rose. Thank you for believing, for showing me how to live fearlessly, and how to leave joy and love in the world long after I am gone. I keep you in every word of these pages. I love you all. This book is for you.

ABOUT THE AUTHOR

Kimberly Garza is a graduate of the University of Texas at Austin and the University of North Texas, where she earned a PhD in 2019. Her fiction and nonfiction have appeared in *Copper Nickel*, *DIAGRAM*, *Creative Nonfiction*, *TriQuarterly*, and elsewhere. A native Texan—born in Galveston, raised in Uvalde—she is an assistant professor of creative writing and literature at the University of Texas at San Antonio. *The Last Karankawas* is her first novel.